THE TREE OF LIFE

ALSO BY JOSH PACHTER

Styx, by Bavo Dhooge with Josh Pachter
(November, 2015)

THE TREE OF LIFE
THE MAHBOOB CHAUDRI MYSTERY STORIES

BY JOSH PACHTER

WILDSIDE PRESS

*This book is dedicated to
my daughter, Rebecca Kathleen Jones.*

*Although she's never been to Bahrain,
her own story began there.*

Copyright © 2015 by Josh Pachter.
Cover art copyright © 2015 by Solodovnikov Alekhander / Fotolia.
All rights reserved.

All of the stories, introductory materials, and afterwords in this book are copyright © 1984, 1985, 1986, 1988, 1991, 2009, 2015 by Josh Pachter. All rights reserved. Reproduction without the permission of the author—except for brief quotations in a review—is prohibited. See "Publication Information" at the end of the book for more details about where each story originally appeared.

Published by Wildside Press LLC.
www.wildsidebooks.com

CONTENTS

Introduction 7

The Dilmun Exchange 11

The Beer Drinkers 22

The Tree of Life 36

The Qatar Causeway 54

ASU 79

Jemaa el Fna 92

The Night of Power 101

Sheikh's Beach 116

The Ivory Beast 132

The Sword of God 152

Publication Information 170

Acknowledgments 171

About the Author 172

INTRODUCTION

"I want you to go to Bahrain next," my boss told me on the WATTS line connecting the University of Maryland European Division's Heidelberg headquarters to the education office at the US Naval Station in Rota, Spain, where I was teaching during that summer of 1982.

"Bahrain?" I said. "What country is *that* in?"

"Bahrain's not *in* a country," David explained. "It *is* a country."

The 10 months I wound up spending in Bahrain changed my life in ways that ranged from small (I discovered the music of Michael Franks) to enormous (I met the woman who four years later would give birth to my daughter Becca). Among other changes, this was the year I came out of retirement as a crime writer.

My first published short story, written when I was 16 years old, appeared in the December 1968 issue of *Ellery Queen's Mystery Magazine*. Over the next six years—while I was graduating from high school in New York and attending and graduating from college at the University of Michigan—I wrote several dozen more stories, selling six of them to EQMM and five others to *Alfred Hitchcock's Mystery Magazine*. In 1973, I was living in Reno, Nevada, and working as a scriptwriter at a tiny mass-media production company. My short stories, I thought, were getting better and better—but the better I thought they got, the less worthy of publication the editors of the magazines seemed to find them. One day, during my lunch hour, I dashed off a silly little story in no time and, for the hell of it, sent it to Ernie Hutter at AHMM … and, to my astonishment, Ernie bought it. Quality fiction I couldn't seem to sell, but *junk* they would buy? In disgust, I quit writing crime stories.

In 1976, I spent nine months traveling around Europe on a rickety Czech motorcycle. While visiting with friends in Holland, I met a Dutch woman, who I married the following year; Lydia and I lived in Pennsylvania for a while, and in 1979 we moved to Amsterdam. The next year, 1980, I spotted an ad for the UMd European Division in the *International Herald Tribune*, and I ultimately taught for them for four months in Germany and Greece that year and for three months in England in '81, right as Prince Charles was getting married to Lady Diana. In '82, Maryland sent me back to Greece, and from there to southwestern Spain, and it was while I was in Spain that I had the conversation with which I began this introduction and learned that my next assignment would be the island emirate of Bahrain, which is located in the Persian Gulf, right off the coast of Saudi Arabia.

I flew to the Middle East as the only passenger on a military cargo plane bringing supplies to the US Navy's Administrative Support Unit in Manama, Bahrain's capital (and only) city. The Department of Defense Dependent School System—which runs elementary and junior high and high schools in locations where American servicemen and servicewomen are permitted to bring their families—had a school in Bahrain, even though assignments to ASU were in most cases what are called "unaccompanied tours." Most of the students at the Bahrain School were the children of American and other-nation diplomats and bankers, and many of the wealthy Bahraini families also sent their kids there, since the quality of the education provided was superior to what was available on the local economy. At one point, the school had been a boarding school, but by the time I arrived it was open to day students only ... and, as the University of Maryland's sole faculty member in residence, I was given the dorm supervisor's apartment in the otherwise unoccupied dormitory to live in.

Hold up your left hand, palm facing away from you, four fingers touching and thumb a little separated from the fingers. Now find that shape on a map of the Middle East, and you'll be looking at Saudi Arabia (your hand) and Qatar (your thumb). Between your thumb and your fingers, you'll see the blue of the Persian Gulf—and, if you look closely, you will (depending on the scale of the map) see a miniscule dot that you might easily mistake for a printing error.

That miniscule dot is Bahrain.

Actually, it's only *part* of Bahrain. The country is an archipelago of several dozen islands, most of them uninhabited and too small to show up on any map showing more of the world than Bahrain alone. When I was there, in 1982, there were a total of 33 islands with a total area of just over 250 square miles; today, land reclamation projects have increased the number of islands to 84 and the total area to a little over 300 square miles. For the sake of comparison, Rhode Island—the smallest state in the US—is a bit over 1200 square miles in area, five times the size of Bahrain when I was there, and the city of Los Angeles, at 502 square miles, is double the size of the Bahrain I remember.

So it's a pretty small place, and it was even smaller in 1982, and smaller still when you consider that the bottom half of Bahrain Island—the main island, the one that shows up on the maps, the one where I lived—was a military area (theirs, not ours) and off-limits to foreigners.

The population was also small, which meant that new arrivals almost automatically became celebrities. Within three weeks of my touching down, I had been interviewed on the national radio station and by both national newspapers, I had been invited to dinner at the homes of the American ambassador and the commander of the US Navy's Middle East fleet, and I'd been asked to give a speech at the British Council. (The Bahraini who called to invite me to speak at the British Council spoke English with a heavy accent, and I was a little surprised when he told me that my audience would consist of about 100 bakers. As small as the country is, I couldn't imagine that there would be a *need* for that much bread. When I arrived to give my presentation, though, I discovered that I'd misunderstood his accent, and the crowd which had gathered to hear me was in fact comprised of about 100 *bankers*. You might think there'd be even less need for bankers than for bakers in a country housing only about a third of a million people, but, since Bahrain doesn't have any oil, the way it kept up with the al-Joneses was by becoming a haven for off-shore banking, and pretty much every major financial institution on the planet had a branch office there!)

It didn't take more than a month or so for the novelty of my arrival to wear off, and once that happened there wasn't really all that much for me to *do* in Bahrain. The *suq*—the ancient marketplace—was fascinating, and there was Sheikh's Beach (which was for foreigners only) and the National Museum, the Suq-al-Khamis Mosque and the Al-Arcen Wildlife Park and a few other sights. The State Department folks and the Bahrain School faculty had dinner parties and cookouts just about every weekend. I had my classes to teach, of course, and I became friendly with some of my students.

But by the time I'd been there for another month, I was spending a fair amount of my time bored.

And eventually I decided that maybe I ought to take this fascinatingly boring place where I was living and use it as the setting for a new short story.

I sent the result, which I titled "The Dilmun Exchange," off to Eleanor Sullivan, the editor of *Ellery Queen's Mystery Magazine*. She bought it, and asked me to turn Mahboob Chaudri into a series character. So I wrote a second Chaudri story, and a third, and I kept on writing them for a while after moving from Bahrain back up to Europe and settling in Germany.

All told, I wrote 10 Chaudri stories—and then, for reasons far too complicated and personal to explain here—I stopped writing altogether.

This time, my "retirement" lasted longer, from about 1988 until 2003, when my daughter Becca, then 17, only half-teasingly said something about how it must have been fun to be able to write publishable fiction, once upon a time.

"I still *can* write publishable fiction, dear," I told her. "I just don't *want* to."

And she gave me a look that said "Sure, Dad," so I figured I'd better prove it to her and came out of retirement yet again. And here I am, once more an engaged member of the crime-writing fraternity—thanks both to Becca, who pushed me to resume writing a decade ago, and to my wife Laurie, who pushes me to continue writing today.

My thanks also to John Betancourt and the folks at Wildside Press, who encouraged me to collect all 10 of my Mahboob Chaudri stories into a single volume. I had fun writing the stories, back in the early and middle 1980s, and I had fun rereading them and writing the Afterwords to them now, 30 years later.

I hope you'll have as much fun with them as I've had.

Josh Pachter
Herndon, Virginia
July 2015

THE DILMUN EXCHANGE

The *muezzin*'s call to dawn prayer echoed sadly down Bab-al-Bahrain Avenue. It was 4 AM, and the long narrow street—the main artery of Manama's old shopping district, the *suq*—was almost deserted. A beggar woman squatted, motionless, beside the doorway of Dilmun Exchange Services and Wholesale Jewelers, completely covered by her black silk *abba*, even her face and her extended palm swathed in black and invisible. Except for her, the road was empty. It would be hours yet before the merchants began to arrive, to raise the heavy metal shutters which protected their shop windows, to unlock their glass doors and switch on their electric cash registers, to look over their merchandise and drink one quiet cup of strong coffee before the madness began.

It was October 1, the first day of the autumn sales. For the next two weeks, by official decree of the Emir himself, every shop in the tiny island-nation of Bahrain would slash 20 percent or more from its prices on all items but food. At 8 AM, the sales would begin, and thousands of Arabs and expatriates would pour into the *suq* from all over the country, showering tens of thousands of dinars on the merchants and artisans, driving home to dinner with the backs of their cars filled with a mind-boggling array of television sets, video recorders, stereo systems, cameras, typewriters, pocket calculators, digital watches, electronic games, refrigerators, air conditioners, washing machines, microwave ovens, furniture, hand-woven carpets, antique pearl chests, bracelets and necklaces of gold and silver, shirts and skirts and shoes and suits and dresses.

But the beginning of the madness was still hours away, and when Mahboob Chaudri turned off Government Road and walked under the tall white arches of the *bab*, the narrow street which stretched out before him was lonely and still, except for the solitary beggar and the dying echoes of the *muezzin*'s call.

Chaudri crossed the small plaza just inside the *bab* and paused to look up at the blue-and-white sign above the doorway of the squat off-white building on the corner. STATE OF BAHRAIN, the sign announced in English and Arabic, MINISTER OF THE INTERIOR, PUBLIC SECURITY, MANAMA POLICE STATION.

Why only English and Arabic? he wondered, as he wondered every morning. *Why not Baluchi and Punjabi and Urdu, since almost two-thirds of us on the police force are Pakistani?*

Then, as always, he shrugged his shoulders, pushed the thought aside, and walked up the three stone steps into the station house.

A small group of *mahsools*, all of them Bahraini, lounged in the hallway, smoking imported cigarettes and talking idly. Chaudri greeted them with deference—he was always careful to be courteous to his superior officers—and walked on back to the locker room.

He was early this morning and no one else was there yet. He unbuttoned his sports shirt and hung it away in his locker, took off his blue jeans and folded them onto a second hanger, and placed his tennis shoes neatly beneath them. Many of the other men came to work in *jutti* and the traditional Pakistani *punjab*—knee-length cotton shirt and baggy trousers, both in the same pale shade of orange or brown or blue—but Chaudri liked the look of Western clothes and wore them whenever he was off duty.

He pulled on his drab-green uniform shirt and pants, adjusted his shoulder braid, knotted his olive-green tie, tucking the bottom half of it away between the second and third buttons of his shirt, and stepped into his sturdy black shoes. Then he faced the mirror inside the door of his locker and positioned his dark-green beret on his head, turning this way and that to make sure it was sitting well.

Satisfied at last, he stepped back from the mirror so he could see more of himself. He liked what he saw: Mahboob Ahmed Chaudri, 28 years of age and not bad-looking, with his deep-brown skin, his regular features, and his immaculate, imposing uniform.

Mahboob Ahmed Chaudri, 18 months a *natoor* on the Bahraini police force and ready any day now for his first promotion. He would be sorry to give up that lovely green beret, but glad to trade it in for the peaked cap of a *mahsool*.

The room was beginning to fill up now, and Chaudri closed the door of his locker and joined one of the half dozen conversations going on around him. It was 4:20 AM, and he still had 10 minutes of his own time left before roll call.

* * * *

By the time his half-hour break began, at 9 AM, the sales were well under way. Bab-al-Bahrain Avenue and the labyrinth of side streets and alleyways branching off from it were inundated with honking cars and bustling shoppers. The air was hot and still, and heavy with the smells of cooking oil and automobile exhaust and sweat, the sounds of humanity and machinery joined together in grating cacophony.

But Mahboob Chaudri walked along with a smile on his face, patiently allowing the throngs to surge around him and jostle against him—small knots of Arab women in long black *abbas*, their faces hidden behind thin veils or the birdlike leather masks called *berga'a*; businessmen in ankle-length *thobes* with red-and-white checkered *ghutras* arranged carefully on their heads; bankers of 40 countries in expensive three-piece suits; expat wives in modest skirts and blouses; Dutch construction workers and Korean longshoremen and British oil riggers in grease-stained jeans; Indian nannies in flowing saris, their midriffs bare or swathed in filmy gauze; children of every color and nationality and description.

Chaudri's monthly pay envelope was in his pocket, he had half an hour free, and he was on his way to the Dilmun Exchange to buy rupees to send home to his wife and children in Karachi.

Outside the money-changing office, the lone beggar woman still sat. Or was this a different one? Shrouded in black, not an inch of skin visible, unmoving, there was no way to tell. Chaudri pulled a 100-*fils* piece from his pocket and laid it gently on her covered, outstretched palm. "*El lo, majee*," he mumbled in his native Punjabi. "Take this, mother."

The woman did not answer him, not even with a nod.

Under that *abba*, she could be fast asleep, thought Chaudri. She could even be dead.

He went into the exchange office. It was a plain room. Behind a wooden counter running along the far wall, a gray-bearded Bahraini in *thobe* and *ghutra* sat working a pocket calculator. Above his head hung a large black board with the day's exchange rates—buying and selling prices for American and Canadian and Australian dollars, French and Swiss francs, Danish, Swedish and Norwegian kronor, British pounds, German marks, Dutch guilders, Italian lira, Saudia Arabian riyals, Japanese yen, and a dozen other currencies. There were a few faded travel posters taped to the walls, an ashtray standing in front of the counter for the use of the clientele, an oversized air conditioner humming morosely, and that was all.

Five men and a woman were waiting to be helped, as the Bahraini made his computations and counted out stacks of 10- and 20-dinar notes.

Chaudri took his place at the end of the line and looked up at the rate board. Almost 30 rupees to the dinar, he read happily. A good rate. Shazia and the children would have a comfortable month.

The first man in line scooped up his wad of bills from the counter, muttered a low-pitched "*Shukran*," and left the office. Chaudri and the other clients shuffled a place forward.

And then the door behind them banged open, and Chaudri whirled around at the noise.

A tall man with dark-brown hair and burning eyes stood just inside the doorway. It was impossible to tell whether he was a native or an expat. A woman's leather *berga'a* hid most of his face, and he did not speak. There was a gun in his hand, a dull-black revolver, and he held it firmly, not trembling.

He stood for a moment, allowing the realization of danger to reach through layers of shock into the minds of his victims, then he reached behind him and flipped the sign hanging inside the glass door to read CLOSED, turned the key in the deadbolt, and pulled down the shade. Only then did he wave his gun at them, motioning them to the side wall of the office.

"Turn around," he told them, "faces to the wall. Hands high above your heads, feet spread wide." His voice was cold and hard; he spoke accented but precise Arabic.

A Yemeni? thought Chaudri automatically, his eyes fixed on a flyspeck on the wall two inches before him. *A Kuwaiti?*

Over the irritated hum of the air-conditioner, he could hear the thief unfold a plastic grocery bag and begin to stuff it with stacks of crisp banknotes. *He'll take the dinars, the American dollars and the riyals,* Chaudri guessed, *and leave the rest of it be—*

"Now listen carefully," the voice interrupted his thoughts, "especially you, *natoor*. Do exactly what I tell you and by Allah's grace no one will get hurt."

"By Allah's grace!" the gray-haired clerk burst out furiously. "How dare you talk about—"

There was a blur of sound as the thief dashed across the room and clubbed the old Bahraini fiercely with the butt end of his revolver.

Chaudri stole a look to the side in time to see the clerk crumple limply to the ground and the masked figure back away.

"Do what he says," Chaudri instructed the rest of them. "Don't speak, don't move, and don't worry. It will be all right."

"Thank you for your assistance, *natoor*," the bandit said crisply. Chaudri could hear no sarcasm in it, which surprised him. *This man is truly calm,* he thought. *He knows just what he is doing.*

"If you follow the advice which the *natoor* has so intelligently given you," the voice resumed, "no one else will have to be hurt. And as you have seen, if you do *not* heed that advice, I will show you no mercy. No mercy at all."

Chaudri listened intently. *If I can't memorize his face,* he thought, *at least I can memorize that heartless voice.*

"In a few moments I will be leaving you," the thief went on. "Before I go, I will say to you the word 'Begin.' When I say that word, you will begin to count aloud, in unison, from one to one hundred. You will keep your faces to the wall and your hands high and go on counting, no matter what happens. When you reach one hundred, you may put your hands down and turn around and go about your business. If any of you should decide to take a chance and come after me before you have finished counting—well, that is a chance I would recommend you avoid. I have a confederate in the street, who is armed and will shoot to kill. Your families will be saddened to hear of your senseless death."

That was a lie, Chaudri was certain. *There is no confederate in the street. This man works alone and will share his loot with no one, I can feel it. But can I afford to gamble my life on that feeling?*

No, he decided. *No.*

"Thank you all for your cooperation," the voice concluded. "And now, you may begin."

"*Oahed*," Mahboob Chaudri said tightly, and the others spoke with him. "*Th'neen, t'lasse, arba'a, hamseh....*"

As they counted, he heard the door bolt being thrown and the door swing smoothly open and then, after soft footsteps passed through it, shut. The temptation to give chase, or at least to raise the alarm, was very strong, but the thief's words rang loudly in Chaudri's ears: *Your family will be saddened to hear of your senseless death.*

"*Thamnta'ash*," he counted grimly, "*tsata'ash, ashreen, oahed ashreen...*"

Suddenly there was the sound of a shot, and glass shattering, and an overwhelming clamor from the startled mobs of shoppers outside.

Chaudri stiffened. *Allah give me strength*, he prayed silently, as he continued to count the Arabic numbers out in the charged atmosphere of the exchange office. Forty, he reached as the bedlam outside swelled riotously, and sixty as it crested, then seventy as it began a slow descent back toward the everyday pandemonium of the October sales, and eighty-five as the strident cries of a dozen police officers became audible above the din, shouting questions and issuing commands to the crowd....

"*Sa'ba'ah watis'een*," Chaudri counted diligently, his palms itching with a feverish ache to be out in the street, "*thamania watis'een, tis'ah watis'een, ma'ah!*"

Before the dull echo of the final number had faded, Chaudri was on the sidewalk outside the Dilmun Exchange, his eyes drinking in the scene before him greedily: a tight half circle of police and passersby across the street gathered in front of the smashed display window of the Akhundawazi Trading Company. Up and down Bab-al-Bahrain Avenue as far as he could see in either direction the shoppers ebbed and flowed, laden with bags and boxes and gaily wrapped packages, an endless tide of bargain-hunting humanity.

"Did you see him?" Chaudri demanded of the black-draped beggar, who had not moved from her perch beside the door. Unlike the first time he had addressed her, he spoke now in flawless Arabic. "The last man to leave this office, mother—did you see which way he went?"

The woman nodded her head stiffly and moved a hand underneath her *abba* to point south.

Chaudri was off at once. "Thank you, mother," he threw back over his shoulder as he ran, his feet pounding against the concrete paving stones, his clenched teeth jarring with every stride.

But it was hopeless, he realized, before he had gone a hundred yards. Completely hopeless. By now the thief could have bolted down any one of a dozen side streets, could have strolled casually into any of a thousand shops, could be trying on a pair of trousers or pricing gold bangles or sipping sweet tea from a gently steaming glass.

What chance did he, Mahboob Chaudri, have of being lucky enough to stumble across a single man with a bag of money, a woman's face mask and a gun, intent on losing himself in the tangled, teeming maze of the old *suq*?

Hopeless, he thought as he ran, disgusted with his caution back at the exchange office, with the cumbersome uniform and clumsy shoes which slowed him down, with the infuriating crowds.

What could he do? What, if it came to that, could the entire 6,000-man Public Security Force do? *One hundred friends are not enough*, as the old Bedouin saying had it, *but a single enemy is too many*.

Yes, they could close off the airport and watch the fishing *dhows* and almost certainly prevent the criminal from leaving the country.

But if the man chose to stay, if he went to ground, say, out in A'ali or Bani Jamra or one of the other villages, if he actually had a confederate, after all, who was willing to hide him, then there was no way they would ever find him. He could disappear into the desert sands of Bahrain, and the country would swallow him up so completely that it would be as if he had never existed.

Chaudri stopped running, leaned weakly against a stretch of wooden scaffolding, and lowered his head, gasping hoarsely and filling his exhausted lungs with air.

Was it but a single enemy he was faced with? What if he'd been wrong, if there *had* been a confederate out in the street? The thief could have passed him that incriminating plastic bag, gotten rid of the money and mask and gun, and melted invisibly away into the crowd.

But that made no sense. Giving the bag to a confederate would leave the thief in the clear, yes, but then what about the confederate? If *he* were found with the bag in his possession, then —

And what was the point of the gunshot? Was it intended simply to draw the crowd's attention away from the thief's escape? If so, then why had he bothered? The shoppers hadn't known that the Dilmun Exchange was being robbed.

Chaudri pulled himself upright and began to retrace his steps. He arranged and rearranged the pieces in his head, manipulating them like the misshapen interlocking loops of the silver puzzle ring he had bought for his daughter Perveen's last birthday, trying to fit them together into an organized, sensible whole.

The Dilmun Exchange. A tall, controlled thief, his identity hidden behind a leather mask. The violent attack on the harmless old Bahraini clerk. "Count to one hundred" ... "Your families will be saddened" ... a gunshot ... the crowds ... the clamor ... the Dilmun Exchange....

And then suddenly the pieces dropped softly into place.

"*Merea rabba*!" Chaudri exclaimed aloud, reverting unconsciously to Punjabi. "Oh, dearie me, of course!"

He was sure of it, he was positive, but before he could prove it there was one question he would have to ask—if only he was not too late! He broke into a jog, weaving carefully from side to side to avoid the scores of shoppers milling in his path.

As he neared the Dilmun Exchange, he saw that the old beggar woman was still there, rocking rhythmically back and forth, her upturned palm—still covered by the black fabric of her *abba*—a silent plea for charity.

He walked up to her, stood over her, looked down at her—and asked her his question: "Tell me, mother, what is your name?"

The black shape that was her head turned up to him, but the woman did not speak.

"Your name, mother," Chaudri repeated. "Tell me your name."

She put a hand to her lips and shook her head.

"Oh, no, mother," said Chaudri, "you are not mute. It is only that you do not wish to speak. And why is that, I find myself wondering?"

Her other hand began to rise, but the *natoor* gripped the wrist firmly and pointed it towards the sky.

"No, mother," he said. "Your friend has already fired one shot this morning, and one shot was more than enough for today."

* * * *

"I was certain the thief had lied when he told us about his confederate in the street," Chaudri admitted to the eager ring of *shurtis* who surrounded him, "but I was wrong. There *was* a confederate, strategically situated right outside the door of the Dilmun Exchange while the robbery took place."

"The beggar woman," supplied Sikander Malek.

"Of course." Chaudri leaned back in his chair and sipped slowly at his tea. He was enjoying himself immensely. "She was out in front of the Exchange very early this morning," he told his listeners. "I saw her there when I reported to work at dawn. And when I went to the exchange office at nine to buy a bank draft to send home to my wife, she was still there. I even gave her a hundred *fils*, laid the coin on her palm and blessed her, and scolded myself for not giving more. She never said a word of thanks, but I thought nothing of it at the time. It was not until later, after the robbery, that I realized the importance of her silence—realized that her silence had been necessary in order to preserve the illusion."

"The illusion?" one of the *shurtis* prompted.

"The illusion that the figure underneath that all-concealing black *abba* was an innocent beggar, an innocent beggar *woman*, no less—when in fact it was a man, our thief's accomplice and brother."

"But how could you have known they were brothers?"

"I didn't know. But when I pulled the *abba* away from him, revealing the bag of money and the mask and the gun, proving his complicity in the crime, he confessed the entire scheme to me and led me straight to the small apartment in Umm al Hassam where they lived together—where his brother, unarmed, was awaiting him."

"And their scheme?"

"A simple plan, devised by simple men, but a clever one nonetheless. As soon as he stepped out of the exchange office, the thief fired a shot across the street, above the heads of the crowd, shattering the window of the Akhundawazi Trading Company. Then he stuffed his gun and mask into the plastic bag which already held his loot, set the bag down next to the black-draped form of his brother, and melted away into the crowd. With a quick readjustment of his *abba*, the beggar woman brother covered over the bag, and that was that. Transferring the incriminating evidence from brother to brother took no more than a few swift seconds and easily went unnoticed in the excitement and confusion that followed the gunshot. Then, when I finally reached the street and asked the beggar which way the thief had gone, 'she' had only to point in the wrong direction—and I, suspecting nothing, chased futilely after a thief who had in truth gone exactly the other way."

"But why did the brother sit there and wait for your return? Why didn't he make good his own escape as soon as you'd gone? No one would have seen the bag beneath the folds of his *abba*."

"A good question, my friend," said Chaudri. "But before I answer it, let me raise another, equally interesting. Why did the thief's brother take up his position in front of the Dilmun Exchange before four o'clock this morning, when his presence there would not be required until after nine? The answer to your question and to mine will seem obvious once you recognize it: the thief's brother arrived at the scene much earlier than he needed to be there, and stayed on well after his role in the commission of the crime was finished, *because he could not risk being seen walking either to or from the Dilmun Exchange*. And why not? Because if he had been seen, it would have shattered the illusion he had created so carefully—shattered it as finally as his brother's bullet shattered the plate-glass window of the Akhundawazi store. They were brothers, you see, similar in appearance and—this is the critical point—almost equal in height. And have you ever seen a beggar woman as tall as our unhappy prisoners? No, he had to get there early, before anyone else was about, and he had to sit there until the streets were again deserted before he could try to escape. Otherwise his height would surely have been noticed."

"One more question," said Sikander Malek. "How did you figure it all out?"

"Ah, now *that* is a question I would much prefer to leave unanswered. Because, you see, I'm not really sure that I *did* figure it out at all. I was thinking over the features of the robbery when the explanation suddenly came to me from nowhere—or perhaps I should say 'by Allah's grace.' The Dilmun *Exchange*: that was not only the scene of the crime, it was the solution to the crime as well. For there *had* been several exchanges, you see: first when the bag of money changed hands and, more importantly, when the thief's brother exchanged his own identity for that of an old beggar woman. I had been running away from the Dilmun Exchange, but the answer was there, back where I had started, all the time."

An appreciative murmur rose from Chaudri's audience.

"When I was a boy in Punjab," he went on, "my grandfather once said to me, 'If you are on the road to knowledge, my child, then you are journeying in the wrong direction. For knowledge is not a place you can get to by traveling. It is a place you come *from*, by standing still and listening to your heart.'"

Mahboob Ahmed Chaudri, *natoor*, smiled broadly and drank the last of his tea.

"Stand still," he repeated contentedly, thinking of the promotion which this day's work was certain to bring him, of the raise in salary that would go along with a higher rank, and of the bungalow back home in Jhang-Maghiana that he was saving to build for Shazia and the children. "Stand still and trust in your heart."

AFTERWORD

In 1982, most of the members of Bahrain's Public Security Force were Pakistanis. Why? Well, as you probably know, Islam is divided into two sects—Sunni and Shi'a—and the members of one don't always get on with the members of the other. The Bahraini government knew full well that a police force comprised of both Sunnis and Shi'as wouldn't have worked well, and putting either group in charge of the police while excluding the other would have been worse. So the Bahrainis came up with a creative solution and basically imported police officers from Pakistan, just as they imported hotel workers from Egypt and construction crews from Holland and so on.

Bahrain's Pakistani police were all men, and many of them had wives and children back home in Pakistan. Their salaries—though low by Western standards—were high by Pakistani standards, and the men received free housing and meals, so they were able to send enough money home to make the long separations from their families economically worthwhile.

The Juffair Police Barracks housed about a hundred of these Pakistani officers, and it was located right next door to the grounds of the Bahrain School, where I lived. So I got to know some of the men—not well, since they tended to be shy and private—but well enough to exchange small talk when our paths would cross.

When I decided to write a crime story set in Bahrain, I sat down with a small group of them and asked them many questions. What would be a good name for a Pakistani man? What would the names of his wife and children be? Where in Pakistan would he come from? The answers came almost faster than I could ask the questions—and I finally realized that they weren't hypothetical answers. In fact, the men were telling me about themselves. So the Mahboob Chaudri I created for my story has the first name of one of them and the last name of another, the wife of a third, the children of a fourth, the home town of a fifth ... and so on.

The geography in this story is accurate—or was, in 1982. The swearing is in Urdu and is, I have been told, particularly filthy. The wise saying Mahboob credits to his grandfather at the end is a paraphrase of a "communication mantra" I still share with my interpersonal-communication students to this day, and relates back to things I read long ago when I found myself fascinated by Zen Buddhism. (See, for example, Sheldon B. Kopp's 1972 book, *If You Meet the Buddha on the Road, Kill Him!*)

When I finished writing the story, I sent it off via international airmail to Eleanor Sullivan at *Ellery Queen's Mystery Magazine*, and she bought it almost by return mail and asked me for a sequel. I celebrated my first fiction sale in a decade by treating some friends to an expensive dinner at one of the better hotel restaurants in Manama, Bahrain's capital city. I especially remember the cobra coffee which finished the meal. Our server carefully peeled an orange and soaked the peel in brandy, then attached one end of it to a tall metal stand which allowed the other end to dangle down into a cup of hot coffee. He touched a lit match to the top of the peel, and a gorgeous snake of fire spiraled down the length of the peel to douse itself in the coffee.

By the time the story appeared in print—in the July 1984 issue of EQMM—I had left Bahrain and was living in Hagenau, a small housing development just outside the village of Baiersdorf, about seven miles north of the town of Erlangen, itself about 14 miles north of Nürnberg in southern Germany.

In her introduction to "The Dilmun Exchange," Eleanor wrote: "It has been over 10 years since we last published a story by Josh Pachter, who wrote his first published story, 'E.Q. Griffen Earns His Name' (EQMM, December 1968), when he was 16 years old. Now, 16 years later, he has created a new detective, Mahboob Ahmed Chaudri, 18 months a *natoor* on the Bahraini police force and ready any day now for his first promotion...."

The next year, Edward D. Hoch reprinted the tale in the 1985 edition of *The Year's Best Mystery and Suspense Stories* (Walker and Company, 1985), with this introduction: "Josh Pachter, an American who has lived abroad in recent years, published his first mystery short story at the age of 16. After too long an absence from writing, he has been active again as both editor and author. His 1983 anthology *Top Crime* has been published in a half-dozen countries, and a collection of his own stories has appeared in The Netherlands. Here he launches a promising new series, set in the little-known Arab emirate of Bahrain, an island nation strategically located in the oil-rich Persian Gulf."

Although I'd been mentioned in Ed's annual Honor Roll before—in the 1973 edition, then called *Best Detective Stories of the Year*, I had three stories listed—this was the first time he chose to reprint something of mine in the book. And the Honor Roll at the end of the collection also lists "The Beer Drinkers," my second Chaudri story, as one of 1984's best.

THE BEER DRINKERS

Mahboob Ahmed Chaudri was bored.

I'm a policeman, not a wet nurse, he thought morosely, *and my place is out on the streets, in the suq, where the action is—not stuck here playing nanny to a pack of silly children.*

It was well that Chaudri kept such thoughts to himself. Were he to give them voice, to speak the frustration that was in his heart, it would mean the end of his right to wear the proud uniform of a *mahsool,* the end of his career, the end of his four-year stay in Bahrain.

For these four boys were no ordinary children. They were the eldest sons of four of the most powerful and influential men in the Arabian Gulf—or "Persian" Gulf, as the Western infidels and the damned Iranians insisted on calling it—and one did not call such boys a pack of silly children unless one was eager to give up the respected position that Chaudri had worked so hard to win and to return in disgrace to the bitter life of a day-laborer in Karachi.

It was the third and final day of the second annual meeting of the Gulf Cooperation Council, and the heads of state of the six member nations—the emirs of Bahrain, Kuwait, and Qatar, the sultan of Oman, the king of Saudi Arabia, and the president of the United Arab Emirates—were cloistered away with their prime ministers, defense ministers, and aides in a magnificently appointed conference room in Manama's shiniest, most elegant new hotel. They had come together to discuss the coordination of security forces in the region, the establishment of "common market" agreements between their several nations, the Palestinian question, the ramifications of the Iran-Iraq war, the advisability of a joint demand for the withdrawal of Israeli troops from Lebanon, the adoption of uniform passports, and other issues of mutual importance.

Four of the senior ministers had brought their first-born sons to Bahrain with them, and it had fallen to Mahboob Chaudri to take care of the boys while Their Highnesses conferred, to tour them around the island's points of interest, and to keep them away from trouble. And, most important, to keep trouble away from them.

It was an important assignment—a vital one, a mark of his superiors' confidence in his abilities. It was also, thought Chaudri, an incredible bore.

Day One of the conference had been filled with arrivals and receptions and parties and dinners. The ministers' children had been included in all these functions, and Chaudri had been but one small cog in the complex machinery of the security arrangements. By Allah's grace, all had gone well. There had been no incidents of any kind—not at the airport, not during the motorcade into the city center, not at the hotel or the various embassies where the welcoming activities had taken place.

On Day Two, the official meetings had begun. That morning, Chaudri had chaperoned the four youngsters on a tramp around the Portuguese Fort and the ruins of the Bronze Age and Stone Age cities, accompanied by a reporter and a photographer from the *Gulf Daily News* and the president of the Historical and Archaeological Society. After a luncheon at the home of the Saudi ambassador, hosted by that dignitary's charming and beautiful wife, they had driven south into the desert for a bus ride through the newly opened Al-Areen Wildlife Preserve. The children had enjoyed themselves immensely, but Chaudri, of course, had been on duty all day and had not had a chance to eat lunch. By the time they reached Al-Areen, he was hot and hungry and tired, and the chatter of the boys and the penetrating stink of the Arabian oryx had given him a headache.

This afternoon, *insh'Allah*, would be the end of it. Another hour or so here at the National Museum and he could herd his charges back across the causeway from Muharraq to the mainland, deliver them safely into their fathers' arms, thank one and all for the honor of having been permitted to serve them, and with a bit of luck catch a ride back to the police barracks in time to take a hot bath before dinner.

Children!

And, to be fair about it, it wasn't only the children. There was also that irritatingly bouncy British reporter with her constant barrage of foolish questions and her obsequious little Indian photographer constantly shooting off his flashbulbs in Chaudri's eyes. And, this morning, the well-meaning but terribly long-winded assistant curator of the museum, Sheikh Ibrahim al-Samahiji, whose lecture on Bahrain's history had been underway for what felt like the last 10 hours and seemed certain to go on for at least the next 15.

"…one of the earliest hymns known to mankind, written over four thousand years ago, when the pyramids of Egypt were new, by a Sumerian in what is today the south of Iraq. It sings the glories of the ancient land of Dilmun, site of the biblical Garden of Eden, whose capital—as the excavations carried out since 1953 have conclusively proven—was here on the island of Bahrain. 'The land of Dilmun is holy,' the hymn begins, 'the land of Dilmun is pure. In Dilmun, the raven does not croak, the lion does not kill. No one says, my eyes are sick, my head is sick. No one says, I am an old man, I am an old woman....'"

The voice droned on and on. Megan McConnell, the reporter, scribbled furiously in her notebook. The Indian photographer snapped exposure after exposure of the assistant curator, the honored guests, the colorful displays of artifacts on the walls. The children themselves, trained since infancy in the art of diplomacy, seemed to be listening attentively, though who knew what thoughts they were thinking as they stood there in their flowing *thobes* and crisp white *ghutras*.

Behind the intent and solemn mask of Mahboob Chaudri's olive face, he was thinking that at least the ethnography room had been worth looking at, with its spears and swords and *khunjars*, its models of stilt houses made all of palm fronds and pearl-divers' boats rigged out with canvas sails, its mannequins in native dress—especially the bride, in her magnificent gold-embroidered *thobe nashel* with its billowing sleeves that folded upwards to cover her head, the elaborate gold ornaments around her neck, the intricately hennaed hands—the camel saddles and tools and pottery and glassware and porcelain, the orchestra of Arabic instruments, the full-size reproduction of the kitchen of a villager's thatched hut and the carpets, mirrored walls, silken pillows, and curtained four-poster bed of the room in which a well-to-do couple would spend their wedding night.

Shazia, his own dear wife, would enjoy that section of the museum, if no other.

Shazia....

It had been almost two years since his last home leave, since he had last heard her speak his name, last touched a hand to her delicate cheek and kissed her lips and felt the soft caress of her sweet and golden arms.

"'Let the sun in heaven bring her sweet water from the earth,'" Ibrahim al-Samahiji's monotone pushed the image of his wife to the far edge of Chaudri's consciousness. "'Let Dilmun drink the water of abundance. Let her springs become springs of sweet water. Let her fields yield their grain. Let her city become the port of all the world.'"

The hymn was over at last, and the assistant curator smiled determinedly and led them off to a small room at the back of the building, a room with a single waist-high display case taking up most of its floor space and old-fashioned black-and-white maps of the Middle East covering its walls.

"About 40 years ago," Sheikh Ibrahim told them, "a small number of a previously unknown type of round stamp seal began to be found both in Mesopotamia and in cities of the Indus River valley. Dating to about 2000 BC, they were clearly 'foreign' among the cylinder seals of Mesopotamia and the square seals of the Indus. No one knew where they came from. But the recent discovery of some 50 seals of this type in the Barbar temples and in Cities I and II at Qala'at al-Bahrain, together with debris of seal-cutting workshops, shows us that this seal type is in fact native to Bahrain. These so-called 'Dilmun seals' are the main evidence for Bahrain's trade connections four thousand years ago with the whole of the Middle East, and they are this country's greatest, most valuable archaeological treasure."

Chaudri leaned forward to see into the case. It was filled with row upon row of small stone buttons, carved with a confusion of geometric shapes, crude human figures, images of goats and gazelles and flowering trees. Beneath each stone was a square of gray clay bearing the impression of the seal that lay above it. A magnifying panel was set into grooves along the top and bottom edges of the case's surface so that the seals could be examined more closely.

But that arrangement was not good enough for the four young boys.

"There's so much glare from the overhead lighting," complained Jamil, the 14-year-old son of a prime minister, "I can hardly see them."

"And the inside of the case is dim," Mohammed added. He was 16, and his father was a minister of defense.

Talal, also 16 and also a prime minister's child, was the one who came up with the idea. "Open the case and take them out," he proposed, though to Mahboob Chaudri's ears it sounded more like a command than a suggestion.

"Yes! Yes!" came Rashid's high-pitched agreement. At 13, though he was the youngest of the boys, he was the most powerful; his father was a crown prince and the heir to his country's throne. "I want to hold them, to feel the texture of them in my hand. If these are Bahrain's proudest treasures, I want to learn to know them."

Sheikh Ibrahim looked staggered. Delicately, he began to explain: "That would be very, ah, irregular. You see, the air in this display case is temperature-controlled and dehumidified. If I open the case, the sudden change in temperature and humidity could damage the seals. And if you were to touch them, the oils on your fingertips and palms could—"

"Well, of course," one of the boys interrupted softly, "if you don't want to give us the pleasure...."

He allowed his voice to trail off and turned away from Sheikh Ibrahim.

The assistant curator swallowed nervously. The small room had gone deathly silent, and the atmosphere was thick and stuffy with tension.

Even the photographer had stopped his incessant picture taking. The dismayed look on Megan McConnell's face was clear: what a story this was, and what a shame that she would never be allowed to publish it. For the first time that day, Mahboob Chaudri found himself truly interested in the events going on around him.

Sheikh Ibrahim took a deep breath and smiled. "The oils on your fingertips and palms might counteract the effect of the changes in temperature and humidity," he went on smoothly, "and I would be grateful for the opportunity to investigate that hypothesis." He pulled a ring of keys from the pocket of his ankle-length *thobe*, selected one of them, and unlocked the back of the display case.

The tightness in the room evaporated, and Chaudri relaxed. He felt that he had at last begun to understand the intricate complexities of statecraft, and the ease with which a simple disagreement between individuals could quickly escalate into an international incident. Instead of feeling sorry for Ibrahim al-Samahiji, for the way the distinguished assistant curator had been put in his place by a child, he found himself admiring the Sheikh's tactfulness and diplomacy.

He remembered an Arabic saying he had heard shortly after his arrival in Bahrain. *Both lion and gazelle may be sleeping in one thicket*, a grizzled graybeard in a teashop on the fringes of the *suq* had told him, puffing wisely at the thin stem of his bubbing *narghile*, the crude clay waterpipe no longer smoked by anyone other than old men, *but only the lion is having a restful sleep*. He had not understood the proverb at first, but he thought he knew now what it was like to be a gazelle amongst the lions.

Sheikh Ibrahim had removed several trays of seals from the glass case in the center of the room and was carefully lifting the stones from their velvet niches and passing them out to the eager boys. Once again the air rang with teenaged chatter, and the photographer's flashbulbs popped almost continuously.

"What's this one?" asked Mohammed, balancing a seal on his upturned palm. "It looks so funny."

Chaudri was standing close enough to make out the design on the stone: two male figures carved in simple outline, seated on identical chairs or stools, the sun shining above them and, strangely, a star at their feet. He had seen this image before, reproduced on countless T-shirts and wooden plaques and gold medallions. It was the only one of the seals with which he was familiar. What made it funny was that the noses of the two seated men were ludicrously long and joined in a V at the top of a large oval shape which hung between them. Each figure held one hand behind him, fingers weirdly misshapen and splayed, and supported his trunk-like nose with his other hand.

"They are called 'The Beer Drinkers,'" Sheikh Ibrahim informed the boys proudly, "and that is the best known and most beloved of all the Dilmun seals. The two men are sharing a skin of mead, drinking it through long spouts or straws—which most people see instead, comically, as enormous noses. Although," he admitted, "there are also those who call this stone 'The Musicians' and claim that the two figures are playing a primitive sort of bagpipes and not drinking beer at all. In any case, I think I can safely say that that small stone which you hold in your hand is the greatest and most important of Bahrain's ancient treasures."

The children were suitably impressed and handled the seal with reverence. Megan McConnell made a swift sketch of it in her notebook, and the photographer finished off a roll of film shooting it from all imaginable angles.

"What were these seals used for?" the reporter wanted to know, her drawing complete. "Were they purely decorative, or were they functional as well?" Her associate was busy changing film, and Chaudri glanced surreptitiously at his watch. Another 20 minutes and it would be time to go.

"Oh, absolutely functional, Miss McConnell." Sheikh Ibrahim rubbed his hands with delight at the chance to launch into another lecture. "Each of the seals is unique. Four millennia ago, they were used as we use our signatures today. A craftsman marked each sample of his handiwork with his own distinctive seal, to show that he had produced it and no one else. A scribe used his seal to sign documents, a nobleman to make his decrees official, a merchant to verify transactions. The poor, of course, had no need for such seals, but anyone with valuable property or possessions would identify them as his own by—"

The bolts of photographic lightning resumed, and the soliloquy went on.

And then, at last, Sheikh Ibrahim began to fit the Dilmun seals back into their velvet trays, matching each with the clay impression just below its waiting position. Megan McConnell snapped her notebook shut and tucked it away in her shoulder bag. The Indian photographer clicked off a few final shots of the group. The four boys milled about impatiently, ready to be under way. Mahboob Chaudri's stomach growled, and he prayed that the rumble had been audible to none but himself.

Then Ibrahim al-Samahiji gasped hoarsely, and, when Chaudri looked, there was stark horror etched into the lines of the assistant curator's weathered face. He was pointing a trembling finger at an empty hole in the last velvet tray.

"The Beer Drinkers!" he cried brokenly. "It's *gone!*"

* * * *

Mahboob Chaudri was no longer bored.

Bahrain's greatest treasure was missing—stolen and not lost, as a careful check around the small room quickly revealed. The prime suspects were four young men whose fathers were so high-placed that even to *question* their sons would be the gravest of insults, and the idea of searching the boys for the stone was absolutely unthinkable. And he had less than a quarter of an hour before it would be time to reboard the bus for the brief ride back to the mainland.

No, Mahboob Chaudri was not bored.

But he would have given a great deal to *be* bored once again, instead of mired in this, the most hopeless, desperate situation of his career.

Sheikh Ibrahim was gaping at him. Megan McConnell had her notebook out again and was scribbling furiously. The Indian photographer was taking pictures of *him* now, and Chaudri could imagine the caption that would appear in the *Gulf Daily News*: "Mahboob Ahmed Chaudri of the Public Security Force," it would say, "baffled by the theft of the most important relic of Bahrain's ancient history."

Luttay gaye, he thought bitterly. *What a disaster!*

The four boys, meanwhile—Jamil, Mohammed, Talal, and Rashid—were talking softly amongst themselves. Chaudri would have sorely liked to have been able to overhear their conversation. The McConnell woman and her photographer had been working all the while that the seals were being handed around; there had been no time for either of them to have pocketed the Beer Drinkers. And it was inconceivable that Sheikh Ibrahim himself had stolen the stone: the thing would be impossible to sell, and if—like certain mad collectors—all he wanted was the knowledge that a unique and priceless piece was in his possession, why, the piece was *already* in his possession, safe in its niche in his museum. There was no reason to steal it: he could enjoy it safely and privately, whenever he chose.

No, the awful truth was that the only valid suspects in the case were the eldest sons of four of the GCC's strongmen, and there was nothing he could do about it. He could not search them, he could not ask them to turn out the pockets of their *thobes*, he could not ask *any* question which implied that one of the boys was guilty while admitting that he did not already know which one. For if the three innocent youngsters saw that their integrity was in doubt, at least one of them would be sure to report the matter to his father.

Chaudri didn't really want to think about the consequences of that.

If only he had been watching more closely, if only he had seen which of the four had taken the stone.

If only....

If only he had a magic box, like the Grand Vizier in the old fairy tale. It had been one of his favorite stories as a child: the Emperor's wonderful golden ring is stolen, and the Vizier is ordered to uncover the identity of the thief. He gathers the suspects outside one of the palace's smaller apartments and instructs them to enter the darkened room individually, unaccompanied by guards. In the center of the room, they will find the Vizier's magic box, and they are to put one hand into that box as deeply as it will go, then leave the apartment by a second door, where the Vizier himself will be waiting for them. The box will have no effect on the hand of an innocent man, but its magic will stain a criminal's skin a damning black.

So, one by one, the courtiers enter the darkened room. One by one, they leave by the opposite door. And, one by one, their hands are examined by the Grand Vizier.

At last: "This is the criminal!" he cries.

"But my hands are clean!" the accused man protests.

"Exactly," smiles the Grand Vizier. For his magic box is not magic at all, merely an ordinary wooden box filled to its brim with soot. The innocent suspects, their consciences clear, have obeyed the Vizier's instructions and come out of the room with blackened hands. Only the guilty man, fearful of the box's magic, has disobeyed, and his immaculate hands reveal him to be the thief.

If only I had a magic box, Mahboob Chaudri thought sadly. *If only I had been* watching!

But—but wait. *He* knew he had seen nothing, but he was the only one in the room who possessed that knowledge. And perhaps they *did* have a magic box of sorts there with them, after all. Yes. Yes. It would be a gamble, but it was all he could think of. And if the Indian photographer was clever enough to catch on and play along, there was a chance it might work.

In any case, it was worth a try. Even if it failed, the situation could hardly get any worse than it already was.

Chaudri drew himself up to his full height, calmly projecting an air of what he hoped would pass for confidence. Less than two minutes had passed since Sheikh Ibrahim had announced the disappearance of the treasured seal. The Sheikh, the boys, Megan McConnell, the photographer—they were all turned toward him expectantly, waiting for him to speak.

He spoke. "I saw who took the stone," he lied. "You thought my attention was elsewhere, but you were wrong. I saw you take it, and I saw where you hid it."

He watched their faces hopefully, praying for the guilty boy to give himself away.

But it was not to be that easy.

And it was too late to back away from it now. He had committed himself. He could only go forward. "Your first mistake," he went on, "was coveting that which does not belong to you—a minor sin, true, but a sin all the same. Your second mistake was stealing the stone, repaying Bahrain for her hospitality by robbing her of her dearest treasure. That, of course, was a graver sin and a more serious error. Your third mistake was larger still: you allowed me to see you as you claimed the Beer Drinkers for your own."

The silence in the room was hot and stifling in spite of the museum's air conditioning.

"But I am only a simple policeman," Chaudri admitted, his voice now humble. "If I accuse you, here or in front of your father, it will be my word against yours. Even if the stone is found in your possession, then perhaps you will say I planted it there in an attempt to discredit you. My word against yours—and your word, obviously, will be worth much more than mine. What I need," said Mahboob Chaudri firmly, "is proof."

Now is the moment, he thought, pausing to let them consider the things he had said. *Understand me, my friend, and give me your help!*

"And I *have* proof," he said, "for you made a fourth mistake, and that was the largest error of all." He whirled to face the stocky little photographer and pointed a finger straight at the man's startled eyes.

"*You,*" he intoned dramatically, his mind imploring the other to comprehend, "you saw the theft take place as well—not only saw it, but snapped a photograph of it with your camera at the very instant it happened."

The Indian blinked nervously, clearly confused.

Don't deny it, Chaudri thought fiercely. *You can help me trap the thief!*

"I—" the man stammered.

It's not going to work, Chaudri realized. *He doesn't know what I'm talking about.*

And then the swarthy Indian countenance cleared. "Why, yes, sir," the man said firmly. "That is completely true. I did."

Chaudri flushed with joy. Praise Allah for those beautiful, blessed words!

"I don't want to cause an embarrassing incident," he told the children confidently. "All I want is for the Beer Drinkers to be returned. So I have a suggestion to make."

He moved to the panel of light switches by the door—the only entrance to the room—and swung the door shut.

"If all four of you will gather around the display case, one on each side of it, I will turn off all the lights in this room. In the darkness, the boy who took the seal can set it back down on top of the case without being seen. I will leave the lights off for one full minute. If the stone is there when I turn the lights back on, then I will return you all to your hotel and nothing further need ever be said about what has happened here today. Sheikh Ibrahim, is that acceptable to you?"

The assistant curator bobbed his head eagerly. "Yes, of course," he agreed. "All I want is the seal!"

"Miss McConnell?"

To her credit, the reporter understood him and nodded her acquiescence immediately. That would mean two marvelous stories lost in a single day, but she was a seasoned enough journalist to recognize that some tales are better left untold.

"And you, Mr.—?"

"Gogumalla, sir," the Indian supplied. "Solomon Gogumalla."

"Mr. Gogumalla, will you swear to say nothing about this incident and to destroy the incriminating film in your camera without developing and printing it if the Beer Drinkers is returned?"

The little photographer swallowed noisily. "Yes, sir," he promised. "Of course. I won't say a word. You can rely on me."

"Well, then." Chaudri turned to the boys.

They themselves seemed willing to cooperate, and Chaudri deferentially arranged them around the sides of the glass display case. Ibrahim al-Samahiji, Megan McConnell, and Solomon Gogumalla he guided to positions along the wall farthest from the case, so they would be well out of the way.

"Now I will shut off the lights," he repeated, "and I will leave them off for 60 seconds."

With hope and prayer in his heart, he hit the four switches and plunged the room into darkness.

* * * *

The room was empty of light and sound. Mahboob Chaudri held his breath and listened for the faint rustle of cloth that would be a hand reaching into a pocket, for the sharp click of stone touching down on glass.

But there was nothing: no rustle, no click, no noise of any kind.

And time floated by, as slow yet intense as one of the emir's golden peregrine falcons drifting steadily across the sky in search of its prey.

Then the sounds began. There was a cough from the corner of the room that could have come either from the assistant curator or the photographer. There was the abrupt crack of a joint flexed after too long a time held stiff. There was a shuffle of impatient feet and a long, tired sigh—and the rapid pounding of Mahboob Chaudri's own anxious heart.

"I will now turn on the lights," he announced, when he judged that a full minute had gone by. He felt for the switches in the darkness and pressed them all at once. When his eyes had readjusted to the brightness, he looked hopefully to the surface of the display case in the center of the room.

There was nothing there.

His bluff had been called.

Disgrace, dismissal, and banishment back to Pakistan. His children would be ashamed of him, his wife would despise him, his friends would abandon him. It was over, all over—his career, his happiness, his life.

He would see his assignment through, of course—escort the children back to their hotel, then go straight to the Police Fort and prepare a letter of resignation. He could at least do that much, and quit before they could throw him out....

No! He was Mahboob Ahmed Chaudri—not a quitter, not a coward. He was a police officer with a job to do, a case to solve, a criminal to apprehend.

His bluff had failed, true—but before he would admit defeat he would play one more card, the only card that was left to him.

He would bluff again.

"Very well, then," he said, "you have chosen to hold onto the stone, which leaves me with no choice at all. I will have that film developed, and I will present the incriminating photograph to your father. Mr. Gogumalla, may I have your camera, please?"

"Certainly, *mahsool*," the Indian replied. "But may I offer you my services, as well? I have a small darkroom of my own, right here in Muharraq. Allow me to develop the roll for you and to make a large print of the picture in question, which I can present to you very quickly and with my compliments."

"A kind offer," said Chaudri, pleased—*and a nice touch*, he added silently. "But in a case like this one, it would be best to have our own men do that job." He put out his hand for the camera, but the photographer held onto it. "Don't worry about your camera," Chaudri reassured him. "Our specialists will be quite careful with it."

Gogumalla shook his head stubbornly and took a step backwards, and at that moment Mahboob Chaudri realized what had really happened to the Beer Drinkers.

* * * *

I should have seen the truth immediately, Chaudri wrote to his wife Shazia late that evening. Usually his weekly letters were filled with questions about the children and wistful dreams of the future, when he would have saved enough money from his salary to return to Pakistan for good. But this week he had news to report.

Miss McConnell and the Indian, Gogumalla, were busy working while the theft was being committed, he wrote, forming the Punjabi words slowly and carefully, *and I was certain that neither of them could possibly have been guilty. Instead of looking only at the fact that they were working, though, I ought to have considered what exactly it was that they were doing. The woman was writing and drawing in her notebook all that time, and the photographer was taking pictures. But at one moment Gogumalla stopped to put a fresh roll of film into his camera, just after shooting a series of exposures of the Beer Drinkers. And, as it turned out, new film was not all that he was loading into the body of his camera—he hid the Dilmun seal there as well, in the hollow cavity inside the lens.*

It was not in his mind to commit a crime when he set out today—he was just a simple photographer on assignment. But when Sheikh Ibrahim explained how valuable the stone was and he saw the opportunity to take it, the temptation was too much for him to resist.

The poor fool—he was too ignorant, Shazia, to know that, for him, the Beer Drinkers had no value at all: unique and instantly recognizable as it is, there is no way he could ever have sold it.

Of course, none of the photographs he was taking after the theft were any good, with the Beer Drinkers lodged between his lens and his film. If I had accepted his offer to process and print the roll himself, he would have gone off to his darkroom, taken the seal out of the camera and hidden it, and come back to me with the sad story that the film had accidentally been ruined. And since he knew that I knew there really was no incriminating picture, he doubted that, once we had left the museum, I would even bother asking him to do the developing and printing. When I carried my bluff to the extreme, though, and insisted on taking the camera myself, he saw that the game was up and confessed.

He is out on Jiddah now, the prison island, in a cell awaiting trial, and I have been commended by my superiors for solving the case without insulting or embarrassing the four boys, who by now are back in their home countries and tucked safely away in their beds. Sheikh Ibrahim has promised me a golden reproduction of the Beer Drinkers as an expression of his gratitude. When I receive it, I will buy a chain for it and send it to you as a memento of your husband's triumph.

Not really a very satisfying triumph for me. If I hadn't happened to remember that old fairy tale and think of the Indian's camera as a modern-day magic box, Solomon Gogumalla would now have the seal and I would be —

Well, the less said about that the better.

It is getting late, dear Shazia, and I must sleep. Kiss the children a hundred times for me and think ever fondly of your own

Mahboob

AFTERWORD

A visitor to today's Bahrain National Museum, which opened to the public in 1988, will find a modern complex of several lovely white stone buildings, erected overlooking the water where the Al Fatih Highway intersects with the Sheikh Hamad Causeway to Muharraq Island.

What's described in this story is the old museum, which has long since either been repurposed or razed. It was much smaller than the new one, much darker—and I imagine quite probably much less interesting. But I loved the original structure, and visited it many times during my year in Bahrain.

The Dilmun seals described here are real, and "The Beer Drinkers" remains the most important surviving artifact of the ancient Dilmun civilization. All of the history presented in the story was carefully researched and is, to the best of my knowledge, accurate.

The story appeared in the December 1984 issue of EQMM, and Eleanor Sullivan introduced it like this: "A lovely second story in Josh Pachter's new series about Bahraini policeman Mahboob Ahmed Chaudri. The illustration of the Beer Drinkers, which really is the best known and most valuable of the Dilmun seals, was drawn from a photograph by Piet Schreuders, a Dutch graphics artist whose book, *Paperbacks USA*, the author translated from Dutch into English."

Like "The Dilmun Exchange," this story also made Ed Hoch's *Best Mystery and Suspense Stories of the Year* Honor Roll. The following year, Bill Pronzini and Martin H. Greenberg reprinted it in their excellent anthology *The Ethnic Detectives: Masterpieces of Mystery Fiction* (Dodd, Mead & Company, 1985). In his introduction, Pronzini wrote: "Mahboob Chaudri is one of crime fiction's most delightful new detectives. 'The Beer Drinkers' and several other of his cases have appeared in *Ellery Queen's Mystery Magazine* over the past two years, and more are planned. Happily, his creator is also considering a Chaudri novel for the not too distant future. A teacher by profession, Josh Pachter has lived in Bahrain ... and writes from first-hand knowledge of the island and its people."

I really *was* thinking about trying my hand at a Chaudri novel at the time, but, when I finally did get around to writing a book-length piece of fiction, 30 years later, it was set in one of the other "B" countries—Belgium, not Bahrain. Of course, I'm still alive and kicking, so who knows what the future might bring?...

THE TREE OF LIFE

This is a privilege, he kept reminding himself as he bounced and jounced and feared for his life. *Oh, dearie me, Chaudri, don't forget it is a privilege!*

Since all of the camels in the tiny island emirate of Bahrain were owned by the royal family, an invitation to ride one as a reward for service to the al-Khalifa government was indeed a privilege.

It was not, however, a pleasure.

Back home in Karachi, Chaudri had taken his children more than once to ride the gaily decorated tourist camels at Clifton Beach, but this was the first time he had ever mounted one of the ugly, sour-smelling beasts himself. The weathered wooden saddle and thin cloth cushion he sat on were intensely uncomfortable, and the creature's clumsy rolling gait jarred his long-suffering head at every stride.

He had been aboard the animal for over an hour now, and he was deeply regretting the chain of events which had put him there. If he had known that the government would bestow this honor on him for preventing the attempted theft of that little bit of stone from the National Museum from turning into an international incident, he might just have let that photographer get away with it. The museum's curator had given him a golden replica of the famous Dilmun seal as a reward for his recovery of the original. That was nice—he'd had one of the Arab jewelers in the *suq* turn it into a lovely necklace for Shazia. But this. This *privilege*. He had managed to put it off for several months with assorted excuses, but his luck had finally run out—and here he was.

Camels! The ships of the desert, they were called, and Mahboob Chaudri could understand why: he felt himself about to become seasick at any moment. *Dear Allah,* he prayed fervently, *if the worst should happen, allow me at least to avoid soiling my uniform and disgracing myself!*

He understood now, too, the truth behind the ancient poet's description of the nomadic Arab tribesmen who had formerly roamed the desert as "the parasites of the camel." As he rode through the scorching heat, Chaudri had frequent occasion to consult the *jirbeh* he had been given, the goatskin bag of sweet water that hung by his side. But the hulking camel plodded on steadily, diligently, not showing the slightest sign of weakness or thirst. Man was not well suited for life in the desert—but with his camels to provide transportation, and milk in times of no water, and meat in times of no food, the Bedouin could survive even this most harsh and desolate of existences.

A sudden crack from below broke the stillness of the afternoon. Chaudri leaned to his left and looked down—to see beneath him the remains of one unfortunate ship of the desert that had capsized in this infinite ocean of sand. Its skeleton had been picked clean by carrion birds and bleached a dusty white by the ferocious summer sun and largely covered over by the ever-shifting sands, but its gently curved jawbone still lay on the surface of the desert, and the hoof of Chaudri's camel had shattered the brittle bone and the oversized ivory teeth loudly.

"Desert driftwood," said Chaudri aloud, though there was no one but the camel to hear. He turned the words over in his mind as his mount moved remorselessly onward, indifferent to the lonely fate of its cousin. The phrase pleased him: those scattered bones, softly sculpted by wind and sand, were indeed the flotsam and jetsam of the arid vastness that made up most of Bahrain's 250 square miles.

He had left the inhabited northern half of the island behind him an hour or more earlier, had passed the national oil company's residential compound at Awali and skirted around the base of the Jebel ad-Dukhan, the Mountain of Smoke. At less than 400 feet in height, it was not much of a mountain, but it was the emirate's highest point, and on a clear day the whole of the country, from al-Muharraq in the north to Ras al-Barr in the south, could be seen from its summit.

Chaudri drank sparingly from the *jirbeh* at his side, then touched the few droplets of water which clung to his upper lip with the point of his tongue so as not to waste even the smallest amount of the precious fluid. His olive-green uniform was itchy and sticky with perspiration. He felt foolish with the traditional red-and-white checkered *ghutra* on his head, but the camel master had insisted he wear it as protection from sunstroke. At least there was no one around to see how incongruous it looked in combination with his uniform.

There was no one anywhere, there was nothing to see and no one to see it. Just Mahboob Ahmed Chaudri and his trusty camel, alone in the middle of an endless expanse of sand and dead or dying brush, the midday sun dizzying his poor brain in spite of the *ghutra*, his aching body numbed by now to the further indignities of the torturous ride.

He would feel it tomorrow, he knew. *O pehan yah geya*, he would feel it tomorrow—unless he was lucky enough to perish today, to tumble insensate from the back of this damnable beast and give up his bruised flesh to the birds and his battered bones to the sun.

"A privilege," he muttered dully, reaching for his half-empty *jirbeh* with a tired hand. "By the beard of the Prophet, it's a privilege."

* * * *

When at long last he saw the Tree of Life take shape through the shimmering haze of heat before him, his first thought was that it must be a mirage. This was his destination, his turn-around point—a sad reminder of the fact that there had once been an underground spring beneath this far corner of the desert. Ancient legend had it that this was the very Tree of Life that the Lord God had planted for Adam and Eve in the Garden of Eden. But this tree was long dead, its trunk wasted, its branches barren—and the Garden of Eden had crumbled to a wilderness of unfriendly sand.

One minute the tree stood there, not a hundred yards distant, and the next minute, mirage-like, it was gone. In its place was an angry tan swirl in the air, and a strange low-pitched whistling that teased Chaudri's ears.

Mirage? he wondered, and then his sunbaked mind shifted back into focus and a different word stabbed horribly at his consciousness.

Shumal!

The deadly scourge of the desert sandstorm!

Instantly alert, the Pakistani's thoughts raced frantically over the available options. Back in the city, the *shumal* was nothing to fear—one simply fled indoors until the raging winds had spent themselves. But out here there was no shelter to be had. And since the wind could carry the suffocating sand in any direction, flight was as likely to be futile as helpful. *More* likely.

Grateful now for the *ghutra*, Chaudri wrapped its long tails across his mouth to keep the choking sand from his throat and lungs. He dug his heels into his camel's flanks and urged it forward, straight toward the spot where he had seen the Tree of Life. If he could find it again, at least be would have something sturdy to hang onto.

And there it was, immediately in front of him! With all his dwindling strength, he pulled back on the length of rope that served him as reins and managed to bring the lumbering animal to a halt. Forgetting the camel master's careful instructions on dismounting, he swung his left leg to the beast's right side and jumped quickly to the sand. He tore the black *agal* that held the *ghutra* in place from his head, figure-eighted it and forced the camel's forehooves into its loops, hobbling the creature to prevent it from wandering away into the storm.

Then he sat down with his back to the tree, settling himself as firmly as possible against it, and squeezed his eyes shut tight. The wind roared furiously around him. Whirling grains of sand stung at the exposed skin of his face and the backs of his hands like a thousand sharpened needles. He thought he could make out the hoarse breathing of the camel through the clamor of the wind, but assumed he was hearing that sound with his imagination, not his ears.

At least he could breathe. The mesh of the *ghutra* was fine enough to filter out the gritty desert sand from the air he drew in with great shuddering frightened gasps.

Merea rabba, he told himself bitterly. *First that miserable ride, and now this.* And today was Friday, supposedly his day of rest, when he could have been back at the police barracks in Juffair, reading a book or chatting with Sikander Malek and the other men from Karachi!

He shifted position irritably, already beginning to feel the soreness in his joints return, and his hand brushed against something hard and smooth and warm, half buried in the sand. More desert driftwood. He lifted the object and held it with both hands in his lap to keep the wind from picking it up and flinging it at him. He could not see it, with the *shumal* raging and his eyes closed, but he traced its bleached surface with his fingertips, comforted by the feel of something firm and unyielding amidst the maelstrom.

It was nearly round—a globe, a skull with the jawbone broken away but the upper row of teeth still in place. The deep eye sockets told him which side was the front. The back of the head was —

It was almost round. And the teeth were much too small.

A camel has teeth the size of a 10-*fils* coin, he remembered, and its head is elongated, not practically spherical.

This was the skull of a human being.

* * * *

"Charming!" exclaimed Dr. Emad Rezk, looking up from his microscope with a glint in his eye and a beatific smile on his oval face. "Perfectly charming. Oh, my fascinating friend, you never fail to bring me the most delightful surprises."

Rezk, an Egyptian, was a professor of science at the Gulf Polytechnic University. He was frequently asked to do lab work for the emirate's Public Security Force, which did not yet have a forensics department of its own, though the Ministry of the Interior had been promising one for several years.

"Human?" Mahboob Chaudri asked the man now.

"Oh, yes," Rezk responded. "Oh, yes, indeed, most definitely human. See for yourself."

As Chaudri bent toward the eyepiece, a spasm of pain clutched cruelly at his lower back. He straightened with a groan.

"Something wrong, my friend?"

The Pakistani smiled weakly. The *shumal* had lasted for almost half an hour, leaving his nut-brown face and hands agonizingly raw. Then had come the endless ride back to civilization, which had been even worse than the trip out to the Tree of Life—though at least the day had become somewhat cooler. When he had finally returned to the barracks in Juffair, he had rubbed a soothing ointment into his tender, wind-burned skin, soaked his aching muscles in a hot tub for an hour, and then gone straight to bed. But this morning he was back on duty, though his body was stiff and sore all over, and the only thing that hurt worse than moving was the torture of sitting or standing still.

"No, no," he lied, "I am quite all right." He was, after all, an officer of the police, and the Security Force's image of impassive strength and dignity must at all cost be maintained. He forced himself to peer at the meaningless jumble of cells displayed in the microscope's field of view, then nodded his head wisely and said, "Yes, I see."

Rezk chuckled. "You are quite all right," he said indulgently, "and you see. Very well, my friend." He grinned mischievously. "Then tell me: what else can you say about the former possessor of this magnificent pericranial specimen, other than the fact that he was human?"

"Ah," said Chaudri sagely, "but that is your specialty, Doctor. I would not want to rob you of your moment of scholarly exposition. And besides, I have not been trained in these matters. I can tell very little, I'm afraid. The skull belongs to a Bedouin, of course, an adult male—that much is obvious. He did not die a natural death. Oh, no: he was murdered. Murdered by strangulation at least 10 years ago. But other than those simple facts I can tell nothing. I depend on you for further enlightenment."

The Egyptian stared at him, dumbfounded. "How—how can you know all that?" he spluttered. "You looked at one preparation only, and at that for but a few seconds! Where did you study forensic medicine, my amazing friend, and why have you never told me that you did?"

Now it was Chaudri's turn to laugh. "I know nothing of forensic medicine," he admitted. "But after five years in Bahrain, I know much of the Arabic way of life. Everything I told you I knew almost as soon as I first discovered the skull, without recourse to your microscopes and preparations."

"But how? Yes, the size of the specimen alone suggests that the victim was an adult, but how do you know he was a Bedouin, a male, and dead for at least 10 years? I can list at least a dozen indications which prove you to be right, but nothing you can have seen without careful chemical testing and a great deal of very specialized knowledge."

"To one who knows a bit about the Arab," Chaudri explained, "this simple skull speaks eloquently. Who but a Bedouin would lie buried beneath the desert sands? A city dweller or a peasant would have a more traditional resting place, in a cemetery in Manama or one of the villages. Only a Bedouin would be left in the desert, and then only if he had died 10 or more years ago, before the government implemented its policy of sedentarization, of settling the various Bedouin clans in villages so that they could be kept track of, controlled, and taxed."

"But how can you say he was murdered—strangled, no less! All we have here is a skull, without a mark of violence on it. And how do you know he was a male?"

"If he had been buried with the usual care and ceremony of a Bedouin funeral, a thousand years of *shumals* would never have uncovered his bones. No, he was buried hastily, without ceremony and too close to the surface of the desert. Why? Because he had been murdered, and his killer wanted to get the body under the sand before the crime was discovered. And if you agree that there was a murder, then it follows that the victim was male and an adult, and that he was strangled, because only a Bedouin would have reason to kill another Bedouin, and a Bedouin would never slay a woman or a child, and when a Bedouin murders he invariably does so by strangulation. As I said, Doctor, it's all quite simple if you only understand the Arab's way of life."

Emad Rezk shook his head in bafflement. "If you already knew all that, my dear Chaudri, then why on earth did you bother coming to me?"

"Because deduction based on a knowledge of the Arab is all well and good," the Pakistani answered, "but police work rests on scientific proof, not confident guesses. I felt certain that my ideas were correct, but I needed your opinion before bringing them up with my superiors."

"Well, I'm afraid that I can't help you as much as you might wish. Yes, the dead man—and it *was* a man—was a Bedouin, perhaps between 30 and 40 years of age at the time of his death, which was at least 15 and possibly as many as 25 years ago. But was he strangled? Was he truly murdered at all? Your deductions sound convincing to me, my friend, but there is no evidence to either confirm or contradict them. Unfortunately, I can tell you nothing more."

"Unfortunately," Mahboob Chaudri scowled, "you have already told me something rather important."

"I have?"

"You have. You've told me that I am likely to be spending a great deal of my time drinking Bedouin coffee over the next few days." He turned to go, then thought better of it and faced his friend Rezk once more. "And I *detest* Bedouin coffee," he complained.

* * * *

Sitting cross-legged on the worn palm-frond matting which covered the floor of the *majlis*, the main living area of Sheikh Mahmood's coral-and-rubble house, Mahboob Chaudri waggled his tiny porcelain cup from side to side to say that he had drunk as much of the cardamom-flavored liquid as he desired. *One more cup,* he thought irritably, his stomach purring with hunger and too much coffee, *and I will float away to sea.*

This was the sixth Bedouin village Chaudri had been to since his session with Emad Rezk the day before. Still sore in every muscle of his body, he had dragged himself down countless narrow alleyways, searching diligently for the identical government-constructed home of each village's sheikh. The sheikh did not "rule" his clan, of course: even though they had been successfully sedentarized, the Bedouins still recognized no power higher than that of each separate individual. The sheikh was, instead, an arbiter, an advisor, a respected figure who exerted considerable influence while avoiding any pretense of actual authority. Still, the sheikh's residence was the logical place for Chaudri to begin his inquiries in each village.

And five times now those inquiries had gone no further. *La,* five sheikhs had told him, after the ritual exchange of formal compliments and the drinking of too many cups of the slightly bitter coffee Chaudri despised, no one of my *qawm* has ever vanished into the desert—not 20 years ago, never. Some have died, of course, and a few of the young have taken jobs in the city or gone away to school. But none have disappeared, none have run away out of anger or sorrow. Our *qawmiya* here, our feeling of unity, is very strong.

This time, though, in this sixth village on Chaudri's tour of the country's Bedouin communities, when the amenities were finally over and the Pakistani posed at last his question, Sheikh Mahmood rocked back on his heels and stroked his white beard thoughtfully.

"Hassan," he said. "It's a long time ago, but yes, it's Hassan you describe. Hassan al-Shama, we called him."

Chaudri had never heard the expression before. "What does it mean, al-Shama?"

The old man smiled. "The city Arabs have always thought of us as lazy wandering gypsies," he said, "traveling only in order to avoid regular work, stealing from the peasants, taking what we can from society and giving back nothing at all. But in truth the Bedouin's life is harsh and always challenging. It takes great skill to survive in the desert, and great courage. During the rainy season, for two months of every year, the desert is Allah's garden. Then we can stay in one place for a while, then our life is less bitter. But for most of the year, we move about because we must. We go where the rain is, since where there is rain there is water to drink and grass for our animals.

"*Shama* is a Bedouin word. It means to watch for flashes of lightning in the distance so as to see where the next rain will fall. So Hassan al-Shama was, for us, Hassan the Watcher. He had marvelous eyes: he knew where the rain would come long before anyone else in the *qawm*. Then we would hurry to the place he had seen and we would stay there until the sun and the wind destroyed the grass brought forth by the rain."

"And you say this Hassan disappeared?"

"Yes." The old sheikh rocked back and forth as he spoke, his voice a crooning murmur. "One afternoon, many years ago, perhaps 10 years before they brought us to this village, Hassan went off alone into the desert to watch. I remember the day very well. It was summer, we had no water at all. We were living off the milk of our camels, and Hassan went off alone to watch. There was a rainstorm that day. It was a miracle, a magnificent downpour at the very spot where we were already camped. By nightfall, there was grass as far as the eye could see. But Hassan did not return. He never returned. His first wife, Aiysha, still waits for him. He will come back when the *qawm* needs him, she thinks. She has been waiting for 20 years."

"And his other wives?"

"He had one other wife, Falila." The sheikh sighed. "It was not a good marriage. That one does not wait for her husband's return: a year after we last saw him, she left the *qawm* with Hassan's younger brother, Ali. They went to live in al-Hidd, near the airport. They are still there, I think. I am told they have a cold store, though I've never been there myself."

"Did you report Hassan's disappearance to the authorities?"

"The authorities," Sheikh Mahmood scoffed. "What have the authorities to do with my *qawm*? We take care of ourselves, we look after our own—we have no need of your laws, your taxes, your authorities. When Hassan the Watcher went off, in the *Aiyamu'l Arab*, the day of the Arab, *we* were the only authorities in the desert—we reported nothing. Today we report, and see what has happened to us."

He waved a feeble hand at the coral walls which surrounded him, their recessed niches filled with the many accoutrements of the settled life. He glared at the wind tower in the corner, at the electric lights above. "We have become weak," he mourned. "We have lost our heritage. The *Aiyamu'l Arab* is at an end."

* * * *

The front door of the house to which Sheikh Mahmood had directed him was wide open. Chaudri stood in the doorway and peered into the gloomy space within. The building—like all of the residences in all of the Bedouin villages he had visited—was built to the same size and general floor plan as the home of the sheikh, but even in the dim sunlight which filtered in through the closed wooden shutters he could see that this home was much more simply furnished than was usual—a plain table bearing a basin and a pitcher of sweet water, a cushioned bench, a chair, *mankur* matting on the floor, a minimum of other odds and ends. The mangrove beams supporting the ceiling were, though attractive, strictly functional. The only decorative touch in the room was the framed photograph on the far wall. Oddly, it was not the standard color portrait of the Emir, but a yellowed newspaper clipping of John F. Kennedy, the American president who had been shot and killed around the time of Hassan's disappearance. He was outdoors, behind a waist-high lectern, in a somber black suit delivering a speech to the great crowd that surrounded him, a broad confident smile on his youthful face.

The face of the woman who sat in the chair by the shuttered window was old, the story of her 50 years in the desert and her decade in this village written across it in tortured lines. She wore a simple red shift, its half sleeves and neckline trimmed with bands of gold, and over it a loose white sleeveless tunic. There were gold bracelets on her wrists and a tiny silver ball affixed to the right side of her nose just above the nostril.

She was sewing the hem of an *abba* with fine black thread, and Chaudri wondered how she could see to work in such poor light. A mangy gray kitten, its enormous ears stiff and pointed like the horns of a devil, caressed her bare foot silently, and the woman absently stroked its fur with her toes. Neither of them gave the slightest sign they were aware of Chaudri's presence in the doorway. He waited there for several minutes, and then he put his fist before his mouth and coughed self-consciously.

The old woman raised her head. "Who is that?" she demanded querulously. "Who's there?"

He took a step forward. "My name is Chaudri," he explained. "I—"

"Chaudri? I don't know any Chaudri. You're not of my *qawm*, are you? Where do you come from? What do you want here?"

What was she babbling about? She could *see* he was not a member of her clan, couldn't she, with his Pakistani features and his Public Security uniform? Unless she was senile, perhaps, or —

Ah, yes, of course. Nothing decorative in the house, except for the single dusty picture which had obviously been hanging there undisturbed, unlooked at, for years. The shutters closed and no artificial lighting, yet the ability to do detailed handwork in the almost darkness of the room. The old woman was blind.

She had lost her sight sometime since the sedentarization of the *qawm*—the photo on the wall told him that she had been able to see for at least part of the time she had lived here—and now he was about to take away from her as well the hope of her husband's return, a hope she had cherished for the past 20 years of her life.

How did one steal a helpless old woman's dream? What words did one use to soften the terrible blow?

"I come from the police," Chaudri said to her tentatively. "I come to speak with you about Hassan."

"Hassan is dead," she replied, with the simple conviction of one who spoke a self-evident truth.

Chaudri was stunned. "But—but Sheikh Mahmood was telling me you believed him still to be alive."

She made an exasperated spitting noise and kicked the scrawny kitten away from her abruptly. With an angry yowl, it bolted through the open doorway and out into the street beyond.

"Sheikh Mahmood is even older than I am," she said. "He is an honest man, and often a wise one, but he sees only what he chooses to see." She touched a hand to her useless eyes. "Even with these, I am not so blind that I cannot tell the difference between reality and a foolish dream."

"I hear no bitterness in your voice," said Chaudri.

"About my eyes, do you mean? Or about my husband? I loved Hassan, and I loved my sight. But there is no God but God, and who am I to question His wisdom?"

There was a serene strength to her which Chaudri had never before experienced in a woman, or in a man either, and he watched with admiration and respect as her nimble fingers worked tight stitches along the fabric of the *abba*. "Tell me about Hassan," he said.

She sighed deeply and set down the cloth, needle, and thread.

"Hassan." The quality of her voice had changed—it no longer fit with the wrinkles etched into her face. It was young and vibrant, the voice of a woman who loved. She thought back across the gulf of years and gathered her memories around her like a warm and comfortable cloak.

"He was not a member of our *qawm* by birth. But when we met in the desert and decided to marry—more than 30 years ago—instead of asking me to leave my family and put on the skin of his clan, he came to us and put on the skin of ours. Ali came with him. Their parents were long dead, there was no other close family, his place was with his brother. Ali was good with the animals—the camels, the sheep, the goats—but Hassan was a watcher. He knew where the rain would fall before anyone else. Some said he didn't need to watch at all, that Allah came to him in the night and told him of His plans for rain."

"And Falila?" Chaudri prompted gently.

A frown flickered across the cracked, pale lips. "Falila was a baby when Hassan and I first met, an infant. Many summers passed and she grew into a complicated child, strong-willed and hot-tempered, but in the end always loyal to the *qawm* and respectful of her elders. She loved Ali even then, I think, but Sheikh Mahmood suggested that it would be good for Hassan to take a second wife, and it was agreed that Falila should be his bride."

Because of her blindness, it was not necessary to look at her while she spoke, and Chaudri's gaze swept the dimly lit room with professional interest. The niches in the walls were mostly empty. A closed door led off to the rest of the simple dwelling. There was an inscription printed across the bottom of the photograph on the wall; the letters were too small for him to make out, but he could see that a few words of Arabic had been handwritten above the typeset line of English text.

"A few more years went by," the woman continued. "Hassan and I grew even closer than we had been before his marriage to Falila. He cared for me with great tenderness. He gave me all I asked him for—all except for one single thing."

"And what was that?"

"He would not treat my sister Falila with the respect she deserved as his wife—and what pained my sister pained me, pained the entire clan."

Chaudri was taken aback. "Sheikh Mahmood did not mention that you were sisters."

The woman's smile revealed a flash of gold at the back of her mouth. "We were married to the same man. That made us sisters."

"Ah. But Hassan favored you."

"He loved me," she said. "And at first he seemed to love Falila, too. But she was still a child when he married her, and his feeling for her faded as she grew into womanhood. The Quran says that a man may take four wives if he so desires, but he must treat them with complete equality. Hassan's only failing was that, where he treated me with kindness and love, he came to treat Falila with nothing more than cold contempt."

Chaudri stood up and moved about the room in a vain attempt to ease the soreness of his muscles. "Why?" he asked. "Why did he hate her?"

Aiysha shrugged her shoulders. "I don't know. She was a good wife to him for a long time after he began to mistreat her. Finally, though, she became resentful. What woman would not?"

There was no way to avoid it any longer. "Might she have become resentful enough to follow him into the desert on the day he disappeared," Chaudri said, "to murder him in anger and bury his body beneath the sand?"

The old woman considered it. "Yes," she said, and there was sudden craftiness in her tone, "she might have."

"Do you think she did?"

The answer, this time, was immediate and forthright: "No."

"No," Chaudri repeated. "But of course she is your sister. If she *did* kill your husband, or if you thought she had, would you tell me?"

She looked straight at him as if she could see him. For a moment, Chaudri glimpsed the spirited nomad she must have been as a girl.

"No," she said again, "I would not. My *qawmiya* runs very deep. And though Falila and Ali have gone to the city, they are still of my clan. My loyalty is to my sisters and brothers, not to you or to the uniform you wear."

Chaudri was standing next to the framed photograph of John F. Kennedy, and as he tried to think of a response he read the line of printing at the base of the picture. It was a quotation he remembered having heard as a child. "Ask not what your country can do for you," the inscription ran, "ask rather what you can do for your country." The word "country" had twice been crossed out, and both times the word "*qawm*" had been written in above it in precise Arabic calligraphy.

Ask rather what you can do for your *qawm*.

The blind woman would not hesitate to withhold information from him. She would not hesitate to *lie* to him if she thought that was needed to protect her clan from danger.

Chaudri did not agree with her attitude. Nor could he approve. But as he looked down at the firm set of her determined old face, he felt in his heart that he understood.

* * * *

A light breeze rippled the emerald waters of the Khawr al-Qulayah as Mahboob Chaudri steered his Land Rover across the narrow causeway to al-Muharraq, second most important of the 33 islands in the Bahraini archipelago. To avoid the twisted labyrinth of the old town, he turned off the Sheikh Salman Road at the end of the causeway, past the bustling shipyard of the *dhow* builders and the Coast Guard barracks and the Abu Mahir fort. He followed the road around the inner curve of the horseshoe-shaped island, along the international airport's perimeter fence and out to al-Hidd.

The cold store was only a few doors down from the al-Khalifa Road police station, within sight of the graceful white minaret of a neighborhood mosque. The shop's windows were piled high with boxes of Omo and Tide, disposable razors in cardboard blister packs, candies and chewing gum and breakfast cereals and bags of British biscuits and American cookies. From a poster advertising cigarettes taped to the inside of the door, a camel regarded him suspiciously with a single narrowed eye. He avoided its steady gaze with a shudder.

The sea breeze that had cooled him while he was driving was gone now, and he was grateful for the air conditioning that greeted him as he entered the store. There were few customers at this time of day: a woman in a black *abba* picking through a bin of tomatoes and muttering irritably to herself as she rejected each of them in turn, two children leafing the pages of an Arabic Sesame Street comic at the magazine rack by the door. A man in a *thobe* was rearranging a shelf of canned goods in the back and a woman in Western clothing sat on a high stool by the electronic cash register, the only modern fixture to be seen. The cashier glanced at him as he crossed to the cooler in the corner, helped himself to a dewy can of Pocari Sweat, ripped off its pop top, and drank deeply, then she went back to her newspaper.

Chaudri waited patiently while the children finished giggling at their magazine, replaced it on the rack, dawdled over the candy display before selecting a brightly colored package of bubble gum and went back out into the street blowing and snapping a series of ever-larger pink bubbles. He waited while the woman in the *abba* finally settled on three small tomatoes and grudgingly paid for them, complaining all the while about their lack of freshness and their price. He drank his Japanese soda and waited until he was alone in the shop with Ali and Falila, the younger brother and second wife of the dead man, Hassan al-Shama. Then he set down his empty can and said the words old Aiysha had said to him but a few hours earlier: "Hassan is dead."

Falila's hands spasmed, ripping her paper cleanly down the middle. Ali dropped a can of fava beans, which knocked over a pile of jam jars, shattering more than one on the cold concrete floor.

A gratifying response, thought Mahboob Chaudri.

* * * *

"Of course he's dead," the woman scowled. The shock of Chaudri's sudden announcement had worn off. "If we hadn't believed him to be dead, we would never have left the *qawm* and begun a new life together. We would have stayed in the desert and waited for him to return." The black kohl that had been applied in a broad band across her eyelids did nothing to conceal the crow's feet at the corners of her eyes. Her powder and lipstick did not disguise the damage time had done to her face. The man in the *thobe* came and stood by her side, with the counter on which customers piled their purchases between them and the Pakistani.

"But why did you believe him dead?" Chaudri wanted to know.

It was Ali who answered, his dark face tight with a blending of concern and anger: "He went away. He was gone for a year. He did not come back. Obviously he was dead. Hassan would never have deserted the *qawm* once he had put on its skin. His *qawmiya* was much too strong."

Chaudri remembered that Aiysha had said almost the same thing about her own sense of loyalty to the clan. "And your *qawmiya*?" he asked, addressing them both. "Why did *you* go away a year after Hassan's disappearance?"

Again it was Ali who spoke. "My brother was not good to Falila," he said. "It saddens me to admit that, but it is true. I was as kind to her as I could be to try to make up at least a little bit for the shame Hassan's behavior brought to her and to the clan. We were close, Falila and I. When Hassan went away, we grew closer. I wanted to marry her, but although the Quran allows a man to take four wives, a woman may have only a single husband. We were certain Hassan must be dead, but our certainty was not enough. In the eyes of the *qawm* my brother still lived, so we could not marry, we could not even allow them to see the love we shared without further disturbing the harmony of the clan." He drew himself up and said proudly, "It was *because* of our *qawmiya* that we came to al-Hidd, so we could live our lives as man and wife without bringing still more shame to our people."

* * * *

Never in Mahboob Chaudri's career had he felt so perplexed. The constant ache in his muscles had dulled by now to a mild discomfort, but his muddled brain was throbbing with the greater pain of confusion.

Hassan had treated Falila badly, that much he knew. Had she killed him for that reason, to free herself from his hatred? Surely not: she had been but a girl at the time. How could she have strangled a full-grown man?

Had Hassan *been* strangled, after all? That conclusion was as yet unproven, was nothing more, really, than the flimsiest of deductions.

Well, then, had Ali committed the murder, to rescue Falila from his brother's grasp? Was Hassan's death the first step in Ali's campaign to win the girl for his own, the girl who already loved him, the girl who he perhaps already loved?

But not only these two had had a motive for following Hassan al-Shama into the desert that day, for robbing him of his life and burying him beneath the sand. Though Hassan had been invaluable to the clan as a watcher, his failure to treat his wives equally, as prescribed by the Holy Quran, had disturbed the effectiveness, the balance, of his *qawm*'s social structure. And to the Bedouins, that balance was all-important: the clan must function smoothly and cooperatively to survive in the unforgiving harshness of the desert. To restore harmony, anyone in the *qawm* might have killed Hassan, even Sheikh Mahmood himself.

Especially Sheikh Mahmood, if it came down to that.

Which of them was guilty? How could he ever answer that question, given the Bedouins' powerful mistrust of the Bahraini government, which had compelled them to give up their nomadic existence—of any government that might challenge their centuries-old autonomy? And, worse, how could he hope to find an answer to this riddle, given the even more powerful stricture of *qawmiya*, the tribal loyalty that made him despair of ever getting the truth out of any of them?

Oh, dearie me, Mahboob Chaudri thought sorrowfully, *my head!*

* * * *

This time, he used the Land Rover to go out into the desert. Beyond the tropospheric scatter stations and the site of Oil Well Number 1, the road ended, but the four-wheel-drive vehicle had been built for the sand, and Chaudri continued on at speed. *The camel may have been the ship of the desert in the good old days*, he thought, *but no more. Today it is this mighty creature which is deserving that title.*

It seemed like no time at all before he reached the Tree of Life, its squat black outline sharp against the burning blue of the sky. He switched off the Land Rover's engine, and an overwhelming silence settled across the desert. From the top of the Jebel ad-Dukhan only a few miles to the north, one could see how small Bahrain truly was. But here, with nothing but a blanket of sand stretching out to the horizon in every direction, the country seemed infinite. Chaudri felt himself no more than the merest speck in the unthinkable vastness of the cosmos.

Why had he come back to this place? To look for more bones, hoping to learn at last the truth of the means of Hassan al-Shama's death? No. The area had been thoroughly searched already—there were no more bones to be found. And besides, he knew, he could feel it in *his* bones, that the man had indeed been strangled.

Had he come, then, expecting the murderer to return to the scene of his crime, as they often did in the detective novels he was fond of reading during his off-duty hours? No. This was reality, not a work of fiction, and it was the Middle East, not the decadent West. And it was 20 years after the fact. There would be no return—not now.

Why, then, was he here, surrounded by emptiness, not a bird in flight, not a clump of scrub brush to be seen, not a sound except the noiseless whisper of the heat?

He had come to visit the Tree of Life, to stand before it and ask it for guidance.

They say that it was God who put you here, he began. He spoke the words in his mind, not aloud, and realized with interest that he was thinking them in Arabic rather than his own native language. He was actually talking to the Tree, he knew then, and not only to himself. *They say that a beautiful garden was built around you, and that you are the Mother of life and death.*

Tell me, then, about the death of Hassan al-Shama. Tell me the truth of what happened here a score of years ago.

And there, alone in the desert, the Tree answered him.

* * * *

Chaudri left his Land Rover and plunged into the maze of narrow streets. He went past dozens of the identical coral houses, their wooden shutters closed against the afternoon's blazing heat, their wind towers pointing like miniature minarets at the sun overhead.

Just outside an open doorway, he stopped. He peered into the room beyond, and, when his eyes at last adjusted to the dimness within, he saw her. She sat cross-legged on the floor, a plump satin pillow on the ground before her. A large round aluminum tray lay on the pillow. There was rice on the tray, and she was cleaning the rice to prepare it for cooking.

Her hands, he noticed then, were very strong.

To the Bedouin, Chaudri thought, loyalty to the clan is all-important. More important, even, than loyalty to a devoted husband. More important even than that.

It had had to be that way, of course, in the days when the nomads had roamed the desert. The life, the harmony, the efficiency of the *qawm* must always be preserved, even at the expense of single individuals within the clan.

Still, it made an incredible motive for murder: to kill a man, not because he treated you badly, but because he treated you better than he did someone else.

Yet the Quran insisted that all a man's wives must be treated equally, and it was a disgrace to violate the Messenger's commands.

Ask not what your qawm *can do for you. Ask rather what you can do for your* qawm. It was a philosophy that applied no longer, now that the

Bedouins had been settled into the relative security of the villages. But 20 years ago, in the *Aiyamu'l Arab*, in the desert, it had been logical and obvious—and right.

In spite of the heat, a sudden chill ran down the Pakistani's spine. He had been five years in Bahrain now, and he was becoming an Arab at last. He did not disturb the old woman at her work. He walked back to his Land Rover and sat there for several minutes, thinking.

Then he turned the key in the ignition and drove away.

AFTERWORD

This is perhaps the most *Arabic* of the Chaudri stories, and it features the most Arabic motive for any of the crimes committed throughout the series. Rereading it now, some 30 years after I wrote it, I'm surprised at how intensely it takes me back to the thoughts and feelings I experienced while I lived in Bahrain.

The details about Bedouin life—about the concept of *qawmiya* and the sedentarization of the tribes—were carefully researched and are accurate. There is some historical evidence to suggest that the original Tree of Life as described in the Old Testament may in fact have been located in what is today Bahrain, but the *Shajarat-al-Hayat*—the tree beneath which Mahboob takes refuge from the desert sandstorm in this story—is apparently only about 400 years old ... and is today a tourist attraction which draws some 50,000 visitors a year. Here is a lovely photograph of it by Harold Laudeus:

All of the camels in Bahrain are (or at least *were* at the time the story was written) the property of the emir, and photographs of JFK are (or were) often found in Bahraini homes. The "cold store" is the Bahraini equivalent of what we would call a 7-Eleven, and Pocari Sweat, as disgusting as the name sounds, is indeed a popular Japanese soft drink.

Egyptian scientist Emad Rezk is named after my Egyptian (now ex) brother-in-law, Mohammed Rezk, and the scene in which he plays Watson to Mahboob's Sherlock Holmes was great fun to write.

In her introduction to the story for the Mid-December 1985 issue of *Ellery Queen's Mystery Magazine*, editor Eleanor Sullivan wrote: "The third in Josh Pachter's appealing new series about Mahboob Ahmed Chaudri, officer on the Bahraini police force, a sensitive man who takes his responsibilities very seriously indeed."

Over the years, some readers have questioned whether or not Mahboob takes his responsibility as a police officer seriously enough at the end of the tale.

I think he does.

THE QATAR CAUSEWAY

Sinterklaas, kapoentje,
Gooi wat in m'n schoentje!
Gooi wat in m'n laarsje!
Dank je, Sinterklaasje!

    The tall, thin man in the long red robe and cotton beard was circled by a ring of gaily dressed children who sang and giggled as they skipped around him hand in hand. His merry eyes sparkled behind the small round lenses of his wire-rimmed spectacles, his bishop's mitre sat snugly on his head, his golden staff glittered cheerfully in the bright fluorescent lighting of the mess room. Outside the ring of children stood half a dozen gangly youths in gaudy pantaloons and floppy felt hats, their faces glistening with coal-black greasepaint, their lips daubed a rich crimson. Each of them held a bulky burlap sack in his ebony hands.
    The bearded figure in the robe was not the only adult present. The parents of the dancers were there, too, clustered in groups of three and four around the walls of the room, sipping strong coffee and watching their sons and daughters enjoy the party. And off in a corner stood a small-framed Pakistani in the olive-green uniform of Bahrain's Public Security Force, listening earnestly to the explanations of the stocky business-suited man at his side.
    The stocky man in the business suit was not a businessman. He was Roelof Smit, a detective lieutenant with the Amsterdam police, and he was visiting Bahrain to observe the workings of the emirate's law-enforcement machinery. Since the abortive coup attempt in 1978, fully two-thirds of the island's security troops were Pakistanis, fiercely loyal to the Arab government that employed them. Mahboob Chaudri, originally from Karachi, was the *mahsool* who had been assigned to work with the Dutchman during the two weeks of his stay.
    Today was December 5th, Sinterklaas, and Smit had brought his host out to al-Qalat—the housing compound of the Dutch construction company Nederbild—for the festivities.
    "What are they singing?" asked Chaudri, his English careful and lightly accented.

Smit's walrus mustache shivered with pleasure. "It's a simple little song," he chuckled, "and typical of the spirit of the holiday. Let's see if I can translate it for you: *Sinterklaas, you little elf*—because, you see, the *tje* or *je* at the end of every line is our way of saying little or cute—*Sinterklaas, you little elf, leave some goodies on my shelf! Leave some candy in my shoe. Thank you, Sinterklaas, thank* you! That's not a literal translation, you understand, but it gives you the general idea of the thing—and at least it rhymes."

"And, lieutenant, is it typical of the spirit of the holiday?"

The Dutchman laughed again. "In most Western countries, Christmas has become so commercialized that it's hard to remember its original religious significance. Well, we Hollanders have our spiritual side, like everyone else, and the spiritualist in us wants to keep Christmas a holy day. But we're a practical people, too, and our practical side tells us that we can't just ignore the commercial aspects of the Christmas season. So we invented Sinterklaas. This way, we can stay quietly religious on *Kerstmis*—in fact, we've even added on a second Christmas Day, December 26th—because we've gotten all the shopping and gift-giving out of our systems three weeks earlier, on the 5th, on Sinterklaas. Like the American Santa Claus, our Christmas Man—the *Kerstman*—is fat and jolly. Sinterklaas is also jolly, but he's much more, ah, *netjes*. 'Distinguished,' that's the word. After all, he is a saint, you know—Sint Nicolaas, which is where the names Sinterklaas and Santa Claus both come from. Every year he travels all the way to Holland from Spain, by steamboat, with his band of helpers—the *Zwarte Piets*, or Black Peters. Foreigners sometimes misunderstand, and object to the *Piets*. But they're helpers, not slaves, and there's really nothing racist about them. Besides, the children love them, and I don't know what would happen if we ever tried to get rid of them!"

The children finished their song to loud applause, with Chaudri and Smit joining in wholeheartedly, then whirled away from Saint Nicholas to face the crowd of Black Peters. Burlap sacks were flung wide, black hands dug deep, and the boys and girls exploded with cries of *"Piet! Piet!"* as the saint's assistants showered them with fistfuls of candy and tiny ginger cookies.

"*Strooigoed* and *pepernoten*," Roelof Smit informed his companion—and then a real explosion sounded from somewhere outside, and every window in the mess hall shattered inward in a horror of screams and flying glass.

* * * *

Sobbing children, panic-stricken adults, the floor littered with a mosaic of candy and glass, the dull reverberation of the blast shaking the walls and deafening the ears.

When at last the first shock faded, Sinterklaas ripped off his beard and mitre and flung away his staff and raced out the back door of the building. Chaudri and Smit were close behind him, their feet slipping on shards of glass and sticking on gooey candy.

At the door, Chaudri grabbed a bewildered father by the front of his shirt. "Sir!" he shouted into the vacant face. "Is there a hospital here on the compound?"

There was no reaction.

"A hospital! A doctor! Some of these children have been hurt! Is there anyone here to help them?" Chaudri shook the man violently until at last he blinked his eyes and nodded.

"A hospital," he repeated flatly. "Yes." A thin line of blood trickled from the corner of his mouth, and he licked it away absently.

"Get someone here to look after these people!" Chaudri cried, releasing him. "Hurry!"

Suddenly awakening, the man muttered, "*Ja, natuurlijk!*" and jumped for a telephone.

With a last look back at the confusion in the room, Chaudri and Smit went out the door.

* * * *

Sinterklaas was standing on the narrow strip of rocky beach that lay between the mess hall and the blue-green iridescence of the gulf. A half-mile to the north, the skeleton of a bridge under construction reached across the water to a small islet not far offshore. A dense cloud of gray smoke billowed up from the point where the bridge met the islet, staining the pale blue of the sky and spreading evilly.

"*Mijn God,*" Sinterklaas whispered, and when Chaudri looked at him, he saw tears in the man's tired eyes. "*O, mijn hemel.*"

"What is it?" he asked. "What's happened?"

"My bridge," Sinterklaas replied. "They've blown it up."

"*They*? Who are *they*?"

The man shook his head. "I don't know. He. She. They. Someone. It doesn't matter who. They've destroyed my bridge."

"What do you mean, *your* bridge?"

At last the man turned towards him. "Come with me," he said, recognizing Chaudri's uniform, "and I'll tell you."

"Where are you going?"

The man in the red robe pointed a trembling finger toward the offshore islet, where heavy gray smoke was draped across the sky like a shroud. "Out there," he said, and his voice was dull and dead.

* * * *

"My name, if you can believe it," the man introduced himself, "is Nicolaas. Nicolaas Sjollema. When I was a boy, the other children used to call me Sinterklaas. I always wanted to play the part for real, and today—today was my first chance."

They were in Sjollema's car, a Japanese import with right-hand drive, barreling along a rough dirt track toward the company harbor. Chaudri, in the passenger seat on the left, found himself automatically trying to brake and steer. In the back, Roelof Smit clenched his teeth on the stem of an ornate meerschaum pipe and jounced.

"I'm the foreman on this phase of the construction project," Sjollema went on. He had taken off his robe, revealing faded denims and a chambray work shirt. "I didn't design it and I'm not paying for it, but I'm in charge of building it. That's why I call it *my* bridge. I've been with the project for three years now—well, almost three years—and I feel as if it's become my child, my son."

"An expensive son to raise," remarked Smit from the rear.

Sjollema smiled grimly. "The second most expensive stretch of highway in the world," he agreed. "Concrete piles sunk into the sea floor, with four-lane slabs of roadbed the length of football fields laid on top of them. About 32 kilometers long from here to Qatar, at a total construction cost of more than half a billion dollars: that's over fifteen thousand dollars a meter. An expensive child, *inderdaad*."

Chaudri's right foot pumped the spot where the brake pedal should have been as the car squealed to a stop inches from a modern pier lined with launches and a long, flat-bedded barge. The only craft showing any sign of life was an old wooden fishing *dhow*, its mast horizontal, its canvas sail spread out as a sunscreen. A powerfully built Arab in a grimy, once-white *thobe*, his *ghutra* wrapped carelessly about his head, was standing in the stern, shaded by the sail overhead and cutting a squid into bait-sized pieces. In the prow a young boy—naked except for worn cut-off shorts, his skin charred black by the sun—sat hunched over a spool of nylon, his fingers moving swiftly as he tied a heavy barbed hook to the free end of the line. Neither of them paid the slightest attention to the dark smoke that still rose from the offshore islet. To see them at work—stolid, emotionless, completely absorbed in their tasks—it was hard to remember that, not 15 minutes earlier, not a thousand meters away, the world had been rocked by a devastating blast. They were living in their own dimension, in another century, where all that mattered was the frantic pull of a 10-pound *hamour* as it strained to loosen the killing barb from its cheek.

"We need to go out there, to Umm as Hawwak," Sjollema told the fisherman, who raised his head slowly and regarded them without interest.

"*La, la,*" the Arab said tonelessly, not singing but refusing. "No, no."

"Police business." Chaudri's Arabic was crisp. "Let's go."

The fisherman shrugged his shoulders and, as Chaudri and the two Dutchmen climbed aboard, put his knife aside and moved to his vessel's primitive controls.

Moments later the engine was growling. The weathered deck boards trembled beneath their feet as the boat pulled ponderously away from the dock.

"At least there's no one working out there today," Sjollema sighed. "I don't want to think about what would have happened if...."

He left the sentence unfinished.

"You shut down construction for Sinterklaas?" asked Smit.

"Oh, no, not that. But this is Friday, the Muslim day of rest. We employ very few Arabs, but we observe their workweek—like all foreign companies in Bahrain. Takes a while for our people to get used to, but it seems the simplest way to schedule in the long run."

The water was made of emeralds, frosted with the pearly turbulence of the *dhow*'s wake and the reflected glitter of the late afternoon sun. Halfway across to Umm as Hawwak, the fisherman's son stabbed a finger to port and cried, "*Uthor!* Look!"

Chaudri spun around in time to see a gunmetal gray tailfin wave a greeting at them and disappear beneath the surface of the sea. "Dolphin," he said. "Do you have them in your country, too?"

Roelof Smit shook his head. "Not like that. Only in the seaquarium, trained to jump through hoops and balance beach balls on their noses."

The *dhow*'s engine stuttered and stopped. For a moment, as they glided the last few meters to the islet's wooden mooring, silence engulfed them. Then they could hear the lapping of waves on the shore and the sad crackle of brush fires dying.

Chaudri ordered the fisherman to wait, and they left the boat for the desolate islet. There was rubble everywhere, blackened clumps of shattered concrete, the ruins of what must have been supply sheds and temporary office space, machinery twisted beyond recognition.

What little vegetation Umm as Hawwak had supported was cinders now; scattered tongues of flame licked hungrily at the last remaining morsels of green. Here and there were geckos—the small, scurrying lizards which the Arabs claimed brought luck to the home. Many of them were missing their tails or heads or limbs; all of them were dead.

"Who could have had a motive for doing this?" Roelof Smit was numb with the horror of the scene.

His countryman shook his head despondently. "I don't know," he said. "It doesn't make any sense. If it had been the Saudi Causeway, which another company is building on the other side of the country, I could understand it. That's a controversial project, and there's been a lot of opposition to it. But if there's anything at all the people of Bahrain are in agreement on, it's that this bridge across to Qatar is a good thing. Trade will be easier in both directions, and the security of both countries will be strengthened. I—"

Sjollema turned away from them and walked off. Roelof Smit hesitated for a moment, then went after him, leaving Chaudri alone in the rubble.

He watched them go, watched Smit catch up to the other man and put a hand to his elbow, watched them reboard the *dhow* and sit side by side in its stern, Sjollema with his head in his hands and Smit with an arm around the foreman's shoulder.

The sea birds were beginning to return to the islet, squawking angrily at the invasion of their privacy. The hum of a motor launch's powerful engine grew louder; by now, several craft were setting out towards Umm as Hawwak from the dock on the mainland.

Mahboob Chaudri hunkered down on the ground, selected a small chunk of scorched concrete from the debris at his feet, and passed it slowly from hand to hand. *This morning a bridge stood here*, he thought, *and now I sit here with its ruined remnants in my hand. Tomorrow the Dutchmen will go back to work, and they will build the bridge again.*

It is a wheel, he decided. *An ever-spinning wheel of life and death.*

He rose, slipped the fragment of concrete into his pocket as a reminder of the day's events, and stepped carefully through the rubble towards the waiting *dhow*.

* * * *

The Bahraini headquarters of Nederbild BV occupied the fifth and sixth floors of a concrete and glass tower in the al-Khalifa Road, in the center of Manama's business district. When Mahboob Chaudri and Roelof Smit stepped off the elevator into the sixth-floor reception area at eight o'clock the next morning, the atmosphere of tension that washed over them was even more noticeable than the chill of the air conditioning.

The blond receptionist was pretty, Chaudri supposed, if you liked European women, but he found her neckline and the tightness of her sweater immodest. She looked shocked when he asked for the firm's managing director and assured them that Mr. Hofstra was much too busy to see them. When Smit explained the purpose of their visit to her in rapid Dutch, though—the only words Chaudri could make out were *bom* and *explosie*—she frowned nervously and ushered them along a carpeted corridor to the executive suite. Her tailored tan skirt ended an inch above her knees, and she wore spiked high heels that accented the firmness of her calves.

Shameful, Mahboob Chaudri thought as they followed her. His own dear wife Shazia would be ashamed to be seen in such garments. He would never understand these Western women, he knew, never.

Hendrik Hofstra's office was a large, plush room with a picture window running the length of one wall and looking out over the *suq*. A second wall was covered with an artist's rendering of the causeway, sketched in bold, confident strokes that contrasted starkly with the smoldering reality of the scene at Umm as Hawwak. A scale model of the bridge stood on a table in the center of the room, complete with tiny vehicles frozen in mid-transit. Hofstra's oversized desk was in a corner by the window, cluttered with papers and books and rolls of blueprints; on the wall behind it were half a dozen framed photographs of a towheaded child of six or seven, sometimes alone and sometimes with a rather plain, large-boned woman who could only be the boy's mother.

Hofstra himself was a middle-aged bantam rooster in a badly cut gray suit, his tie pulled loose and his collar button undone. What he lacked in stature, though, he made up for in temper.

"Hofstra," he introduced himself abruptly. He offered them neither a handshake nor a seat. "I've got almost 200 meters of downed roadway to rebuild, gentlemen, and I need to get that done in about one week and without spending a *stuiver* if I want to keep this project on schedule and under budget. What do you want?"

"Information, sir," Chaudri began. "About the bombing. I am Mahboob Chaudri, and this is Lieutenant Smit of the Amsterdam police."

"The *Amsterdam* police?" Hofstra roared. "Listen here, Mr. Tawdry, or whatever your name is: I've got a 25-man security team out there on Umm as Hawwak right now, turning that little islet upside down. They don't need any help from you, and they *potverdorie* don't need any help from the Amsterdam police!"

"Lieutenant Smit is here only as an observer, sir," said Chaudri implacably, "and as for me, when the crime of industrial sabotage is committed on Bahraini soil, our Public Security Force is charged with conducting a complete investigation of its own. As I was on the scene at the time of the explosion, my superiors have assigned me to the case."

"The case," Hofstra fumed. It was clear that he realized he was in the wrong, and equally clear that he was unhappy about it. "All right, then. Ask your questions."

"Our explosives experts were on the islet within an hour of the blast yesterday afternoon. They report having found traces of at least nine separate charges and possibly more, spaced 10 to 20 meters apart and simultaneously detonated by a single timing mechanism which was put in place beneath the roadway no more than 24 hours before the explosion. Several indications lead to the conclusion that the charges and timer were set by a single individual."

"I got that information from my own people last night, Mr. Tawdry, now—"

"The name is Chaudri, sir. Excuse me."

"Mr. Chaudri, then. Now, what do you want?"

Chaudri pulled a notebook and a pen from the pocket of his uniform shirt. "I would like to know who had access to Umm as Hawwak during the 24 hours that preceded the blast, Mr. Hofstra. I would like to know who had the opportunity to set those charges."

"*Getverdemme.*" Hofstra ran a hand through his close-cropped graying hair. "The islet was not guarded, Mr. Chaudri. Night before last, any *uilskuiken* with a boat could have gone out there completely unobserved."

"A half-billion dollar project and you leave it unguarded?" Smit was incredulous.

"*Left* it unguarded. We won't make that mistake again."

"But you made it once," the Dutch policeman observed.

Hofstra answered through clenched teeth. "Yes, Lieutenant Smit, we made that mistake once. This is Bahrain, Lieutenant, not the Zeedijk in Amsterdam. We were led to believe that the local police"—he glared angrily at Chaudri—"had created a climate of order here where we wouldn't need to worry about theft or sabotage. Do you have any further questions?"

"You suggested that the charges could have been set on the evening of the 4th of December," said Mahboob Chaudri, "or in the early morning hours of the 5th. What about the afternoon of the 4th, a full day ahead of the explosion?"

"We had a crew working out there from 8 AM until 6 PM. Anyone crawling around setting explosives would have been seen."

"But what about the crew themselves? Could one of them have done it?"

"How would I know? I wasn't there, I was here. Ask Nick Sjollema that kind of question. It's his job to know who's where at all times. Anything else?"

Chaudri looked up from his notebook. "One possibility, Mr. Hofstra, is that the bridge was blown up by a former employee, someone nursing a grudge against Nederbild. Have any of your people been let go recently?"

The director glanced impatiently at his watch. "Mr. Chaudri," he said slowly. "Nederbild BV has over 1200 employees in Bahrain, from cleaning ladies through senior executives here in this building, from gate guards and maintenance men to a 24-hour child-care center at the al-Qarat housing compound, and from construction workers all the way up to Nicolaas Sjollema on site. I direct the entire operation from this office, yes, but I do not keep my fingers on the names and work histories of all 1200 of those employees. You can take that question down to the fifth floor, where you will find our Personnel department. Do you have anything else you would like to ask *me*, Mr. Chaudri?"

"Yes, sir," the Pakistani said promptly, "I do. I didn't notice you at the Sinterklaas party yesterday. Why weren't you there?"

For the first time, the fight drained out of Hofstra's face, leaving him looking tired and old. "I have no children, Mr. Chaudri. There was no reason for me to be there."

Chaudri glanced quickly at the framed pictures on the wall. "No children?" he mused. "Then—"

"My son," said Hofstra, his voice hoarse. "Three weeks ago—20 days ago—my son Pieter was playing on the beach, behind our house at al-Qarat. His mother was in a deck chair, knitting, and Pieter strayed away from her while she was absorbed in her work. When she noticed he had gone, she went to look for him. She found him in—in the water. He was dead, Mr. Chaudri. He had drowned."

* * * *

Down on the fifth floor, as they were heading for the Personnel office, Chaudri and Smit met Nicolaas Sjollema coming out of Purchasing. He looked haggard and harried, but his drawn face lit up when he saw them.

"I've been wondering how to reach you," he greeted them. "I thought you'd like to know about the people at the party. I checked with the compound hospital after I dropped you yesterday, and then again later on last night, and there were no serious injuries at all. Minor cuts from the flying glass, several of the adults who were closest to the windows required some stitches, a few of the children were pretty badly shaken up—but that was the worst of it. Everyone was home in time for dinner, *Godzijdank*."

"Indeed, that is good news," Chaudri grinned. "And you've saved us a trip out to Umm as Hawwak. We need to ask you a question about your crew, if you can spare us another minute."

"Yes, of course. They're sweating this morning, I can tell you that: I've got every laborer on the payroll out there cleaning up the islet today, loading rubble onto company barges and dumping it out in the Gulf. If they can finish up by tonight, we'll be able to start right in on the reconstruction. That's why I'm in town now, trying to rush-order enough supplies and tools to get us rolling again." Sjollema seemed about to go on, but changed his mind. "You don't need to hear about my problems," he said. "What was it you wanted to ask me?"

"Your crew," said Chaudri. "Could one of your men have placed the explosives that blew up the causeway during the afternoon of December 4th, during working hours, without being observed? He would have needed an hour or more for the job."

"No." Sjollema's answer was immediate and definite. "Impossible. I was on site all day, running our standard weekly inspection. I would have seen him."

"*U bent er absoluut zeker van?*" Roelof Smit put in.

The foreman answered in English for Chaudri's benefit: "Yes, Lieutenant, I'm positive. Those charges were not set during working hours on Thursday. It had to have been done after we'd all left for the day, after six. I'd swear to that in court."

* * * *

Nederbild's personnel manager was a severe woman in her mid-40s, dressed simply in a long black skirt and plain white blouse. She wore her hair frizzed in that strange style that never lasted more than a few months but was called—for some reason which was not clear to Mahboob Chaudri—"permanent." A pair of eyeglasses was suspended around her neck by a thin silver chain; when the two policemen approached her, she put them on and eyed them carefully. There was a clipboard in her left hand.

"Gentlemen," she said. "I am Annemieke Stutje. I manage this office. You are the police. You want to know the names of Nederbild employees who have recently been fired." It was a statement, not a question, and it took them by surprise.

"You've just spoken with Mr. Hofstra?" Chaudri guessed.

"I have not."

"Then how did you—"

"How did I know what you want?" She put a forefinger to the bridge of her spectacles and pushed them a millimeter higher. "I am not a fool, gentlemen. Someone blew up the Qatar Causeway yesterday afternoon. Perhaps it was a disgruntled former employee. I expected a representative of the police to call on me this morning, and here you are. I have already gone through my files for the information you need."

She riffled through the pages on her clipboard and selected one of them, a half sheet of yellow flimsy. "Yes, I have it here. Within the last 30 days, only two of our employees have been dismissed. On November 26th, a Korean laborer named Kim Lee Kwan was fired for attempting to steal sweet water from the Umm as Hawwak site."

"He was fired for stealing water?" Smit looked amazed.

Mevrouw Stutje adjusted her glasses again and peered at him. "You are new to Bahrain," she decided. "As I said, Mr. Kim was fired for stealing sweet water, which is pure spring water and the only water in this country that is fit to drink. It is used on site for mixing concrete, and Mr. Kim was caught trying to sneak a large jug of it back to his barracks. Sweet water is rather expensive here, and neither Nederbild BV nor the Bahraini government is prone to tolerate thievery: Mr. Kim's visa was immediately revoked, and he was on a plane to Seoul that same evening. I checked with the authorities at the Immigration and Passports Directorate earlier this morning, and he has not returned to Bahrain."

"And the second former employee?" Chaudri asked, scribbling furiously in his notebook.

"Ebezer Kwaja," the woman read, "Indian, employed as a clerk in our Purchasing office until his dismissal four days ago, on December 2nd. He is still in the emirate, working at the Central Market. He has a cousin who sells fruits and vegetables there, and who took over sponsorship of Kwaja when we let the man go."

Chaudri looked up. Annemieke Stutje had omitted something, which seemed out of line with her usual brisk efficiency.

"Why was Kwaja fired?" he asked.

She hugged her clipboard to her chest. "I don't know," she admitted, plainly troubled. "I *should* know, but I don't. No explanation was given. That is unusual for Nederbild BV."

"Whose decision was it to get rid of him?"

She pulled her spectacles down to the tip of her nose and appraised him silently over the rims. At last she spoke. "The order came down from the sixth floor," she said. "From Mr. Hofstra personally."

* * * *

Manama's Central Market is a huge gray barn that sits just outside the western edge of the *suq* between the Naim Hospital and the Budaiya roundabout, within sight of the Gulf. It is an ugly, windowless, characterless structure, whose metal walls trap the stifling heat all summer and the odors of meat and fish the year round. Shopping in the tangled maze of the old produce *suq* had been an adventure, but shopping at the new Central Market was a chore.

When they entered the vast fruit and vegetable hall, Roelof Smit was overwhelmed by the enormity of it. It was as if a half dozen copies of Amsterdam's outdoor Albert Cuypmarkt had been laid side by side, with four drab walls and a high ceiling thrown up around them.

They were instantly surrounded by a gaggle of grinning Indian and Pakistani boys with wheelbarrows, who followed closely behind them, eager to carry their purchases for a few hundred *fils*.

But Smit and Chaudri walked down the seemingly endless rows of merchants—all males, from young boys in blue jeans to toothless old men in threadbare *thobes*, each sitting patiently on a tall stool, surrounded by his mountain of goods —without buying. They were not looking for tomatoes or eggplants or cabbages from Jordan, for cucumbers or lettuce or sweet peppers from Cyprus, for hot peppers or okra from India, for onions from Pakistan or cauliflowers from Australia or potatoes from Egypt or garlic from Thailand, for bananas, pears, oranges, mangoes, guavas, kiwis, or African lemons the size of grapefruit. They were not looking for local produce, either, or for an infinity of burlap sacks overflowing with peas, rice, raisins, flour, lentils, fava beans, pumpkin seeds, peanuts, pistachios, walnuts, almonds, chickpeas, red peppers, kidney beans, popcorn, or shredded coconut.

They were looking for Ebezer Kwaja, and at last they found him. His cousin had allowed him a brief rest period, and he was sitting on a pale blue wooden bench along the north wall of the cavernous building, holding a small glass of steaming tea in both hands and watching the tide of buyers and sellers and wheelbarrow boys flow by.

"Mr. Ebezer Kwaja?" Chaudri approached him.

The man eyed them curiously. He wore a satiny long-sleeved shirt in a loud floral pattern and navy blue slacks with gray pinstripes, tightly cut but flaring widely at the ankles. His deep brown forehead glistened with perspiration; his dark hair was styled but greasy.

"Most certainly," he said. "If you are looking for Mr. Ebezer Kwaja, then I am most certainly the Mr. Ebezer Kwaja you are looking for." He raised his glass of tea to his lips and blew on it, then lowered it untasted. "But why, I am asking myself, are you looking for Mr. Ebezer Kwaja at all?"

Mahboob Chaudri was not a tall man, but standing over the seated Kwaja in his immaculate uniform, with his gun on his hip and his black-peaked cap and the military braid on his shoulder, he was an impressive figure. "Until recently," he said, "you were employed as a purchasing clerk at the Nederbild headquarters in the al-Khalifa Road. Four days ago, on December 2nd, you were fired. Why?"

The Indian's jet black eyes gleamed. "Ah," he said, nodding his head sagely, "I am waiting for this very question to be asked. I am waiting every day to be asked why big man from the distant Netherlands is dismissing humble Mr. Ebezer Kwaja from his post. And now, at last, you have come." He paused for a sip of his tea, then looked up at them with a broad smile on his face. "Big man is dismissing Mr. Kwaja," he continued, "because Mr. Kwaja is knowing the truth. Yes, indeed, Mr. Kwaja is knowing too much truth."

"Too much truth about what?" Chaudri asked patiently, amused by the man's air of self-importance.

"Too much truth about his baby," Kwaja announced. "Too much truth about the—"

A muffled report sounded from somewhere behind them, and the look of pride on the Indian's face warped into a mask of shock and pain. The glass of tea dropped from his hands and shattered on the concrete floor. He slumped back against the pale blue bench and clawed weakly at his chest, where a crimson blossom grew quickly among the flowers of his shirt.

"Water!" he gasped, and his clear black eyes were glassy now, and filled with tears. "Water!"

A minute later, someone came forward with a paper cup of water for him, but by then it was too late.

* * * *

"*Jeetje mina!*" Roelof Smit wheezed huskily. "This is *hot!*"

They were sitting in a curtained booth at the Star of Paradise, a small Pakistani restaurant not far from the police barracks in Juffair. Mahboob Chaudri was enjoying a large order of brain masala, but the Dutchman was having trouble with his bowl of beef rogan josh.

Smit filled a tumbler from the metal pitcher in the center of the table, and drained it in one noisy swallow. "I don't understand how you can eat this *spul*," he complained. "*'s Niet te geloven!*"

"I am glad you took my advice and ordered your dinner mildly seasoned," Chaudri chuckled. "If you had gone ahead and asked for it spicy, I'm afraid I would have had to carry you back to your hotel. Here, let me pour you some more sweet water."

Smit took another long swallow and wiped the back of his hand across his bushy mustache. "Why *sweet* water?" he wanted to know. "It tastes like ordinary drinking water to me."

"The word 'Bahrain' is Arabic for 'two seas,'" Chaudri explained, "which is a reference to the Gulf on the one hand and the fresh-water springs that lie beneath the island on the other. Compared to the brackish salt water of the Gulf, the spring water is sweet indeed."

"And expensive, like the Stutje woman said?"

"Oh, dearie me, yes. In fact, until the last round of increases in the price of oil, the service stations here in the emirate would wash the windows of your car with gasoline because that was cheaper than using sweet water." He ripped a large piece of bread from his bubbly round chapati and sopped up curried gravy from his plate. "You're not eating, Lieutenant."

"I've had enough," Smit sighed, pushing his plate away and shaking his head sadly. "Anyway, I don't want to eat, I want to talk."

"You talk," mumbled Chaudri around a mouthful of brains, "and I will eat for both of us."

The Dutchman settled back in his chair. "All right," he said, "I'll talk." He leaned forward, elbows on the table and chin cupped in his hands. "We're dealing here with four separate incidents: the drowning of Hendrik Hofstra's son, the dismissal of Ebezer Kwaja, the explosion at Umm as Hawwak, and Kwaja's murder. Each of these incidents gives rise to one or more questions. Was the death of Hofstra's child an accident, for example, as Hofstra himself told us—or was it something else? Was Kwaja really fired because of what he knew about the drowning—as he told us—or, if the boy's death was accidental, was there some other reason? Who blew up the Qatar Causeway, and why? And, again, why and by whom was Ebezer Kwaja killed?"

Mahboob Chaudri nodded attentively, but his eyes never left his plate.

"Finally," Smit pressed on, "what relationships exist between these various events, if any? Was Kwaja fired because of what he knew about the drowning—and, more important, was he killed to keep him from passing that knowledge on to us? Did Kwaja take revenge for his dismissal by blowing up the bridge, or was the explosion nothing at all to do with him? Were the blast and the drowning connected, or the blast and the murder—and, if so, how?"

Chaudri set down his knife and fork and poured himself a glass of water.

"We need to talk with Hofstra again," Smit suggested. "We need to know his explanation of the firing of Ebezer Kwaja, and why he sent us down to Personnel instead of telling us about it himself, and where he was this afternoon when the Indian was shot. We need to know more about young Pieter's death, too—perhaps a conversation with Mrs. Hofstra would be worthwhile. And we need to find out who might have had a motive for setting those explosives. What do you think our next move should be, *mahsool*?"

Chaudri said nothing. He was staring, transfixed, at the glass of water in his hands.

"*Mahsool*?" said Smit, more loudly. "*Mahsool*?"

Startled, Chaudri looked up. "Oh, Lieutenant," he said. "I'm sorry. I was just thinking."

"About what?"

"About what?" he repeated slowly. "How strange, Lieutenant. That is exactly what I asked Ebezer Kwaja a moment before he was shot." He shook his head and took a small sip of water. "I was thinking about a book I have been reading to practice my English, a book of the many adventures of your great European detective, Mr. Sherlock Holmes. 'You *see*, my dear Watson,' Mr. Holmes chastised his friend in one of the stories, 'but you do not *observe*.' And now I am chastising myself. Sometimes, my dear Lieutenant, it seems that I *hear*—but I do not *listen*." A dazzling smile suddenly illuminated the nut-brown face. "But what was it you were asking me while my thoughts were far away in Victorian England?"

"Our next move," the Dutchman supplied. "What do you think our next move should be?"

"Aha!" said Mahboob Chaudri. "Our next move, I think, should be to order some khulfi for dessert. It is a combination of vanilla ice cream and spaghetti and you will almost certainly hate it, but it is very typical of my country and I would like for you to try it."

"You're avoiding my question. I mean, what's our next move about the case?"

Chaudri beckoned to a white-jacketed waiter. "Ah, yes," he said indulgently, "the case. Well, my friend, there's nothing more we can do tonight. Tomorrow morning, when the university opens, we have a delivery to make, and then we shall see what develops."

* * * *

"We haven't got a forensics laboratory of our own yet," Chaudri explained as he steered the dusty blue Public Security jeep into the main parking lot of Gulf Polytechnic's Isa Town campus. "So when we need lab work done, we bring it out here to one of the professors. Usually they are able to help us. *Insh'Allah*," he added automatically.

"That's not the first time I've heard that word," said Smit, swinging out of the vehicle and following Chaudri up a covered walkway towards the science department's modern building. "What does it mean?"

"*Insh'Allah*?" Chaudri smiled. "It is the Arab's constant prayer. 'Tomorrow it will be cooler, *insh'Allah*.' 'Your car will be fixed by this afternoon, *insh'Allah*.' 'Their marriage will be a happy one, *insh'Allah*.' It means: if Allah is willing. If Allah is willing, anything can happen."

"We might even solve this case," the Dutchman grimaced.

"*Insh'Allah*," laughed Mahboob Chaudri.

They found Professor Emad Rezk in his classroom, going over his notes for the day's first lecture. Rezk, an Egyptian, had been with Gulf Polytechnic since the establishment of the school several years earlier. He was a talented chemist and had held a tenured position at the University of Cairo, but the offer of a substantially higher salary, a house, a car, and complete academic freedom had lured him—along with a large number of his colleagues—to the Gulf. Though his thoughts were always perfectly organized, Rezk's exterior was usually disheveled. His white lab coat showed acid burns in various places, his fingers were permanently yellowed from exposure to caustic chemicals.

"Mahboob Chaudri!" he exclaimed with delight as they edged between two rows of students' desks. "And a friend! How charming it is to see you both!"

Chaudri introduced Roelof Smit to the Egyptian, then pulled a small package wrapped in brown paper from his pocket. He unwrapped it carefully, to reveal the chunk of rubble he had taken away from Umm as Hawwak two days before. "How soon can you analyze this for me, Professor? It is, I believe, quite important."

Rezk took the rock from Chaudri's hand and squinted at it. "Concrete," he said simply. "Is that soon enough for you, my impatient friend?"

Chaudri rolled his eyes comically.

The professor pushed back the right sleeve of his lab coat and checked his watch. "I have a class in 15 minutes," he said. "Second-year students. Hopeless cases, most of them, but they are trying. *Very* trying, much of the time, I'm afraid. They visit with me for one hour. When they leave, I will have time to apply myself to your intriguingly important mixture of cement, mineral aggregate, and dihydrogen monoxide. What, if I may ask, am I to analyze it *for*?"

"If I'm right," said Mahboob Chaudri cryptically, "you will know it when you see it. May I phone you in, say, two hours?"

* * * *

"Back to Personnel?" Roelof Smit ventured, as they stepped off the elevator at the fifth floor of the tower in the al-Khalifa Road.

"Not this time," said Chaudri. "This time we are here to pay a call on the Purchasing department, where the late Mr. Ebezer Kwaja was employed as a clerk."

The director of Purchasing, Egbert Merkelijn, received them in the cubbyhole that had been partitioned off in a corner of the large workroom to provide him with a private office. The space was barely big enough for his desk, two filing cabinets and the man himself: Merkelijn was no taller than Mahboob Chaudri, but he weighed at least 250 pounds. His tiny eyes were sunk deep in layers of fat; in spite of the air conditioning, his puffy face was flushed and damp. He seemed broader than the entrance to his cubicle, and Chaudri wondered if he was able to leave it at day's end, or if the partitions had been erected around him and had trapped him there.

There was nowhere for Chaudri and Smit to sit, so they stood in front of the desk and spoke down at him.

"Did you know Ebezer Kwaja?" Chaudri began.

"Yes, of course," the fat man rasped. "He worked here in my department."

"What can you tell us about him?"

"About Kwaja? He was quiet, he was respectful, he did his work efficiently."

"Then why was he fired?"

Merkelijn jutted out his lower lip and exhaled noisily through his nose. "I don't know. I had no complaints. But the order came down from the sixth floor: get rid of him."

"How long had he worked for you?" The question, this time, came from Roelof Smit.

"*Ach, ja*, a year, perhaps a bit longer. I'd have to look it up."

"What was his job?" asked Chaudri.

"He processed purchase orders. When an order was submitted from any of the other departments, it went to Kwaja. He countersigned it, and made out an authorization for disbursal of the necessary funds."

"Would it be possible to see some samples of his work?"

Merkelijn grunted and swung ponderously around to the file cabinet nearest him. He slid open a drawer, drew out a thick file folder, and laid it on his desk. "That contains all the purchase orders we have handled so far this quarter," he said, "in chronological order with the most recent on top. You'll need to go back a few days before you reach the last of the ones that went through Kwaja."

Chaudri leafed quickly through a dozen or more sheets, most of which had been filed that morning by Nicolaas Sjollema, then slowed down and began to examine each page individually.

"There are three signature lines," he commented. "The first signature is apparently that of the person requesting a purchase, then underneath that is Kwaja, and then comes the first signature again."

The fat man nodded. "That's right, verifying that the monies requested have been paid out—either directly to the supplier or, in some cases, to the person submitting the request for transfer to the supplier—and that the merchandise ordered has been delivered."

Chaudri flipped deeper into the sheaf of papers, found a sheet that interested him and paused to make a note. He continued in this way through the entire pile, glancing at most of the order forms cursorily, stopping occasionally to jot down a line on his pad.

When he finished, he straightened up the papers and handed the file back to Merkelijn. "Yes," he said, "this seems to be in order. May I use your telephone?"

Egbert Merkelijn waved a pudgy hand at the instrument, and Chaudri picked up the receiver and dialed the number of Gulf Polytechnic. He asked the operator for Emad Rezk, and waited patiently as the call was switched through.

"Professor Rezk?" he said at last. "This is Mahboob Chaudri speaking. Have you had a chance to examine that specimen I brought you?... Yes?... Yes?... Yes, that's exactly what I expected. And what would the consequences of that be?... Can you estimate how long that process would take?... About five years, you think, or perhaps a bit more or less.... Yes, I see. Very well then, professor, I thank you for your time.... No, no, thank *you*." He cradled the phone.

"Well?" said Smit, recognizing the grim satisfaction etched across Chaudri's face. "What did he tell you?"

"He told me why the Qatar Causeway had to be destroyed, and why Ebezer Kwaja had to be silenced," Mahboob Chaudri replied. "And he told me who it was who committed both of those crimes."

* * * *

Hendrik Hofstra and Nicolaas Sjollema were huddled over Hofstra's model of the causeway when Chaudri and Smit walked into the office without knocking.

The director was furious. "What's the meaning of this?" he demanded. "This is a private office, Mr. Chaudri. You can't just barge in here unannounced!"

"*Rustig aan*," Sjollema soothed him. "They wouldn't have done it if it weren't urgent. Would you like me to leave, officer?"

"I'd rather you stayed," said Chaudri. "What I have to say concerns you, too. Sit down, gentlemen—this may take some time."

Hofstra growled under his breath, but he did not argue.

The four men settled themselves into comfortable armchairs, and the Dutchmen turned expectantly to Chaudri.

"First," he began, "a question. Mr. Hofstra, you personally ordered the dismissal of Ebezer Kwaja from your Purchasing department on December 2nd, just under a week ago. Why did you issue that order?"

"I—" The director glanced quickly at Nicolaas Sjollema, then turned back to Chaudri. "My reasons have no bearing on your investigation," he said gruffly.

"Your reasons, if you will excuse my saying so, do not exist," Chaudri corrected him. "You gave the order to get rid of Kwaja, true, but I suggest that you did so at the instigation of someone else. Kwaja knew who was truly responsible for his dismissal: the 'big man,' he told us, 'from the distant Netherlands.' He said that the big man had fired him because he—Kwaja—knew too much about the big man's baby. We assumed that he was speaking figuratively when he said the words 'big man,' and that he was speaking literally when he referred to the big man's baby: the big man, we thought, was the big boss—you, Mr. Hofstra—and the baby was your son Pieter."

"My son was not a baby," Hofstra objected. "He was six years old, almost seven."

"Exactly. Ebezer Kwaja was speaking figuratively when he used the word 'baby.' He was not referring to the death of your child. But he spoke literally when he said that a 'big man' had fired him. And you, Mr. Hofstra, are hardly big. Who, then, was the big man who convinced you to dismiss Ebezer Kwaja, for reasons that were clear to the Indian if not to you? Who was the big man whose 'baby' Kwaja knew too much about? Who was the big man who killed him in order to keep him from telling us what he knew?" Chaudri paused for a moment, observing Hofstra closely. Then he went on: "You do not seem surprised, Mr. Hofstra, to hear that Ebezer Kwaja is dead."

The director's aggressiveness seemed to have melted away from him, leaving him tentative, confused. "No," he said, "I—I'm not surprised. Nick told me, shortly before you burst in here."

"Ah," Chaudri nodded, "now that is very curious. Because Kwaja's murder has not been mentioned on the radio news, or on television, or in this morning's paper. Which leads me to wonder, Mr. Sjollema, how you could possibly have known about the killing? Unless, of course, you were there at the Central Market when it happened. Unless, in fact, you murdered Ebezer Kwaja yourself."

Nicolaas Sjollema eyed him narrowly. "You're crazy," he said. "I barely knew the man. What possible reason could I have had for shooting him?"

"*Shooting* him, Mr. Sjollema? Oh, dearie me, and I am *quite* certain I never mentioned that Mr. Kwaja had been shot. 'Killed,' I said, and 'murdered,' but never 'shot.'"

"Nick," Hendrik Hofstra said angrily, "what is all this? What's he trying to say?"

"I am not *trying* to say anything, sir," Chaudri told him. "I am *saying* that your foreman, Nicolaas Sjollema, shot and killed Ebezer Kwaja at the Central Market early yesterday afternoon."

"But why, dammit? *Why?*"

Chaudri sighed. "Kwaja told that as well, though I am afraid we didn't understand him at first. He said that he had been fired because he knew too much. 'About what?' I asked him. 'About his baby,' he replied, speaking figuratively. 'About the—' And then the shot was fired, and he gasped the word 'water' twice, and died. We thought that, in his final moments, he was asking for something to drink. He was not. He was finishing his sentence. 'About the water,' he was saying. He was fired because he knew too much about the water."

"I still don't understand," said Roelof Smit. "What *about* the water?"

Chaudri ticked the points off on his fingers. "The Qatar Causeway is made of concrete. Concrete is mixed with water, pure water—in Bahrain, with *sweet* water. Nicolaas Sjollema needed money—or wanted money—and he saw a way to amass quite a bit of it. He ordered sweet water for the project, ordered it frequently and in large quantities—I have the dates and amounts right here." He patted the pocket of his uniform shirt. "But he built the Umm as Hawwak section of the bridge with ordinary tap water, and kept the money he was to have paid out for the sweet water for himself."

Sjollema sat there, impassive, motionless, silent.

"Then things began to go wrong. A few weeks ago, a Korean laborer named Kim Lee Kwan stole a jug of Mr. Sjollema's tap water from the site, but Mr. Sjollema caught him in the act. Perhaps Kim tasted the water, and realized that there was a swindle going on. Perhaps he never had the chance: Mr. Sjollema had him on a flight out of Bahrain that very same day. For a while, he must have felt safe again. Then Ebezer Kwaja became suspicious. The Indian was not under Mr. Sjollema's supervision, so Mr. Sjollema could not get rid of him directly, but he went to you, Mr. Hofstra, with some vague, trumped-up story—"

"He said he'd heard the man was working out a method of siphoning money away from the company." Hofstra filled in the details dully. "He had no evidence, so I couldn't come out and make a direct accusation. But since it was Nick, I—I believed him. And I had Personnel let him—Kwaja—go."

Chaudri drew a breath and went on. "Mr. Sjollema expected that the Indian would be deported, as was Kim Lee Kwan. He hadn't counted on Kwaja's having a cousin here who would take over sponsorship of his visa. And, meanwhile, he realized that the Umm as Hawwak section of the bridge would have to be destroyed. Made of concrete mixed with brackish tap water, he knew that it would last only a few years, perhaps half a decade. Then it would collapse—there would probably be loss of life, there would certainly be an investigation, and the truth would be discovered. No, it was better to sneak back out to the islet late at night on the 4th of December, after work, and to set the charges that would rip the structure apart on Sinterklaas, while Sjollema himself was in full view of dozens of impeccable witnesses."

At last the accused man stirred. "You have no proof," he said. His voice was flat, emotionless.

"I have your signatures on the purchase orders," Chaudri replied, "requesting the purchase of thousands of liters of sweet water. And I have Ebezer Kwaja's signatures, authorizing the monies to be paid to you, rather than directly to a supplier. Which, of course, is why you finally decided that you had to kill him: so he would never reveal what he suspected about your bridge—your 'baby'—and about your phony purchases of sweet water. Then I have your signatures again, confirming that the sweet water Nederbild paid for was in fact delivered."

"It *was* delivered," Sjollema snarled. "I ordered sweet water, I paid for sweet water, I *got* sweet water, and I built that roadbed with nothing but pure sweet water. And you can't prove otherwise, Mr. Chaudri: after the explosion, I had my crew dump every last bit of rubble so far out to sea that you'll never be able to find it."

"A clever move," Chaudri admitted. "But what you do not know, my clever Mr. Sjollema, is that I happened to pick up a small piece of concrete debris when I was out at Umm as Hawwak that day, after you and Lieutenant Smit went back to the fishing *dhow*. I had it analyzed this morning. And according to that analysis—"

But there was no need for Chaudri to continue. Nicolaas Sjollema put his head in his hands and began to sob.

* * * *

At Roelof Smit's insistence, they had dinner that night at Mansouri Mansions, where it was possible to eat a Western meal and drink large mugs of foaming Dutch beer.

"So the analysis showed that the concrete had been mixed with tap water," Smit said, wiping suds from his bushy walrus mustache contentedly, "which was enough to prove Sjollema a crook even without his confession. But there's one thing I still don't understand. Right after the explosion, when we rushed out of the mess hall to the beach, I saw him standing there crying, and he was crying real tears. Was he so upset about the destruction of his bridge, even though he'd blown it up himself?"

Chaudri shook his head. "Mr. Sjollema stopped caring about the causeway the day he began building it with worthless concrete. It was not his baby when he killed it, not any more."

"Then why the tears?" Smit frowned.

Chaudri picked up his hamburger and bit into it hungrily. "You know quite a lot about police work, Lieutenant," he said, "but you must learn to pay more attention to human beings. Mr. Sjollema planned the blast for a day when no one would be working out at Umm as Hawwak, a day when he could devastate the bridge without hurting any people. Yet he needed to ensure that the contaminated section of the structure would be completely destroyed, so he used a very large amount of explosive. Much more, as it turned out, than was needed."

"You mean—?" Smit's face cleared.

"The children," Mahboob Chaudri nodded. "Sinterklaas cried because he hadn't meant to hurt the children."

AFTERWORD

Having lived in Holland from 1979 through 1982, I decided to give Mahboob a case that would take him into Bahrain's Dutch community. At the time, a Dutch construction company was nearing completion of the most expensive stretch of roadway anywhere in the world, a seven-mile causeway connecting Bahrain to Saudi Arabia, and I decided to blow the bridge up and have Mahboob investigate the crime.

So the story's original title was "The Saudi Causeway," and that was the way I sent it to Eleanor Sullivan at *Ellery Queen's Mystery Magazine*. Eleanor —who'd bought and published all three of my previous Chaudri stories—liked this one, too, but she told me it was far too long for EQMM and asked me to cut it down to about half of its original length.

I suppose I could have done that, but I really didn't want to, so I asked Eleanor how she'd feel about my submitting it as is to Cathleen Jordan at *Alfred Hitchcock's Mystery Magazine,* which had been under independent ownership until 1975, when Davis Publications bought it and made it EQMM's kid sister. Eleanor graciously agreed, and Cathleen also liked the story—but she was uncomfortable with the idea of my destroying an actual bridge that really existed in the real world, so she asked me to shift the causeway project to another Bahraini location. There's only one other place where a bridge connecting Bahrain to the mainland could *go,* though, and that's why the published version of the story is called "The Qatar Causeway." (My fictitious construction project is referred to in the story as "the second most expensive stretch of highway in the world," which was a tip of the hat to the actual Saudi Causeway.)

Often in my fiction, I name my characters after people I know. Here, Emad Rezk, who is named after my ex brother-in-law, makes his second appearance in the series, having first shown up in "The Tree of Life." Similarly, I knew people in Holland named Merkelijn and Stutje, and I borrowed both of their names for minor characters. I even gave myself my second-ever Hitchcockian cameo. When Mahboob and Dutch policeman Roelof Smit have dinner together at the Star of Paradise, the Dutchman orders a bowl of a well-known Kashmiri dish: beef rogan josh.

When I first started selling my short stories, the sale itself was an incredibly exciting honor for me. As I placed more and more stories in more and more magazines and anthologies, though, the sale itself became—I'm not going to say *un*exciting, that never happened—but certainly *less* exciting, and the bigger excitement came at those rare times that my name appeared on the publication's cover. The first time that ever happened to me was in 1972, when mine was the ninth of ten names listed on the front cover of the September issue of EQMM. I made the cover of EQMM several more times over the next couple of years, but in those days AHMM didn't feature author's names on its covers. They started to do so when they were bought by Davis, and I was listed second of four names on the cover of the issue containing this story.

Also something of a rarity for me is to see my stories illustrated, but I just love the drawing Jim Odbert did for the first page of "The Qatar Causeway," and I'm delighted to share it with you here:

The Qatar Causeway
by Josh Pachter

One criticism I've had regarding this story is that, in its final scene, Roelof Smit is drinking a mug of beer in a restaurant—while "everyone" knows that the serving of alcohol is prohibited in Arabic countries. That prohibition is not, however, absolute. In fact, a running joke when I lived in Bahrain is that the country got its name—which is pronounced *Bar-rain*—because of all the bars in and around the *suq*. Mansouri Mansions was in 1982 one of my favorite Manama restaurants, and they did indeed serve big mugs of foamy beer. (According to *booking.com*, the place still exists, although it's now called Mansouri Mansions Hotel, and it has "a wine bar and an Irish pub, with billiards and darts.")

A word about cursing. In English, we sometimes euphemize swear words to tone down their impoliteness, so that "fucking" becomes "fricking" or "frigging" and "Goddammit" becomes "goshdarnit" or "goldangit." The Dutch do the exact same thing: *"Godverdomme"* is a very very nasty thing to say, but *"getverdemme"* and *"potverdorie"* are socially acceptable variants.

In his Honor Roll at the end of *The Year's Best Mystery and Suspense Stories* (Walker and Company, 1987), Ed Hoch acknowledged the work of 66 crime writers. Only nine of those writers had multiple stories on the list, and I was proud to be one of that select group, with both "The Qatar

Causeway" and "The Night of Power"—another Chaudri story, which appears later in this collection—singled out for inclusion.

ASU

"And one more thing," Captain Craft told them. "You're not in San Diego or Norfolk any more. You're going to find out right quick that the folks out here have got some different values from the folks back home. When you were stationed stateside, going off base on liberty meant you could loosen up and relax for a while. But when you go out on the economy here, you've got to be twice as careful as you are on post. The locals are fine people as a rule, but there are things that might be second nature to you and me which are downright offensive to them. That means no drunkenness, no fights, no wisecracks, and no uniforms.

"You men: I don't care how hot it gets out there, you wear long pants and a shirt at all times unless you're *on* the beach. And you, Miller: no sleeveless tops or low-cut necklines, nothing tight or see-through, and you either wear slacks off base or keep your hemlines at the knee or lower. These people are more modest than you ever thought was possible, and they don't want to have to look at your uncovered skin." The captain paused to check his watch. "Well, that about wraps it up," he said, "unless there are any questions?"

The four new men—one of them, Miller, a woman—exchanged tentative glances. It had been a huge amount of information to absorb at one shot: the briefing had lasted a little more than an hour. The one black sailor in the group half raised his hand.

"Sanders?" the captain recognized him. "Let's go, mister, sing it out."

"Well, sir," the youngster began, "I'm kinda proud to be serving here in the US Navy and all that, you know? So I don't understand how come we're not supposed to wear our uniforms when we go off post."

"Your pride is noted and appreciated, mister. But nobody's asking you to *understand* the policy. I am *ordering* you to *remember* it, that's all. Do you understand *that*?"

Sanders looked stricken, and Craft realized that perhaps he'd been a bit too hard on him. After all, it was the kid's first day at a brand-new duty station. Maybe he'd better unbend a little, not come across the complete ogre right off the bat. What was the boy's first name again? Bill? No, that was Garripy, the new postal clerk. Tom, that was it.

"Listen, Tom," he said more gently, "the local government wants us to keep our military presence here in the emirate as low-key as possible. I'm not sure *I* understand it, either. Hell, I'm not sure the admiral does, or even the ambassador. But part of the agreement that entitles us to maintain an Administrative Support Unit here in Bahrain, and to dock and fuel our ships out at the Mina Sulman harbor, is that we're not supposed to flaunt the fact that we've got 70-some naval personnel stationed at ASU. And that's why, any time you go out that gate and into town, the requirement is that you wear your civvies. You with me, son?"

Sanders managed a weak smile. "Yes, sir."

"Very well."

The Miller woman shot up a hand.

This one was going to be trouble, Craft thought. He'd felt sure of it the moment he saw her march down the C-130's boarding ladder out at the airport on Muharraq this morning, strutting her stuff like she owned the damn plane. He was all in favor of equal opportunity and all the rest of it—hell, if a lady service member was willing to go into *combat* with the men, *he* didn't see any reason to stop her—but Miller was going to have to learn that the Middle East was a far cry from the Midwest she'd grown up in, and she was going to have to modify her aggressive behavior a tad if she wanted to make it through her tour of duty here without some serious problems. He nodded at her, and she jumped into her question just as brash as can be.

"Sir," she said, "I'm a little worried about the possibility of sexual harassment while I'm here. What am I supposed to do if I'm downtown and one of these ragheads starts—"

"Young lady!" the captain roared, and whatever Miller had intended to say died stillborn in her throat. "The piece of cloth our hosts wear on their heads is a *ghutra*, not a rag, and the men who wear *ghutras* are known as Arabs. If I hear the word 'raghead' out of your mouth again, I can assure you you'll be much too busy peeling potatoes for the rest of your stay on this island to have to worry about sexual harassment."

The woman gaped at him, speechless.

"Have I made myself *clear*?" Craft barked.

"Aye aye, sir!"

"Very well. And in answer to your question, Ensign, in the unlikely event you should ever find yourself in a situation where you feel you are being harassed, you get yourself *out* of that situation and report the circumstances either to me or to the XO and let us take care of it. But I'll tell you what, Miller: with your attitude, I don't think you've got much to worry about. Any other questions?"

There were no other questions.

"Very well," said Captain Craft. "I wish you all an enjoyable year in Bahrain. Dismissed."

* * * *

"Hey, Sanders, wait up," a voice behind him called, and when he turned he saw Miller jogging toward him, a bulky canvas carryall banging her hip with every step. She came up to him breathing hard and put a hand on his shoulder to steady herself as she caught her breath. "You heading into town?"

"Name's Tom," he said, shifting his leather camera bag out of her way. "Yeah, I figured I'd take me a little look around. Captain really chewed you out back there."

"You, too. I guess he doesn't much care for women or blacks, huh?"

"He's not so bad, I guess. Just runs a tight ship, that's all. I seen worse. What's your name?"

She brushed the question aside. "Miller's fine. You mind if I come along with you?"

"Suit yourself. But I can't go calling you Miller. My stepdaddy's name's Miller. What's your first name?"

"Oh, hell." She shrugged. "It's Dolly. My damn name's Dolly."

The boy smiled. "Dolly. That's a *fine* name. Pleased to meet you, Dolly."

She smiled back at him, and they shook hands solemnly.

As they approached the thin wooden railing that separated the base from the outside world, a small man in an unfamiliar olive-green uniform stepped out of the guard shack next to the barrier.

"Good afternoon," he greeted them pleasantly. His English was lightly accented, and his lively chocolate eyes regarded them with friendly interest.

"Hello, yourself." Sanders returned the smile. "How come they got a Bahraini soldier here on the gate instead of a US Marine or somethin'?" He pronounced the word "BAH-rainy," putting the emphasis on the wrong syllable and missing out on the gutteral *hr* most Westerners had so much trouble with.

"I am Pakistani," the man explained, "not Bahraini—and a police officer, not a soldier. The Bahraini government's Public Security Force supplies the guards for this gate, and most of us on the force come from Pakistan. In other countries, your own men stand the watch?"

"Men and women," Dolly Miller corrected him. "Aren't there any women on your security team?"

"No, I'm afraid we have no women—not in uniform, at any rate. This is an Islamic country, and such positions are held only by men."

Miller seemed about to express her opinion of a system that excluded half its population from *any* type of position, but her companion cleared his throat.

"We were gonna stroll into town for a while," said Sanders, "look around a bit. Can we go on through?"

"You are new here," the Pakistani deduced. "Welcome to Bahrain. You will find it's rather longer than a stroll from here to Manama, especially in this heat." He nodded at the line of a half dozen red-and-white cabs parked beyond the wooden railing, their drivers—all in flowing *thobes* and checkered *ghutras*—lounging in a circle on the cracked sidewalk, conversing lazily in liquid Arabic. "You will enjoy yourselves much more if you take a taxi. And most certainly you may pass through—today and tomorrow, at any rate. But I will have to ask you to open up your camera bag and your purse for a moment before you go."

"Why's that?" asked Miller. "And what happens after tomorrow?"

"Someone has been smuggling spirits out of ASU, and this gate is the only way on or off the base. I am supposed to catch the criminal and put a stop to his activities. It is a matter of some urgency, I'm afraid. The government will not tolerate crime involving the non-Arab community, and, if the smuggling has not been stopped by midnight tomorrow, my superiors have been instructed to seal off this gate and allow no one on or off ASU until the situation has been satisfactorily resolved."

Sanders let out a low-pitched whistle. "That's heavy stuff. You're talkin' about holdin' the US Navy prisoner here?"

"It is indeed a most serious state of affairs," the policeman agreed soberly. "But I am hoping that I will be able to find out who is smuggling the spirits before my deadline is reached."

"Spirits," Sanders repeated. "You mean liquor."

"The demon rum, I believe you call it. Dark rum, from a lovely tropical paradise some 20 times the size of Bahrain."

"Jamaican rum," said Miller. "And somebody's smuggling it off base? Why bother? Captain Craft just told us this place is so liberal compared to the rest of the Arab countries you can walk into your neighborhood package store and buy whatever you want."

"So you can. But the prices are quite high—much higher than in your American Class VI store here."

"Still, how much money can a smuggler figure to make?" Tom Sanders asked him. "I mean, our booze is rationed, you know? You can't buy but one bottle of the hard stuff a week. I don't care *how* much you can sell it for outside, you can't make enough of a profit on a bottle a week to make the risk worth takin'."

"Ah, but our information is that the smuggler is taking two or three bottles of dark rum away with him per *day*. Or, perhaps"—he made a graceful gesture toward Dolly Miller—"with *her*. But I don't want to hold you back from your excursion, especially since this may be your last opportunity to leave ASU for some time. May I?"

The Pakistani looked quickly but carefully through Sanders' camera case and Miller's shoulder bag, then raised the wooden barrier for them. "Your driver will tell you the ride downtown costs two dinars or perhaps even more," he called after them as Miller pulled open the back door of the first vehicle in line. "They always try that, though the rates are fixed for journeys within the Manama area. Don't pay him more than one dinar, whatever he asks."

"Thanks!" the woman called back. "Hey, I'm Miller and this here's Sanders! What's *your* name?"

"Chaudri," the little policeman said. "Mahboob Chaudri. Have a pleasant afternoon!"

* * * *

Their afternoon was far better than pleasant. It was fascinating. They roamed the twisted alleyways of the *suq* with the eager excitement of adventurous children. This was the first time outside America for both of them, and they were determined to soak up as much of the strange Arabic culture as they could. They watched gray-bearded tailors hand-stitch jet-black *abbas*, sitting cross-legged on the wooden floors of "shops" barely three feet wide and deep. They wandered down streets lined chockablock with gold merchants and tinsmiths and incense sellers and dealers in redolent herbs and spices. They passed open-air teahouses whose pale-blue benches were filled with grizzled old men puffing dreamily on tall glass water pipes. They saw beggar women swathed in black on every street corner and heard the babble of a dozen unfamiliar languages everywhere they turned.

It was a day of enchantment until, over milkshakes at the Aradous Coffee Shop, Dolly brought up the thought that had been troubling the back of both their minds.

"This thing about the smuggler," she said. "You know, if we could catch him before that deadline tomorrow night and turn him over to the captain, I bet that'd go a long way toward making up for the kimshee we got ourselves into this morning."

Sanders looked up from his half empty glass. "Him?" he said, a twinkle in his eye.

"All right," she blushed, "him or her. Whoever. But what do you think? We could sort of nose around, ask some questions, see what we could dig up. We've still got more than 30 hours before the deadline. What do you think?"

"I think you gone crazy, Dolly, that's what I think. You reckon we're in trouble *now*? Well, you just go out there and start playin' detective, girl, you're gonna get us both in some *deep* kimshee and that's for sure."

Miller's excited expression sagged. She lowered her head to her straw and sucked on it dismally.

"Hey," said Sanders softly. "Hey, Dolly."

When she looked up, she saw him beaming at her. "What the hell," he said. "Let's go for it."

* * * *

When their cab dropped them back at the ASU gate, there were four Pakistanis lined up on the other side of it, waiting to be searched so they could leave the base. Although they were all in civilian clothing, it was as if they were uniformed: all four wore tailored long-sleeved shirts and dark pin-striped trousers with widely flared cuffs, all were of medium height and thin, all had dark-brown skin, short black hair, and lively brown eyes, and each one carried a five-liter water jug of red plastic.

It was obvious there was nothing concealed beneath their tight-fitting clothing, but as Sanders and Miller paid off their driver and headed for the gate they saw Mahboob Chaudri unscrew the cap from the first man's jug and pour a thimbleful of its contents into a clear plastic cup.

"You checking for that demon rum?" Miller asked.

"Yes, indeed," the policeman replied. "But as you can see, I am finding nothing but ordinary water." He spilled the sample into the dirt and went on to the second man's jug. "Every non-American working here at ASU is permitted to bring one jug of sweet water home with him each day," he explained. "That is what I think you would call a fringed benefit of their employment. Outside, they would have to pay for sweet water—which is the only water in Bahrain that is pure enough for drinking—but because they work at ASU they may get it here for free."

He recapped the third jug and opened the last one. "This would be the simplest way to move the dark Jamaican rum off the base, which is why you are finding me checking. Without luck, though, I'm afraid. Everything is as it should be." He threw the fourth small sample of water into the dust at his feet, capped the jug, and raised the wooden barrier to let his countrymen out and the two Americans in.

"Well, listen," said Sanders, "it can't be a non-American doing the smugglin', anyway, can it? I mean, liquor's rationed here on base and only Americans have got ration cards."

"Your reasoning is certainly persuasive," Chaudri agreed, "but I must check everyone who leaves the base through this gate. This crime, you see, is not a logical one, and *how* the criminal is smuggling the rum away from ASU is only one of the mysteries I have been instructed to solve. There is a larger puzzle."

The young newcomers leaned toward him.

"Our information is that the dark rum appearing on the market here in Bahrain is definitely coming from ASU," Chaudri told them. "But there *is* no dark rum available at ASU. The only rum sold here, even to the American holders of ration cards, is *light* rum...."

* * * *

The Class VI store was closed when they went there after leaving Chaudri, a heavy iron gate swung across the pale-green door and padlocked, so Miller and Sanders put off the inquisition they'd been planning and had dinner together instead. They ate at the Two Seas, a cafeteria-style restaurant where Pakistanis did the cooking, bussed the tables, and ran the cash register. There was no mess hall at ASU, so most of the military personnel ate their meals there. The food was good, the prices were low—and it was the only place on post that served food. Which made it the only place where any of them would be eating for an indefinite time, unless the smuggler could be apprehended within the next 28 hours.

Both Miller and Sanders were eager to get started with their investigation, but since checking out the Class VI seemed to be the obvious first step, they separated after dinner with an agreement to meet again in the morning.

In-processing kept them busy for several hours after reveille, but they joined up at 1100 hours and headed for the Class VI. The store turned out to be a smallish room, the walls crowded with shelves of canned goods, snack foods, and such basic items as paper plates, plastic utensils, zip-lock bags for storing leftovers, shaving gear, toothpaste, and a modest array of over-the-counter medications. There was a single deep freezer packed with an assortment of frozen foods and a cooler for cheeses, lunchmeats, and chilled beverages. An even smaller second room held cases of beer and soda and several well-stocked shelves of wine and liquor. In one corner was a towering jumble of empty cardboard boxes and unopened cartons of surplus goods for which there was no display space available.

The clerk was one of the four Pakistanis they had seen leaving the base the afternoon before, and—after browsing around for a while and verifying that there was indeed no dark rum being offered for sale—they walked to the counter where he stood writing a letter in a strange script that made no sense to either of them. A hand-lettered sign taped to the cash register identified him as *Mr. Owais Gujarit, Manager*.

"Is that Pakistani you're writing there, Mr. Gujarit?" Dolly asked him.

The man looked up at them and grinned. "It *is* Pakistani, I suppose you could say, but it is not *called* Pakistani. It is called Urdu."

"Urdu," she repeated, tasting the unfamiliar word and finding it somehow pleasing. Then she remembered the task at hand and let what she hoped would pass for a look of cool indifference wash across her face as she framed her first question.

* * * *

"I'll get this one," said Sanders and held up a hand to cut off Miller's protest. "No, you bought dinner last night. Now it's my turn." He ripped open the velcro seal on his wallet and fished out a five-dollar bill.

"One Cornish hen, one cordon bleu, two salad, two cola," the young Pakistani behind the register chanted rapidly, keying in prices with a stabbing motion of his right forefinger. "Four dollar sixty, sir," he announced, an instant before the total appeared on the machine's digital readout screen in bright blue figures.

Sanders dropped his change in the glass jar next to the register and they carried their trays across the busy dining room to the only remaining empty table.

The room was filled with whispered conversations—most of those Miller and Sanders could hear were worried discussions of the government's threat to close the base off from the outside world in only 12 more hours. The two ensigns ate their lunch in silence, chewing over the information they had just received as they chewed their food—Owais Gujarit, the Class VI manager, had been cooperative but hadn't had much of interest to tell them. New stock came into the store once a month, on the same C-130 flight that had delivered Sanders and Miller to the island the day before. Each month's shipment included two cases of light rum, but there had never been any dark rum delivered in all the four years he had worked there.

"The thing's impossible," Sanders complained at last. "There's no dark rum on sale over there in the first place, and even if there *was* there's no way anybody could buy more than a bottle a week—and even if they *could* there's no way to smuggle it out past that man Mahboob on the gate. I tell you, Dolly, it's impossible."

Miller set down her fork. "No, it's not," she said calmly. "I know where the stuff's coming from, I know how it's getting off-base, and I know who's doing the smuggling. What say we step over to the Captain's office and see if he's around?"

* * * *

But as luck would have it Captain Craft was having lunch with the admiral aboard the Navy flagship out at Mina Sulman, so, an odd glint in her eye, Miller suggested they stroll down to the gate and share her theory with Mahboob Chaudri instead.

"Ensign Miller here's solved your case for you," Sanders greeted the Pakistani as he emerged from the guardhouse.

"Has she indeed?" An air conditioner rumbled loudly inside the shack, but Chaudri's forehead glistened with perspiration. "I am delighted. I have not been pleased about the approach of my deadline. Closing down access to ASU would be making for a very uncomfortable situation here, one I would be happy to avoid. And although I have been enjoying my time here, I must admit I am ready for a more *active* assignment."

Miller licked her lips nervously. "You mean this isn't your regular job?"

"Oh, dearie me, no. This duty generally falls to a *natoor*—what you, I believe, would call a patrolman. I am a *mahsool*, a detective. I was placed here when we first learned about the smuggling, and I will be reassigned as soon as you tell me who I am to arrest and explain the reasoning behind your accusation."

But a look of agonized embarrassment stole across Dolly Miller's face.

"What's the matter?" Sanders turned to her in concern.

She was hiding behind raised hands now and shaking her head.

"Ah, I believe I understand," Chaudri smiled. "I'm afraid Ensign Miller was about to name *me* as the ASU smuggler."

* * * *

"It's really the most logical solution," he said, pushing steaming cups of tea toward them. They were sitting around a plain deal table in the cramped guardhouse, and the air conditioner's roar almost overwhelmed his comforting voice. "Unless you happened to know that I did not report to ASU until after the smuggling had already begun. Without that one vital piece of information, it must have seemed obvious that I was the only person with access to the base who could leave it without being searched."

Miller lifted her head from her hands. "Thank heaven the Captain was out when we checked his office," she said. "I feel like a big enough fool right now with you two knowing about this."

"What I don't get," said Sanders, "is how you figured Mahboob here was gettin' his hands on all that rum in the first place if he's stuck up here in this shack all day and he hasn't even got a ration card."

Miller sighed. "I thought he had an accomplice, maybe—somebody who sneaked the stuff to him so he could take it away every evening when the gate closed down for the night and he went off duty."

"But they've only got *light* rum here on base and it's *dark* rum that keeps turning up outside."

Dolly's eyes lit up. "Well, that's the part I was positive I had all scoped out. It came to me while we were eating lunch just now. I was wondering why they call it *cordon blue* when there isn't any blue in there at all. I thought maybe it starts out sort of blue and changes color while they're cooking it."

"I took French at school," Sanders said. "*Cordon bleu* means 'blue ribbon,' and the idea is—"

"Changes color," Mahboob Chaudri repeated slowly. He set down his cup and addressed Dolly. "Excuse me, please, Ensign, but are you saying that—?"

"I'm saying I figured you were taking light rum away from the base and adding some kind of coloring to it to make it look like dark rum later on."

Chaudri washed a hand across his face. "In that case," he said pensively. "In that case." Suddenly he jumped to his feet. "Can you be back here at five o'clock this afternoon? Both of you?"

"Well, sure," said Sanders.

"I can," Dolly nodded. "But why?"

Chaudri flashed them a brilliant grin. "Because you have earned the right to be present when I expose the *real* ASU smuggler," he said. "Is that reason enough, my friends?"

* * * *

Miller and Sanders were back at the guardhouse at five sharp. Mahboob Chaudri was waiting for them alone, but he refused to explain. "Allah is with those who patiently persevere," he told them with a sparkle in his eye.

A quarter of an hour later, the four Pakistanis they had first seen the day before approached the wooden railing. Once again, each of them carried a red plastic jug of sweet water. The ensigns recognized two of the men as busboys who worked the luncheon shift at the Two Seas cafeteria. The third man was Owais Gujarit from the Class VI store, and the fourth was unknown to them.

As he had done the day before, Chaudri poured a small quantity of the liquid from each jug into a clear plastic tumbler. This time, though, he seemed vastly more confident, and, rather than simply *looking* at his samples—assuming because they were crystal clear that they were in fact sweet water—he sniffed at each of them delicately and tasted them, knowing that one of the four would turn out to be not water, but colorless light rum. And yet, one by one, the four samples proved to possess the no-smell and no-taste of pure water.

"May we go now?" said the fourth man.

Mahboob Chaudri seemed not to hear him. "Impossible." He shook his head stubbornly. "This is impossible. There is no other way for the rum to be leaving ASU, I would swear it. If the smuggler is not bringing it out in these jugs—"

Then, all at once, the little policeman's querulous expression cleared. "Ah," he sighed. "Ah, dearie me, of course. I'm afraid that I will have to trouble you further," he told the Pakistani civilians. "I must ask you to empty your jugs entirely."

One of the busboys said a word in a language neither of the Americans had heard before. Miller wondered if it might not be Urdu. Chaudri answered him in English, for their benefit. "I want to compare the weight of the empty jugs," he explained. "I want to see if one of them isn't rather heavier than the others. When I am finished, you will have to go back and fill them all over again. I apologize for the inconvenience, but I have had an idea, and I must know whether it has any validity."

With shrugs of exasperation, three of the four men uncapped and upended their jugs, spilling the expensive sweet water in the dirt at their feet.

The remaining Pakistani stood there silently, making no move to comply with the *mahsool*'s instruction.

"And you, *sahib*?" Chaudri prompted him.

The man raised his plastic jug slowly, as if preparing to uncap it, and then with a frightened cry he swung it at Chaudri's head, knocking him to the ground. He ducked under the wooden railing and raced off down the dusty road.

Tom Sanders was after him in an instant. Before they had passed the far end of the line of taxis outside the gate, he had brought the man down with a flying tackle. He rolled the prostrate figure onto its back, his fist clenched and ready.

But there was no fight left in the slight man cowering on the ground. Staring up at Sanders with terror in his eyes was Owais Gujarit, the Class VI clerk.

* * * *

"When Mahboob poured the water out of the jug," Dolly Miller explained, "we could hear something still sloshing around in there."

They were in Captain Craft's austere office in the Admin Building, and Mahboob Chaudri—with a cold compress held gingerly to the side of his head—seemed content to allow the Americans to do all the talking.

"The way he worked it was simple," Sanders told his superior. "Every afternoon after closin' up the shop, he stuffed one of those big plastic baggies into his water jug, leavin' the mouth of the baggie stickin' out of the mouth of the jug. He filled the baggie with rum, then fastened it shut and filled the jug the rest of the way up with water."

"How was the man covering up all that missing rum?" Captain Craft asked. "And what was he doing with it once he got it off the base?"

"He explained that while we were waiting for the Public Security wagon," Sanders replied. "There was a foul-up in last month's cargo shipment: the C-130 brought in 20 cases of rum for ASU instead of the two we were supposed to get. Gujarit was the only person in a position to spot the mistake, and when he did he hid the extra cases under a pile of other cartons in the back of the shop and started smugglin' it out a little at a time. He smashed the empties and got rid of them with the store's daily trash. Outside, he colored and rebottled the rum and pasted on phony labels he had made up at one of the print shops in town."

The Captain swiveled his chair to face Mahboob Chaudri. "We'd better get a medic over here to take a look at that bump of yours."

"Not necessary," the Pakistani protested. "Back in Karachi, where I come from, my family has a long history of hardheadedness. But there *is* one request I would appreciate your granting me."

"Name it, *mahsool*. We're in your debt. I hate to think about the international repercussions if you hadn't managed to clear up this business in time to prevent your government from actually shutting down our base."

"Not in *my* debt," said Chaudri. "Oh, no, indeed not. I would never have solved this case without the invaluable assistance of Ensigns Miller and Sanders, whom I overheard a short while ago hoping that the events of this afternoon might help to raise them a bit in your estimation. I'm not at all sure what they meant by the phrase 'deep kimshee,' Captain, but I would be most grateful if you would lift them out of it, whatever it is."

The room was silent for a moment. Dolly Miller and Tom Sanders looked as if they were wishing they had somewhere to hide.

But Captain Craft surprised them. "Very well," he said, with a smile that remained on his face until the meeting was adjourned a few minutes later.

AFTERWORD

The Administrative Support Unit in Bahrain has since been renamed, but it's a real place as described in the story, and I spent quite a bit of time there during my 10 months in Bahrain. The Class VI store, the Aradous Coffee Shop, the red plastic "sweet water" jugs, the Cornish game hens and cordon bleu in the Two Seas restaurant on post—that's all real. Even Miller and Sanders are named after real sailors, although the Miller I knew was male, not female, and the Sanders I knew was white, not black.

This is the second consecutive Chaudri story in which *water* plays an important role, and that too is authentic. Bahrain is an island nation, completely surrounded by water, but the water that surrounds it is seawater and therefore undrinkable. The country itself, however, is mostly desert, and the presence or absence of potable water is a life-and-death matter for everyone who lives there.

When the story was published in the April 1986 issue of EQMM, the table of contents gave its title as "Asu," and that's how it's listed in various online mystery databases. The correct spelling, though, is "ASU," which is pronounced as three separate letters ("A-S-U"), not as the words "ass-you" or "as-you."

Rereading the story now, 30 years after I wrote it, I was struck by Mahboob's statement that "Allah is with those who patiently persevere" and wondered if that was something I made up or something I researched. Google tells me that, sure enough, the second chapter of the Quran, which is called the *Surat al-Bakarah*, includes this passage at line 153: "Oh, you who have believed, seek help through patience and prayer. Indeed, Allah is with the patient."

"ASU" was originally written as a standalone, but I eventually wrote a sort of sequel, "The Ivory Beast," in which Miller and Sanders make a brief cameo appearance at the beginning. (You'll find a photograph of the real Miller and the real Sanders—and the real me—in that story's Afterword.)

JEMAA EL FNA

"*Biqam?*" asked Mahboob Chaudri, holding the ceremonial Berber belt in his hands and gazing admiringly at its bold colors and long tassels and glittering bits of mirror. "How much?" The belt would be an extravagance at any price, but Chaudri had promised himself an extravagance this day, and, after hours of searching through the *souks* of Marrakesh, he wondered if this might not at last be it.

"No, no, my friend," the merchant smiled, wagging a chiding finger at the Pakistani and his companion, fellow Public Security Officer Sikander Malek. "How much you like to pay?"

Chaudri had already bought souvenirs for his children and his wife, spending—after much bargaining—some 50 *dirham* on each of them. Now he had a last 50 *dirham* set aside for himself. He had long since grown tired of the ritual haggling. It was clearly expected of him, though, so he fingered the belt with apparent indifference and began the game with an offer of 15 *dirham*.

The Arab laughed. "This is a very fine piece," he explained. "*Very* fine. But because you are visitors to my country, I make you a special price: two hondred *dirham*."

Chaudri and Malek had arrived in Marrakesh four days earlier as part of the 12-man security team accompanying His Highness the Minister of Defense and his staff. Today was the first time the duty rotation had allowed them a day of rest, and it was to be their only time off of the trip: the Conference of Non-Aligned Nations which His Highness was attending was due to end within 24 hours, and the Bahraini contingent would be flying back to Manama as soon as the final session was over.

"Two hundred *dirham*?" Chaudri feigned shock and laid down the belt. "*La, la, da hrali awi.*"

The merchant scooped it up again and held it out to him. "No, my frien', it's not too much. Look, you pay hondred-fitty *dirham*, okay?"

Chaudri waved away the offer. "Thirty *dirham*," he said firmly, with the voice he used to interrogate a suspect.

The Arab pressed the belt into his hands. "Not thutty," he compromised, "not hondred-fitty. We say hondred-thutty *dirham*, you happy, me happy."

"*Da akhir taman?*" the Pakistani asked. "Is that your lowest price?"

The smile disappeared from the merchant's face. The foreigner in the olive-green uniform had asked that crucial question much too soon. *He will never pay my final price*, the Arab saw, *and I will make no profit if I give it to him for his*. He shook his head sadly and took back the belt, folded it together, and returned it to its place. The game was over, and both of the players had lost.

Disappointed, Mahboob Chaudri shook the brown hand the merchant held out to him and turned away from the shop. The Berber belt would have looked beautiful hanging above his bed in the police barracks back in Juffair, but —

"Never mind," Sikander Malek consoled him. "Perhaps you will find something even better when we get to the Jemaa."

"These Moroccans are amazingly clever," muttered Chaudri as they strolled beneath the green canvas awnings which protected the *souks* from the fierce heat of the afternoon sun. "Somehow—I don't know how—they seem to know who will be buying and who will not. They are, I think, the finest observers of human nature I have ever seen. They would make excellent policemen, all of them—or excellent criminals."

They twisted and turned through the tangled maze of bustling alleyways and finally broke out of the coolness of the Medina into the bright pandemonium that was the Jemaa el Fna, Marrakesh's main square, an enormous tent city where each of the tents was a self-contained shop and hundreds of Arabs too poor to afford even a tent prowled up and down the haphazard arrangement of aisles with their entire stock of merchandise draped carefully over their shoulders and arms.

Teenaged boys in tattered shorts and nothing else offered fists full of hand-carved hash pipes with fragile clay bowls. Grizzled old men sang the praises of "antique" daggers, which were turned out by the thousands by craftsmen from the Middle Atlas mountains, and cheap woolen blankets their wives and unmarried daughters toiled over in their ramshackle cottages in the poorest sections of town. Water sellers in tasseled red hats and red jackets studded with coins from around the world poured sparkling spring water from the bulging goatskins slung over their shoulders into shining brass drinking bowls, and dirt-caked gypsy girls were half hidden beneath their collections of hand-woven wicker baskets. Ancient crones sat cross-legged in the dust, knitting bright skullcaps with nimble fingers and looking up now and again to wave their work-in-progress at the passersby and yell "Three *dirham*! Three!"

But the Jemaa el Fna was not just a place for shopping. Shoeshine boys clustered wherever one turned. There were guess-your-weight men with heavy old scales and fiery preachers with nothing but an upturned orange crate and a mission from God. There was a long row of tents which served as restaurants, where Berber chefs kept aromatic stews bubbling in heavy iron pots and spicy skewered meats roasting over open fires. There were beggars everywhere—crippled, diseased, one-eyed, blind—crying for alms and offering nothing in return save the knowledge that the giver had fulfilled the third of the five Sacred Pillars of Islam, *Zahat*, which is the command to be charitable to the unfortunate.

More than anything else, there was entertainment. Not even in the streets of Karachi had Chaudri and Malek seen such an abundance of jugglers, dancers, singers, musicians, storytellers, fire eaters, magicians, and acrobats. They watched, entranced, as a snake charmer flung away his wooden flute, grabbed up three monstrous hooded cobras and stuffed them down the front of his baggy white pantaloons. With a piercing scream, the man dropped to the ground and writhed in wonderfully overplayed agony, clutching wretchedly at his groin and pleading for mercy in a comic mixture of Arabic, French, and English.

For more than an hour they roamed around the square, pausing to hear snatches of a speech or a song, to see trained monkeys with faces almost human in their intensity perform simple tricks at the ends of their thin red leashes, to watch children act out elaborate playlets while the youngest member of the troupe approached each onlooker with an upturned palm and a look of forlorn entreaty.

At the edge of the Jemaa, they found a small knot of men gathered around a cardboard carton, buzzing with excitement and waving 100-*dirham* bills eagerly. The group's attention was focused on a young man in a yellow-and-brown-striped *djelleba* in the center of the circle who was busily arranging a length of cord on the upper surface of the carton to form two small loops, with some 10 centimeters of cord left over at either end. The loudest of the spectators slapped his money down next to the pattern, then stabbed a forefinger into one of the loops. There rose a mixed chorus of groans and approval, and then the crowd fell silent as the young man in the striped *djelleba* took one end of the cord in each hand. With a dramatic flourish, he pulled the cord taut, and the loop snapped closed around the other man's finger. Happy cheers rang out, and the young man released the other's finger and returned his wager—along with a second 100-*dirham* note from the pocket of his *djelleba*.

As they watched, Chaudri and Malek saw that the rules of the game were simple. If a gambler selected the correct loop, the cord would trap his finger when pulled and he would win 100 *dirham*. If he picked wrong, the cord would pull free and he would lose his bet.

After watching the sequence repeated several times, the Pakistanis turned to go. But suddenly there were hands tugging at Chaudri's sleeves, and the players were urging him back toward the cardboard carton.

"*La, la,*" he said politely, holding up his hands in a gesture of refusal, but the young man in the *djelleba* waved his hesitation away and grinned, "No money! No money! Just for try!"

Chaudri glanced back over his shoulder at Sikander Malek, who shrugged as if to say *Do not be asking me, my friend.*

"Well, all right," Chaudri decided, handing over his armload of parcels to his companion. "Just for try."

Encouraging noises bubbled up from the crowd. The cord was arranged on the surface of the carton and then there was silence as Chaudri studied the simple arrangement of loops. "I see," he murmured at last, and confidently touched a forefinger to the center of the smaller circle.

There were cries of agreement, there were cries of dismay, and then again there was a hush of eager expectation.

The young man in the striped *djelleba* pulled on the loose ends of his cord, and as the larger loop shrank and disappeared the other caught Chaudri's finger tightly.

The crowd exploded with glee, and with an incredibly swift movement of his hand the proprietor pressed a 100-*dirham* note into Chaudri's palm.

"Oh, dearie me, no," Mahboob protested. "No money, do you not remember? Just for try?"

But the man in the *djelleba* would not accept the return of the bill. "You win! You win!" he chanted as if the words were a prayer, and the other players nodded their heads and jabbered their agreement in liquid Arabic syllables. Even Sikander Malek shouted over the din, "Why do you argue, my friend? You've won. Keep the money!"

"Absolutely not," said Chaudri firmly. "The man said just for try and I consented. If I had guessed wrongly, I would not have paid him. Guessing rightly, I may not profit."

The proprietor recognized his determination. "You keep half," he suggested. "I give you 100 *dirham*, you give me back 50. Then we both win, yes?"

At that, Chaudri's jet-black eyes gleamed with understanding, and he pulled his wallet from his hip pocket and fished out a crisp new 50-*dirham* note. The young man in the *djelleba* snatched it from his hand—and as if some powerful *djinn* had performed a feat of magic the Pakistanis found themselves alone at the edge of the Jemaa el Fna. Proprietor, gamblers, length of cord—all vanished so abruptly that their very existence might have been nothing but the memory of a dream were it not for the sagging cardboard carton left behind and the 100-*dirham* bill in Chaudri's hand.

"Fascinating," he said softly, looking around in vain for any other trace of the scene they had just been part of. "Most fascinating. How many gentlemen would you say were here just now?"

Malek frowned. "How many? Eight, perhaps, including the man with the cord. Eight or nine."

"Eight or nine. That means, say, 10 *dirham* for him and five for each of his accomplices. Not bad for only five minutes' work."

Sikander Malek was staring at him. "What is it you are saying, Chaudri? I am not understanding you at all."

Chaudri smiled. "Ah, my friend, I apologize. I assumed that you saw it, too."

"Saw it? Saw what, man?"

"The arrangement of the cord. No matter which of the loops I had chosen, the cord would have caught around my finger when pulled."

"You mean—you mean they *wanted* you to win?"

Chaudri clapped his companion on the shoulder. "Yes, of course. That was why they were here in the first place, pretending to play their most fascinating game. They were waiting for us to come along—or someone like us—waiting for the chance to let me win, 'just for try.'" He chuckled at the thought. "These men make their living with this little game of theirs. They set up their carton here and play, and, when the right tourist comes along, they urge him to enter their game."

"The *right* tourist?"

"Indeed. I was saying it earlier. These people can judge a man's character as expertly as others we have seen today can guess his weight. *You* would have kept the 100 *dirham*, my friend, where I would not. That is why they chose *me* to play their game instead of you. They saw that I am a man who would refuse to keep the full amount pressed into my palm, but who could be persuaded to take half in the spirit of fairness."

Malek seemed more perplexed than ever. "But you say they make a living at this game? How can that be? The man gave you 100 *dirham* and took back 50. He lost 50 *dirham* in the exchange!"

"No, no," Chaudri shook his head. "He took 50 *dirham* from me, and in return he gave me this." He handed the 100-*dirham* note to Malek, who examined it briefly and then looked up with comprehension dawning in his eyes.

"Counterfeit?"

Chaudri nodded. "A trifle, worth nothing at all. Perhaps they make them themselves, perhaps they buy them for a *dirham* or two. Either way, they sell them to unsuspecting tourists for 50 *dirham*, almost all of which is pure profit."

"But you were *not* unsuspecting—you knew what they were up to all the time!"

"Yes, I did. I was certain it was a con game even before they invited me to play. It all seemed too smooth, too carefully rehearsed to be spontaneous."

"Then why did you agree to take part?" Malek demanded. "Why did you give them your money?"

A broad grin spread across Mahboob Chaudri's nut-brown face.

"For 50 *dirham*," he said happily, "we have had the opportunity to participate in Moroccan street theater at its finest. But there is something more important than that." He took the counterfeit bill from Malek's fingers and held it up between them. "For 50 *dirham*," he said, "I have bought myself the souvenir I was searching for, a souvenir which will forever remind me of our afternoon in Marrakesh."

AFTERWORD

This is, I think, the most autobiographical story I've ever written. In 1984, while I was living in Germany, I spent two weeks in Morocco on vacation, including several days in Marrakesh—where I actually bargained for and bought the "ceremonial Berber belt" with its "bold colors and long tassels and colorful bits of mirror" which Mahboob regretfully passes up as too expensive, and I watched in fascination the workings of the con game by which Mahboob willingly allows himself to be victimized. I wanted to write about the city, so I sent Mahboob there as part of a security detail accompanying the Bahraini Minister of Defense to a Conference of Non-Aligned Nations, gave him a day off to explore, and then just reported very directly on my own experience.

I'd love to show you a picture of the belt, but I unfortunately lost it in my 1991 move from Europe back to America. (Long story.) I wish I *could* show it to you, since it looked every bit as beautiful hanging on my bedroom wall as Mahboob knew it would look on his. But the best I can do is show you a similar belt, so at least you'll have a general idea of what it looked like:

As you've noticed, I've peppered the Chaudri stories with occasional Arabic words and phrases—and with Mahboob's occasional swearing in Urdu. The Arabic alphabet is different from ours, though, so when I use Arabic words in the Chaudri stories, I have to transliterate them from the Arabic alphabet to ours. In the stories set in Bahrain, I consistently use the spelling *suq* for the old marketplace in the center of Manama. Depending on where you look, you may find the same word transliterated in a number of other ways, such as *sook* and *suq*. When this story was published in EQMM, the spelling used was *souk*, which is the English transliteration often used in Morocco. For the sake of consistency, I thought about changing that to *suq* for this collection, but ultimately decided not to. To emphasize the difference between Mahboob's usual stomping grounds and the setting of this story, I decided to let the marketplace in Marrakesh remain the *souk*.

You probably know that some English-language words vary depending on which country or which *part* of a country you're in—American cars have "hoods" and "trunks," for example, while British cars have "bonnets" and "boots," and a carbonated soft drink would be called a "soda" in New York but a "pop" in Michigan—and the same applies to some Arabic words and phrases. For example, the traditional checkered men's headdress which in Bahrain—and, therefore, in the Chaudri stories—is called a *ghutra* is in other parts of the Middle East called a *keffiyeh* (by Palestinians), a *shemagh* (by Jordanians), and so on. Similarly, the traditional ankle-length garment worn by men is called a *thobe* in Bahrain, while in Morocco it's a *djelleba*.

Parenthetically, the Bahraini *thobe* is usually (but not always) a solid color, generally white, while the Moroccan *djelleba* is usually (but not always) striped and dark. Here, have a look:

And, since I've used the terminology in many of the stories, this is perhaps a good time to identify the red-and-white checked headdress the man on the left is wearing as a *ghutra* and the black band used to keep it in place on his head (also useful for hobbling camels in a desert sandstorm!) as an *agal*.

Original EQMM editor Fred Dannay was notorious for changing his authors' titles, but I had much better luck with Eleanor Sullivan. She left all of my Chaudri titles intact—except for this one. *My* title, "Jemaa el Fna," was way cool: how could a reader see the word "Fna" on the page and not be sucked right into the otherness of the world of the story? But, for reasons of her own, Eleanor changed this one story's title to "The Exchange." I loved Eleanor dearly and still love her memory—but "The Exchange" is not only boring and bland, it's almost identical to the title of the *first* Mahboob story, "The Dilmun Exchange," which had appeared in EQMM only two years earlier! So the story is published here for the first time under its original title.

THE NIGHT OF POWER

The burning in his lungs was a hawk with sharpened claws, and it tore at his flesh with cruel anger.

Ana aouz cigara, he thought, his throat parched, his breathing hoarse. *I must have a cigarette!*

But it was Ramadan, the month of Saum, and the Holy Quran commanded all able-bodied adult Muslims to "eat and drink until so much of the dawn appears that a white thread may be distinguished from a black, then keep the fast completely until night."

The sick were temporarily exempt from fasting, as were nursing and pregnant women and travelers making long journeys, though they were all obliged to make up any of the 30 days they missed for such reasons as soon after the end of the month as they were able. Only the very young and the very old were fully excused from participation.

He had no reason not to fast, so he tasted no food in spite of his hunger, his cracked lips touched no water in spite of the heat of the day, and—worst of all—the packet of cigarettes in the pocket of his *thobe* remained unopened, and its cellophane wrapper crinkled in laughter at his suffering as he caressed it with longing fingers.

He looked out the plate-glass windows of the great Presidential Hotel, past the green-tiled roofs and golden central dome of the Guest Palace to the sea, where the sun's nether rim flamed but a centimeter above the slate-gray waters of Gudabiyah Bay. He watched without appreciation as the fireball extinguished itself in the Gulf and brilliant streaks of salmon and orange and brightest yellow washed across the ivory sky. He clenched his teeth and waited impatiently as darkness fell, and the *imams* peered solemnly at their white and black threads in the gathering dusk.

Then at last, at 8:07 PM, the signal canon sounded. Almost instantly there was a cigarette between his lips and he was drawing its soothing smoke deep within himself, blessing the Almighty for having given him the strength to conduct himself faithfully throughout the day.

Praise Allah, he thought, *only three days more and I am free of this torture for another year!*

When he had smoked his cigarette down to the filter, he stubbed it out in an ashtray and crossed the lobby to the doors of the Al-Wazmiyyah

Coffee Shop. The room was already crowded, but he filled a plate with *mezzah* and *ouzi* and *kofta kebabs* from the *Iftar* buffet and found an empty table by the window. He ate slowly and sparingly and drank three glasses of cool spring water, then he left the restaurant and, after a brief stop to pick up the object he needed, rode the elevator to the sixth floor of the hotel.

The corridor was deserted—all the Presidential's guests but one, he felt certain, were downstairs at the buffet, even the Westerners, who had been cautioned not to eat in public during the daylight hours as a sign of respect to Ramadan and to the Muslims observing the fast. He walked quickly down the hallway to the fire door, let himself through it, and climbed the last two flights of stairs to the hotel's top floor.

Here, too, there was no one to be seen, no one to see him as he crept along the thick brown carpeting to the door marked 613. He put his left ear and the fingertips of his right hand to the wood and listened intently. There was nothing to be heard from within. His hand darted into the pocket of his *thobe*, not for his cigarettes this time but for the ring of keys, which he clasped tightly in his fist to keep them from jangling as he drew them forth.

He selected one key from the dozen on the ring and fitted it soundlessly into the lock set into the doorknob. He held his breath as he turned the key, turned the knob, and swung the door inward just enough to allow himself to slip through the opening and ease it shut behind him.

The room was dark, illuminated only by the faint glow of the hotel's exterior lighting that filtered in through the drapery covering the single window.

He waited. The only noises in the room were the gentle hum of the air conditioner and the deafening pounding of his heart. When his eyes had adjusted to the almost-blackness, he was able to make out the shape in the left-hand bed, imagined he could actually *see* the one thin blanket rising and falling with the breathing of the figure who lay there asleep.

He stole across the room to the side of the bed and reached once more into his *thobe*'s deep side pocket.

When his hand reappeared, he was holding neither cigarettes nor keys. He was holding a small black revolver that glittered evilly in the diffused light admitted by the curtains, and his hand was steady as he touched it to the temple of the sleeping man in the bed.

* * * *

Mahboob Chaudri's temples throbbed and his pulse raced with exasperation as he stood looking down at the dead man.

"Where in the name of the Prophet is his clothing?" he demanded of no one, though there were four other people in the room to hear him. There were angrier words in Chaudri's mind, but he was able to bite them back before they escaped his lips. *Fasting is only one half of faith*, he reminded himself. During the month of Saum, hostile behavior was also to be avoided—as were lying, backbiting, slander, the swearing of false oaths, and the glance of passion. So it was written, and—a devout believer—so Mahboob Chaudri would comport himself, the better to avoid distraction from the pious attention to God that was the meaning of Ramadan. It was not easy for him to calm his thoughts, but he held them inside his mouth with the tip of his index finger as he returned his gaze to the bed.

The dead man was completely naked, covered only by a light blanket of a blue several shades paler than his eyes. He was a Westerner, a Caucasian, but his skin was richly tanned. He had close-cropped blond hair, a fine Roman nose, and what Jennifer Blake under happier circumstances would have called a dishy moustache. There was a small black hole just above his left temple, and the blood that drenched his pillow was still damp.

The Pakistani turned away in disgust. In spite of the air conditioning, he was hot and sticky in his olive-green Public Security uniform. There was a line of perspiration on his upper lip.

"Where are his *trousers*?" he exclaimed, fighting to keep his voice below a shout. "His shirt? His shoes and stockings? Where is his billfold? Where are his *papers*?"

"The murderer—" Abdulaziz Shaheen began, but Chaudri cut him off.

"Yes, yes, of course. The murderer has taken everything away with him, including the gun and the keys they used to let themselves into this room."

"But, *why?*" said Jennifer Blake, a willowy brunette in a trim gold-and-white suit with a nametag on one lapel that identified her as the hotel's night receptionist.

"So that we would not be able to determine the victim's identity, of course." Chaudri had been called away from his *Iftar* meal at the Juffair Police Barracks to investigate a report of a gunshot at the Presidential Hotel, and he was tired and hungry after a long day of fasting.

"That's not what I meant." The Blake woman frowned, her cultured British tone beginning to broaden under the strain of the evening's events. "It's bloody well obvious that's why his kit was taken off, excuse my French. What I meant was, why was he *here?*"

"Yes," said Mirza Hussain from a straight-backed chair by the low couch where the receptionist, Shaheen, and an elderly woman bundled up in a terrycloth bathrobe were all sitting. "That is exactly what I have been asking myself all along. Why was this man sleeping in room 613 in the first place? Why, for that matter, was he in the hotel at all?"

"He was not a guest?" asked Chaudri.

"I never checked him in," Jennifer Blake said firmly. "Not tonight nor any other night."

"Mr. Hussain? Mr. Shaheen?"

Although the Presidential was part of a large American chain, it was—like all major hotels in the emirate—run by Bahrainis and staffed by a mixture of British expatriates, Indians, and Pakistanis. Mirza Hussain was general manager, Abdulaziz Shaheen chief of security.

Both men were native Bahrainis, both now wore the traditional Arabic long white *thobes* and red-and-white-checkered *ghutras*, but there the resemblance between them ended. Hussain was built along the lines of the country's ruler, Sheikh Isa bin Sulman al-Khalifa; he was small in height but rather portly, with golden skin, a graying moustache and chin beard, and wise black eyes behind the glittering lenses of a pair of spectacles with thin golden rims. Shaheen was muscularly built and clean shaven and olive-complected, a decade younger and a full head taller than his superior.

"I have never seen him before," said Hussain, with an uncomfortable glance at the lifeless figure on the bed. "Perhaps Miss Ramsey or Miss Messenger checked him in during one of the other shifts."

The security chief shook his head. "I don't think he was a guest," he said, and paused to draw deeply on the cigarette held between the thumb and index finger of his right hand. When he spoke again, wisps of smoke puffed from his mouth along with his words. "But of course I can't be certain. It should be easy enough to find out."

"You yourself do not recognize him?" Chaudri persisted.

"No. I have no idea who he was. But whether he was a guest here or not, he had no business in this particular room, that much is certain."

"And why is that?"

It was Mirza Hussain who answered. "Standard hotel practice, *mahsool*. Sometimes important visitors drop in on us unexpectedly. We must always have space available to accommodate them. So, no matter how fully booked up we may be, we keep this one room vacant in case of an emergency. It is never rented out in the ordinary way."

Chaudri made an irritated grimace and turned back to the dead man in the bed. "Then what were you doing here sleeping?" he muttered. "What is it you were doing in room 613, where you ought not to have been at all, asleep so early on a Ramadan evening? And who is it who shot you, by all that is holy? Why were you here, and why were you killed, and by whom?" He curled his nut-brown hands into fists and rubbed wearily at his eyes. "All right," he sighed, "let us begin at the beginning. Frau Jurkeit?"

The older woman in the bathrobe stirred restlessly on the green leather sofa. "I am in ze room next door," she said, her English heavily accented. "Room 611. I am here in Manama wiss ze trade delegation from Bonn. We were to meet in ze coffee zhop downstairs for dinner at 8:30, but I twisted my ankle as I was dressing and decided to dine alone in my room. I ordered a—how do you say it?—a cutlet from room service." She glared disapprovingly at Mirza Hussain. "It was undercooked. Tomorrow I shall recommend zat we try ze Hilton instead. Just after nine o'clock I heard ze shot from zis room."

Chaudri took a pad from the pocket of his uniform jacket and made a note. "And what did you do then?"

"I called down to ze desk and reported what I had heard to, I assume, zis young woman."

"You did not look out into the corridor?"

"Certainly not!"

"Ah, yes," Chaudri remembered. "Your ankle."

"*Mein Gott*, it had nuzzing to do wiss my ankle! Someone is shooting a gun, do you sink I am sticking my head outside for a better look?"

"No, no," he said quickly. "Of course not. Miss Blake?"

The receptionist brushed a stray lock of hair into place and took up the story. "It was three past nine when I spoke with Frau Jurkeit, I checked the time as I hung up the phone. I immediately rang Mr. Shaheen's office, but he wasn't there at the moment. Then I tried Mr. Hussain, but he didn't pick up, either. So I did what I ought to have done straightaway, I expect—"

"You rang up the Manama Directorate," Chaudri completed the woman's sentence for her. "And the officer you spoke with reported to the Investigation Officer, and the Investigation Officer sent for me. And by the time I arrived here at the hotel, you had located Mr. Shaheen and Mr. Hussain, and you gentlemen had already come up to this room and let yourselves in, and discovered...."

He let his voice trail away and indicated the body in the bed with a wave of his hand. He worked his jaw thoughtfully from side to side and went on. "And discovered a naked man in a room where he ought never to have been, shot to death by an unknown assailant who then took all the victim's clothing and other belongings away with him when he left."

"It seems incredible," said Abdulaziz Shaheen. "What will you do now, *mahsool*?"

The Pakistani clapped his hands together decisively. "Now," he said, "I will begin to earn the salary which the Public Security Force is so generously paying me."

* * * *

It was almost midnight, and Mahboob Chaudri was alone in the room with Abdulaziz Shaheen. Mirza Hussain had gone down to his second-floor office, where he had promised to keep himself available in case his further presence should be required. Jennifer Blake was back at her post. In a few moments, she would be relieved by Gillian Messenger, who would be on duty at the reception desk until 8 AM. Frau Jurkeit had long since returned to her own room next door. Even the body of the murder victim was gone.

Much had happened during the last two hours. Two and three at a time, the Presidential Hotel's entire night staff and those members of the daytime and graveyard shifts the security chief had been able to reach by phone had paraded in and out of room 613 for a look at the dead man. Yousif Albaharna, the daytime doorman, thought he might have seen him entering the hotel that afternoon, but all Westerners looked more or less alike to him, he admitted sadly, and he could not be sure. No one else could remember ever having seen the man before, and both Gillian Messenger and Leslie Ramsey were certain they had not checked him in as a guest.

The Forensic Medical Officer had arrived shortly after 11, had examined the body, had confirmed that death had resulted from a single shot to the head from a small-caliber weapon, had grudgingly agreed that the victim had most probably been asleep at the time the shot was fired, had stood around impatiently while the final groups of hotel employees filed past the corpse, and then at last had instructed two uniformed *natoors* to carry it away on a stretcher. He would perform an autopsy in the morning, he announced, and then he was off.

Mahboob Chaudri had been kept almost continuously busy. He had interrogated the staff. He had conferred with the FMO. He had supervised the activities of the team of photographers and fingerprint men sent out by the Criminal Investigations Division. He had gone down to the lobby and verified that both of the keys to room 613 were present in the room's mail slot on the wall behind the reception counter, where they belonged. There were several sets of passkeys available to the maids, and the manager and security chief each had a set of his own, of course, but these, too, he had been able to account for.

It seemed improbable that the dead man and his murderer had entered the room together. A more likely explanation of the sequence of events was that the victim had let himself in, either with a skeleton key or by springing the lock with a strip of celluloid, and had then undressed and gone to sleep. The murderer had followed some time later on, had committed his crime and gone away with the dead man's belongings, unaware that there was anyone next door to hear the fatal gunshot and report it.

Thus far Mahboob Chaudri had proceeded with his investigation and with his thinking, and now he sat with Abdulaziz Shaheen and sipped gratefully at the strong Arabic coffee that Mirza Hussain had sent up for their refreshment. There was a bowl of fresh dates next to the fluted *dallah* on the room-service dolly, and the fruit had happily dulled the edges of Chaudri's hunger.

The security chief lit a cigarette from the butt of his last one and slipped the almost-empty packet back into the pocket of his *thobe*. "If only we could put a name to the man," he grumbled. "If we knew who he was, that might tell us why he was here in the hotel, in this room. And if we knew why he was here, that might tell us why he was killed, and who it was who shot him."

"In the morning," said Chaudri, "we will circulate his photograph around the embassies, the banks, the Western companies, and hopefully someone will recognize him. But all that must wait for business hours. If only there was something else we could be doing *now*."

"What a night to feel powerless," Shaheen growled, "on this, the most powerful night of the year."

Mahboob Chaudri looked up from his thoughts. In the flurry of activity surrounding the murder, he had forgotten that this 27th night of Ramadan was *Lailat al Qadr*, "the Night of Power," when the first teachings of the Holy Quran were revealed to the Prophet of Islam for the guidance of his followers.

"This night better than a thousand months," Chaudri quoted, "when angels and spirits descend to the Earth, and it is peace until the rising of the dawn."

He got impatiently to his feet and began to pace the deep golden carpet, his hands clasped fitfully behind his back.

"Well, for once the blessed Book is mistaken," he said. "There has been no peace for *me* this night, oh, dearie me, no. And there will *be* no peace for me, not until I locate the gun and identify the villain whose finger pulled its trigger, not even should all the angels and spirits in Heaven choose this very moment to begin their descent."

And at that very moment, Mahboob Chaudri ceased his restless pacing. "To begin their descent to Earth," he said slowly, staring down at the faint impression in the empty bed that showed him where the dead man had lain.

Then, to the amazement of Abdulaziz Shaheen, he grabbed up his peaked uniform cap from the nightstand between the two beds and dashed from the room without another word.

* * * *

Milling crowds of men in long white *thobes* and women in veils and long black *abbas* thronged the Baniotbah Road as Chaudri wheeled his dusty Land Rover out of the Presidential Hotel's parking lot and headed north toward the Muharraq Causeway. Andalus Park was filled with picnickers, and children splashed in the fountains as wide awake and gleeful as if it were the middle of the afternoon rather than the middle of the night. But this was Ramadan, and Bahrain's Islamic population would celebrate with food and drink and gaiety till long after dark, then sleep for several hours and arise to celebrate again until *Sahari*, when the first light appeared in the east and the *muezzin*'s call to dawn prayer announced that it was time to resume their fasting with the ritual of *Niyya*, the renewal of intention.

The crowds thinned out as he swung across the Khawr al Qulayah waterway, then picked up once more when he reached Muharraq Island. He left the Land Rover in a no-parking zone at the entrance to the International Airport's main terminal building and welcomed the rush of cool air that greeted him as he stepped through the glass doors.

As always, the terminal was buzzing with activity. Day and night had no meaning here: Bahrain was a refueling point for flights connecting the Western world with the Far East, and there was a constant ebb and flow of transit passengers whiling away the hours between legs of their journeys, in addition to the frequent takeoff and landing of planes beginning or terminating their runs in the emirate. As Chaudri paused in the teeming passenger hall to get his bearings, the information boards above his head showed the arrival of a Korean Airlines flight bringing construction workers from Seoul and the imminent departure of an Air France 727 returning bankers, corporate executives, and diplomats to Paris.

When he found the small glass-walled checkpoint he was looking for, a solicitous *natoor* listened to his request and handed him a thick bundle of white cards. He went through the stack carefully, and when he had examined them all he shuffled back to the middle of the pile and removed a single card. He read it again, and a third time, and then he put it in his pocket and returned the rest of the cards to the *natoor* and drove back into Manama to the Police Fort at Al Qalah, where he closed himself up in a tiny investigator's cubicle and placed a long-distance telephone call to a distant city where it was still late the previous afternoon.

* * * *

"I appreciate your staying on so late," said Mahboob Chaudri, as they stepped off the elevator into the quietly tasteful lobby of the Presidential Hotel. "So early, I suppose I should be saying—it will be dawn in another few hours. Which way is it we are going?"

"This way." Mirza Hussain led him past the entrance to the Al Wazmiyyah Coffee Shop (still open, but practically deserted now), past the reception desk (where Gillian Messenger stood diligently at her post), and down a broad corridor lined with boutiques, a newsstand, a hairdresser, all dark and long since closed for the night. "I am responsible for whatever happens at this hotel," he said as they walked. "Never before has such a terrible thing taken place here. Naturally I stayed."

"It is almost over now," Chaudri told him reassuringly. They were at the end of the corridor, facing a heavy wooden door marked "Abdulaziz Shaheen, Chief of Security" in both Arabic and English.

Chaudri knocked loudly, then twisted the doorknob and walked in without waiting for a response. The Presidential's security chief was seated behind a cluttered desk, a half-smoked cigarette in his hand. He had apparently been reading through the contents of the file folder lying open on the desk before him, but he closed it at their entrance and pushed it casually off to one side. His dark face was drawn and tired, and there were shadows beneath his deep-set black eyes.

"Mr. Shaheen," said Chaudri, "we've come to talk with you about the murder."

Shaheen nodded silently and waved them to a pair of chairs. He put his cigarette to his lips and inhaled deeply.

"According to the stories of Frau Jurkeit and Miss Blake," Chaudri began, "the death shot was fired at approximately nine o'clock last evening. Now, of all the puzzling questions this crime presents, the question which has been interesting me the most is this one: why was this man in bed, probably asleep, at that rather early hour of the evening? The simplest answer would be that he was in bed because he was tired. But why was he tired? During Ramadan, both Arabs and nonbelievers keep late hours as a rule—and even were it not Ramadan, nine o'clock is rather early for a man of that age to be sleeping, isn't it?"

"Not necessarily," Mirza Hussain frowned. "If he had had a busy day, he might well have decided to go to sleep early. But why here in my hotel? He was not a guest. He had no business here. He most certainly had no business in room 613."

"Yes, yes," said Chaudri. "But still the question bothered me. Then, an hour ago, you said something which supplied a possible answer, Mr. Shaheen."

"About the Night of Power, you mean?"

"Indeed. You reminded me that tonight, the 27th night of Ramadan, is *Lailat al Qadr*, and it struck me that perhaps our victim had just recently descended to Earth, like the angels and spirits written of in the Holy Quran—not in a winged chariot from Heaven, no, but in a silver bird from some other time zone. Though it was only nine in the evening to us when he died, if he was a new arrival from, say, the United States or Canada, his inner clock would have insisted that it was, for him, the middle of the night. Perhaps that was why he was in bed when his murderer found him in room 613."

Abdulaziz Shaheen stubbed out his cigarette carefully and took a fresh packet from the top drawer of his desk. He left the drawer open, Chaudri noticed, stripped off the cellophane and peeled back the foil, and tapped the packet against his forefinger. "So you think he was a newcomer to Bahrain?" he asked, as he flicked a thin gold lighter into flame.

"I know he was. When I left you in such a rush, I drove out to the airport and found the officer in charge of Customs and Immigration. He gave me all of the disembarkation cards filled out by the passengers who arrived in Bahrain yesterday afternoon. Those cards are containing quite a bit of information: name of the arriving passenger, home address, employer, reason for visit to the emirate, and so on. One of yesterday's cards caught my eye. It was made out in the name of Stephen Kimble, an American, and his employer was given as Presidential Hotels International, with an address in California, in the USA."

Abdulaziz Shaheen breathed out a cloud of smoke that masked the expression on his face for a moment.

"I placed a phone call to the Presidential chain's Los Angeles headquarters," Chaudri went on. "It was still daytime there, and I was able to speak with a Mr. Deming, who recognized my description of our unfortunate corpse and identified him as a company executive named Stephen Kimble and told me exactly why Mr. Kimble had been sent to Bahrain."

It happened so swiftly that, had Mahboob Chaudri not been waiting for the movement, he would certainly have missed it. Abdulaziz Shaheen's hand darted into his opened desk drawer and came out holding a .25-caliber Browning automatic pistol. His dark face was cold and hard as he jumped up from his chair with the gun in his fist.

"I must insist that you keep both your hands in sight," he said, his voice tight and strained. "I'm sorry, Mr. Hussain, but I really must insist."

Mirza Hussain sat very still, one hand in the pocket of his *thobe*. His eyes told a tale of infinite weariness and sorrow. At last, with a deep sigh, he took his hand from his pocket. He was holding a packet of cigarettes and a plastic lighter. He lit a cigarette for himself and held out the packet to Chaudri.

"No, no," the Pakistani shook his head. "I am not a smoker. It is, I think, an evil habit. But it does not seem to have interfered with your reflexes, Mr. Shaheen. I'm glad I stopped in to see you on my way up to the second floor and warned you of what to expect from this visit. Now, if you will give me your pistol, I will hold it while you are seeing what else is to be found in Mr. Hussain's cavernous pockets."

"You are thinking of the murder weapon?" Hussain smiled grimly. "I don't have it here, gentlemen. Perhaps I should have brought it with me, after all. But it is back in my office, in my closet—in Stephen Kimble's suitcase."

* * * *

"You were embezzling money from the hotel," said Chaudri flatly, when Abdulaziz Shaheen had confirmed that the manager's pockets were indeed empty, save for a ring of passkeys and a handkerchief.

"Yes. Never very much at a time. Always small amounts, small amounts. But over the last three years I have diverted almost fifty thousand dinars into my private account. I was very careful. I thought it would be impossible for anyone to discover what I had done. Apparently I was wrong."

"Embezzlement," remarked Mahboob Chaudri, "is also an evil habit. More evil than smoking, since it does harm not only to oneself but to others as well. But I am interrupting. Please forgive me and go on with what you were saying."

Hussain told his story matter-of-factly. There was nothing in his manner to indicate that he saw anything out of the ordinary in the events he was describing. "Kimble flew in yesterday afternoon," he said. "He took a taxi from the airport and came directly to my office without stopping at the reception desk. We spoke for a few moments only. He was exhausted from his journey, and I took him up to 613 and let him in with my passkey. He did not tell me why he had come—we would talk further in the morning, he said—but I knew. The home office had found out about the missing money. He had come to investigate, and he was sure to learn that I was the thief. If only I could have another few days, I thought, I could get my affairs in order and get out of the country before anyone was the wiser."

"So you killed him," said Abdulaziz Shaheen.

Hussain looked down at the glowing tip of his cigarette. "Yes. I waited until *Iftar* was well under way, when I could be certain that the sixth floor would be deserted, then I went upstairs and let myself back into the room. It was dark, he was sound asleep. I shot him. Then I gathered his belongings and put them in his suitcase with the gun and brought it down to my office."

"You realized that if we knew who he was," Chaudri suggested, "we would quickly learn the reason for his visit to Bahrain. And that would tell us it was you who had the only motive for killing him."

"I thought I was safe. Unless room 613 is in use, the maids clean it only once a week. It would be days before the body was discovered, I felt certain, and by then I would be safely away. It never struck me that there might be anyone else on the sixth floor when I fired the shot. I never stopped to consider that you would be able to trace him through Customs and Immigration without his papers. I must have been mad. If I had thought of that, I would never have killed him. I would have dropped everything and fled."

Mahboob Chaudri got to his feet. "But criminals never think of everything," he said. "Not even wise men think of everything. Perhaps it is their remembering that fact which makes them wise."

* * * *

"In another hour it will be *Niyya*," said Mirza Hussain, lighting a cigarette. "I'd better smoke now, while it is still permitted."

Chaudri marveled at the state of the man's mind, at the idea that he felt it acceptable to embezzle money during the month of Ramadan, felt it permissible to commit murder then or at any other time, but would be careful to avoid food, drink, and tobacco during the daylight hours as if he were truly a devout Muslim.

They were standing in the warm night air in front of the Presidential Hotel's main entrance, waiting for a Public Security van to come and take Hussain away. The streets were almost empty, the city was asleep. But shortly the Islamic population would begin to awaken, in time to enjoy another meal before the time of fasting began.

"Listen to me, *mahsool*," said Mirza Hussain softly. "I have perhaps ten thousand dinars hidden away at my home. If we were to go there, you and I, I could give you half of that money and use the other half to make my escape. You could say that I broke away from you, that you chased after me but lost me in the darkness. No one would ever know the truth."

Chaudri did not respond.

"Five thousand dinars," the murderer continued. "That is a great deal of money, *mahsool*. It is, I imagine, more than your beautiful green uniform earns you in an entire year. Does my proposal not even tempt you?"

Chaudri considered the question. In fact, five thousand dinars was slightly more than he earned as a policeman in *two* years. It was enough to make the down payment on the bungalow in Jhang-Maghiana he was planning to build for Shazia and the children. It was enough to allow him to return to Pakistan much earlier than he had ever dreamed possible.

Was he tempted? Was he resisting temptation now, or was his mind truly pure?

The answer came to him with the clarity of polished crystal.

"No," he said firmly, truthfully. "Your proposal is not tempting me, Mr. Hussain. It is not tempting me at all."

It was still quite dark, but soon the sky would begin to lighten. Soon it would be possible to distinguish a white thread from a black, soon the *muezzin* would call the faithful to the renewal of their fast, soon the Night of Power would draw to a close.

Mahboob Ahmed Chaudri took in a deep breath as he stood there before the great hotel with his prisoner at his side. He could feel the power enter his body, his lungs, his very being—the power of a thousand months. He raised his gaze to the heavens and offered up a silent prayer of thanksgiving and joy. As his lips formed the unspoken words, a shooting star arced across the sky and lost itself in the velvet infinity of the night.

A great sense of peace descended around him and into him, a peace Mahboob Chaudri knew would last until—no, *beyond*—the rising of the dawn.

AFTERWORD

This, in my opinion, is one of the best of the Mahboob Chaudri stories—possibly *the* best—and it was the last to appear in the pages of EQMM.

All of the background information about Ramadan and *Lailat al Qadr* is accurate—if memory serves, I did more research before writing this story than for any of the others. The Presidential Hotel doesn't really exist, but there were quite a few American-owned hotels like it in Manama when I was there.

In preparing this collection of the Chaudri stories, I reread them all, some for the first time since their original publication. It was tempting at times to polish them for this new incarnation, but for the most part I've left them as they originally appeared. Here, though, I've made one change I'd like to explain.

In the version of this story that was published in the September 1986 issue of EQMM, Mahboob Chaudri and Abdulaziz Shaheen drink coffee at one point from what I referred to as "a fluted *qraisheih*." In preparing this volume for publication, to make sure I had the unusual spelling correct, I checked it online—and came up completely empty. Perhaps it's a term that has fallen out of fashion, or perhaps my original use of it was simply a mistake. In any case, I've replaced it with the word *dallah*, which seems to be the contemporary name for the fluted metal Arabic coffee pot I meant to include in the story. Here, to give you the idea, is a photograph of the one I bought a quarter of a century later, when what was by then renamed the University of Maryland University College sent me back overseas to spend a summer teaching on a US Army base in the middle of the Kuwaiti desert:

I don't think I ever actually knew anyone named Gillian until I came to work at my present position at Northern Virginia Community College, where Gillian Backus is a member of the biology department, but I note that, in the 1980s when I was originally writing these stories, it seems to have been a name I considered typically British, since I used it both for

Gillian Messenger in this story and—as you'll see—for Gillian Steele in the next one, "Sheikh's Beach."

"The Night of Power" was one of the 13 stories Ed Hoch selected for inclusion in his 1987 volume, *The Year's Best Mystery and Suspense Stories* (Walker and Company), where he introduced it like this: "The exotic area of Bahrain on the Persian Gulf is well known to Josh Pachter, who lived and worked there before moving to his present home in West Germany. Pachter's name can be found these days in all the American mystery magazines, and I think his most successful stories to date have been those involving his sleuth Mahboob Chaudri in the mysteries of a region still too little known and understood by the Western world."

SHEIKH'S BEACH

"Look, Mum, bang ahead there!" Jeremy Steele stabbed excitedly at the windscreen. "It's a camera tree, see it?"

"Cama tee," baby Adam echoed from the rear of the battered old canary-yellow station wagon, waving his stubby forefinger in eager imitation of his older brother.

Gillian Steele hunched forward over the steering wheel and peered through the dusty glass. A magnificent date palm marked the end of the road some 50 yards on, and its broad trunk seemed indeed to be overgrown with a lush crop of cameras of assorted shapes and sizes. "Odd," she murmured, more to herself than her children. "Perhaps it *is* a camera tree, at that."

"Cama tee, cama tee!" Adam bounced gleefully in his car seat. At 24 months, he was thoroughly entranced with the sound of his own voice, a development which thrilled his father but often left his mother exhausted by day's end.

"Cameras don't really grow on trees, Mum, do they?" asked Jeremy.

"I'm quite sure they don't. We'll see what this soldier says, then, shall we?"

A small-framed dark man in an olive-green uniform and peaked black cap stood by the side of the tree, and as they approached him he held up a hand and signaled Gillian to stop. Now that they were closer, they could see that the cameras had been hung by their straps from nails driven into the trunk of the palm.

Gillian rolled down her window and switched off the noisy air conditioning. "I still haven't gotten used to driving on this side of the car," she announced, as if the man had asked her a question.

He smiled at her, and his nut-brown skin made his teeth seem dazzlingly white. "You are from England, then, madam?" he deduced.

"Yes, London, actually. We've only just arrived this week and our own car won't be here for ages, so my husband hired this wagon from a place called Darwish Rent-a-Dent. What a lovely name, don't you think? Well, anyway, it was quite cheap, really, nothing at all like one would have to pay in London." She blushed prettily. "I'm talking too much, aren't I? We haven't met anyone yet, you see, and with Jeffrey at work all day that leaves me alone with the children. I'm afraid I'm rather desperate for conversation."

"Ask him about the camera tree, Mum," Jeremy whispered fiercely, and baby Adam shrilled "Cama tee!" from the back seat as if on cue.

"Quietly, please, Adam," said Gillian. "And Jeremy, love, you are big enough to ask the gentleman yourself."

"Please, sir," the boy said shyly, and the man in the green uniform drew closer to the open window, "are you a Bahrainian soldier?"

"Not at all, my young friend. For one thing, I am a police officer, not a soldier. And for another, I am from Pakistan, not Bahrain. Now perhaps you should be telling me a bit about yourself, Master—?"

"Steele, sir. Jeremy Steele. I'm eight years old."

"Jemmy," little Adam confirmed joyously. "Jemmy, Jemmy, Jemmy!"

"And that is—?"

"Adam, sir. My brother. Don't mind him, he's just a baby. Why's that tree got all them cameras on it?"

Gillian Steele raised an eyebrow. "*Those* cameras, Jeremy."

"*Those* cameras. Why has it?"

The Pakistani hunkered down for a better view of the station wagon's passengers. "This is a private beach," he explained. "It is owned by Sheikh Abdulaziz bin Yousif al-Sayed, one of the wealthiest men in Bahrain. Sheikh Abdulaziz has made the beach available for the exclusive use of Westerners—no Arabs are allowed here, except for the Sheikh himself and his family."

"He's a bit eccentric, then," said Gillian, "isn't he?"

"But why are all them—sorry, Mum—*those* cameras hanging there?" the boy insisted.

"Sheikh Abdulaziz does not care to be photographed by his guests. And since he is quite influential in the government of Bahrain, a police officer is stationed here at the entrance to his beach during its open hours. Our job is to ensure that no Arabs violate the Sheikh's privacy, and to see that no cameras are brought inside the grounds. Do you have a camera with you, madam?"

"Ah, yes, we do, actually." The woman turned around to fetch it from the back seat. "Oh, Adam, look what you've done! Jeremy, be a love and find the camera for the officer while I wipe this up, please?" She shook her head sadly and reached for a cloth.

"It's a silly rule, that's what I think," her older son complained, rummaging about in a canvas bag filled with diapers and packets of sandwiches and tubes of sun lotion. "I don't see why we can't take photos if we want to."

"You will find," said the policeman kindly, "that many of the rules here in the Middle East are different from those you are used to. The customs, the traditions, the language—even the alphabet itself—all these are things you must come to understand and accept, if you are to be happy while you reside in Bahrain."

"Here, Jeremy, let me have that." Gillian Steele plucked a small Kodak from the bag and handed it to the Pakistani.

"Jemmy," baby Adam pouted from the rear. "Jemmy, Jemmy!"

"How will you ever remember which of them's ours when we leave?" Jeremy demanded.

"I will be counting on your assistance, my young friend. Though I may indeed have forgotten which of these cameras is yours by the time you are ready to leave this place, surely you will help me to remember." He hung the camera from a vacant nail and turned back to them. "You may proceed," he smiled. "You will find a parking area not far ahead, and from there you will see the Gulf before you. I trust you will enjoy your visit to Sheikh's Beach."

Gillian thanked him and turned the key in the ignition and rolled up her window and drove off, leaving the Pakistani alone in the morning heat.

Some of the men enjoyed this duty, would rather stand here quietly in the shade than trudge endlessly through the sweltering maze of the *suq* for the eight hours of their shifts.

Mahboob Chaudri was not one of them. He preferred the liveliness, the activity, the vitality of his regular beat. Oh, yes, he appreciated the opportunity to exchange pleasantries with charming families like the Steeles, but that was the only aspect of this assignment he valued. Otherwise, he found it a chore better suited to the talents of a hat-check girl than a policeman.

He was a loyal member of the Public Security Force, though, and on the infrequent occasions when he was scheduled to spend a day on guard at Sheikh's Beach he did not protest.

Not that it would do him any good if he *did* protest. He remembered a story Sikander Malek had told him on the very day of his arrival in Bahrain. It was not, perhaps, a true story, but it had made an impression on him all the same. It was the story of an impertinent *natoor* from Baluchistan who, when he was as new to the emirate as Chaudri himself, regularly challenged the orders of his commanding officer. "But, sir," he argued hotly, when he was finally called to task for his arrogance, "surely you were not rising to your esteemed rank by meekly obeying every order ever given to you by a superior, without even pausing to question its wisdom?" The Deputy Director nodded slowly. "You are correct," he admitted. "That is not how I rose from *natoor* to my current position. It is, however, how I rose from *natoor* to my first promotion."

Chaudri stepped into the shade of the camera tree and wiped his forehead with a damp white handkerchief and sighed.

It was 10:24 AM, and the temperature was 87 degrees. It would reach 100 by noon.

* * * *

A cooling shadow fell across Gillian Steele's legs, and she looked up from her book to see a man towering over her—a very brown man, browner even than the Pakistani who had taken their camera, in baggy burnt-orange trousers and a loose shirt of the same color whose absurdly long tails hung far below his knees.

"I pray that I did not startle you," he said, his voice deep and resonant.

She adjusted the shoulder straps of her bathing suit and sat up, tipping back the broad brim of her straw hat so she could see him more clearly. "Yes?"

"I fear I have interrupted your reading."

"What, this rubbish?" Gillian closed the book and tossed it to the sand. On its lavender cover, a blonde in a white dress was running away from an onion-domed mosque in the dead of night with a look of unspeakable terror on her lovely face; a single light gleamed mysteriously from atop the minaret which stood beside the mosque. "Interruption quite welcome, actually. I've never tried a romance before, but a woman at the British Club recommended this one because it's set right here in Bahrain. I've read about 30 pages, and it's really just too awful. Damn!" She slapped irritably at a loud buzzing on her arm. "If it wasn't for these bloody flies, this place would be smashing."

The stranger bowed his head respectfully. "They are indeed an irritation. But perhaps I can offer you at least a temporary respite. You have noticed the golden beach house of Sheikh Abdulaziz?"

The beach was a strip of perfectly manicured sand, sandwiched between the palm forest that concealed the parking area and the brilliant iridescence of the Gulf. Southward, it stretched beyond the horizon, but a hundred yards to the north the vista was broken by a white pier jutting out into the water and a large, square two-story structure that was more yellow than gold. Gillian had assumed it was an office building, though why anyone would locate their offices so far from the city was a question it had been too hot to ponder.

"Yes, of course. It's a lovely home."

"The Sheikh will be delighted to know that you think so. He wonders if you would care to join him for tea?"

Gillian flushed. "Oh, my! That's frightfully kind of him, but I—I'm afraid I really couldn't." She rolled onto her side and fumbled unnecessarily with Adam's sunbonnet. "My son's asleep, you see. I couldn't possibly leave him alone, and I'd hate to wake him, now that he's finally gone off."

"Ah, of course. The Sheikh will be most—"

"Mum, Mum, look at this!" Jeremy came running up in a spray of sand, an open bottle of soda held tightly in his fist.

Gillian got to her knees and brushed sand from his hair. "Not so loud, love, your brother's in the middle of a kip. Where did you get that, then?"

"There's a little hut back there in the trees, and the man said I could have whatever I wanted. Shall I fetch you one? They've got Pepsi and strawberry and—"

"It is quite all right," said the stranger. "The Sheikh is pleased to provide soft drinks for the refreshment of his guests."

Jeremy hugged his bottle to his pale white chest and examined the man critically. "Who are you?"

"My name is Naveen Jayasinghe. I have the honor to serve His Excellency Sheikh Abdulaziz bin Yousif al-Sayed."

"Are you from Pakistan, like that policeman when we came in?"

"Oh, no, I am an Indian."

Jeremy shook his head. "You're not an Indian. Where's your tommy hawk, then?"

Jayasinghe smiled. "I am not a cowboys-and-Indians Indian. I am an Indian from India. There is quite a large difference. Now, if you would be so good as to excuse me, I shall return to—"

"No, wait!" The words popped out of Gillian's mouth before she could stop them. "Jeremy, sweet, Mr. Jayasinghe came over to invite me to meet the Sheikh, but I didn't like to leave Adam alone. Now you're here, though, stay and look after him for me for a bit, will you, love?"

"But, Mum, I was just going in for a swim!"

"Yes, well, the sea will still be there in half an hour, stubborn. Do this for me, Jeremy, please? How often do you think one gets a chance to have tea with a sheikh?"

The boy dropped to the blanket with a disgusted mutter and took a sip of his soda. "Right, then. I'll just sit here and mind the child, shall I?"

Gillian chucked him under the chin. "There's my very best helper. I'll be back before you miss me. Right with you," she promised the Indian, and reached for her skirt and blouse.

* * * *

"And what are his duties there?" Sheikh Abdulaziz asked, and sipped from the delicate porcelain cup cradled protectively in his hands.

"Well," said Gillian, "one of the Council's most important activities is teaching English as a second language to Arabs and other non-native speakers. There are eight lecturers at the moment, and Jeffrey's been brought in to coordinate the entire program."

"It is, then, a position of great responsibility."

"Oh, yes, it's frightfully important. Ever since your country became independent in—'72, was it?"

"The 14th of August, 1971," the Sheikh murmured.

"Yes, of course, '71. Well, since then, the British Consul has been England's primary representative in Bahrain. And since the British Council's closest contact with your people has been through its language program, the coordinator's job carries quite a bit of weight. The previous bloke, Brian Stevens, couldn't handle the pressure, apparently, so they demoted him to lecturer and brought Jeffrey in to replace him."

"And I am certain your husband will acquit himself admirably." The Sheikh raised his index finger a fraction of an inch, and instantly a servant appeared at his side to refill his cup from an ornate brass pot with a long fluted spout. "Mrs. Steele?"

The tea was strong and rather bitter, but Gillian was certain it would be impolite to refuse. "Yes, please. It's lovely tea."

The Sheikh had not risen from his chaise at her approach, but he had leaned forward to offer her his hand. She had thought him rude at first, then reminded herself that he was a member of the royal family and suspected that it was she who had committed a gaffe by her failure to curtsy.

He was a tiny man, surely no more than five feet tall, and he seemed even smaller in his voluminous gold-trimmed *thobe*. The folds of his long white *ghutra* framed a friendly olive face; his nose was wide and flat, his lower lip full, his mouth kind between a thin black mustache and a graying chin beard. Framed by wire spectacles that glittered in the sun, his enormous brown eyes were intelligent and curious. Two steps behind him, an impassive Indian in a white turban stood with a broad palm frond in his hands, noiselessly fanning it up and down to produce a wonderfully cooling breeze.

From the patio where they sat, they looked out over the calm green sea and the crowded sand. They were too far away from her blanket to see what the boys were up to. Several attractive Western women in bikinis lay much closer at hand, and Gillian wondered how she had been selected for the honor of this audience. Did Naveen Jayasinghe do the choosing, or did the Sheikh have a telescope hidden away on the upper floor of his golden beach house? She was tempted to ask, but could such a question possibly be permitted? Surely not. There must be some official protocol specifying how one was to behave in the presence of Arabic royalty, but she had no idea what it included. Perhaps Jeffrey would know.

She realized that Sheikh Abdulaziz was speaking and managed to set her thoughts aside for the moment and return her attention to him.

" ... being planned as a resort area," he was saying, "with restaurants and other amenities. There is no such thing as tourism in Bahrain as yet, but I am hoping that, as we develop more of our beaches and continue with our program of archeological excavation, we will be able to—"

A sudden noise came from behind her, and the Sheikh's brow furrowed with surprise. Gillian turned in her chair to see her older son racing toward them across the patio, his bare feet slapping the warm yellow tiles in soft explosions.

"Jeremy, what on earth are you doing here? I thought I told you to stay with your brother!"

He stood before her, panting, his right palm pressed tightly to his heart. "I know, Mum," he gasped. "I'm sorry. I was wrong. I shouldn't have done it."

"Shouldn't have done what?" Gillian Steele felt her throat constrict. "Jeremy, please, what's happened?"

Hot tears welled up in the boy's eyes and spilled to his cheeks. "It's Adam, Mum. He's gone!"

* * * *

"I thought I might find some seashells," Jeremy sobbed. His face was twisted with grief. "Adam was sleeping, and I thought perhaps I'd find some pretty ones he could play with when he woke up. I only went down to the edge of the water. I only meant to be gone for a moment."

"And what happened?" asked Mahboob Chaudri gently. They had placed themselves around the perimeter of the Steeles' brightly colored beach blanket—Jeremy, Gillian, the Pakistani and the Sheikh—and an outer circle of curious sunbathers had formed beyond them. Jeremy's rubber sandals, denim shorts and rolled-up T-shirt held the blanket's four corners in place; a canvas tote bag rested in the sand to one side, and Gillian's book lay where she had thrown it. The center of the blanket was very empty.

"A man," said Jeremy. "He took him. I saw it—I shouted at him to put him down, but he ran away."

"Can you remember what the man looked like? Was he a dark man, like me?"

"No, sir. I was only down at the water, so I could see him clearly. He was a white man, his legs and chest were very pale."

Chaudri nodded approvingly. "He was wearing only a bathing costume, then?"

"Shorts, sir. Khaki shorts. I noticed him walking along the beach earlier, but I didn't pay much attention to him. I mean, he was just a man, I didn't have any reason to be interested in him. But then he snatched up my brother and ran into the trees, toward the parking area."

"And what did you do?"

"I chased him, shouting and shouting. Some people came to help, but they were too late: the man put Adam in the back of his car and drove away. It was a white car, I don't know what kind." Jeremy put a fist to his mouth and spoke through it, his voice tortured. "I shouldn't have gone off! He's going to hurt him, I know he is, and it's all my fault!"

Gillian knelt beside her son and put her arms around him, tousled his smooth brown hair with a comforting hand. "Hush, Jemmy," she crooned. "Hush, now, we'll find him. He'll be fine. Everything will be fine."

But her eyes shone with the desperate fear of an animal in a trap.

"There is only one way out of this compound," the Sheikh said softly. "You must have seen the car, *mahsool*."

"Indeed," the Pakistani frowned. "But many automobiles have come and gone today, and many of them have been white. If only I had noticed the little one and recognized that he was being taken away in a different car than the car he arrived in. But I did not notice, and now we have nothing, no slightest clue."

"A clue, sir?" Jeremy Steele looked up from his mother's embrace. "Would the license number of the car be a clue?"

"The license number? Most excellent child, did you see the license number of the car? Not the letters, the letters are the same on every Bahraini license plate, but the Arabic numerals? Is that what you saw? Can you remember?"

"Yes, sir. I memorized it, sir, that's what they always do on the police programs on the telly. I didn't really memorize it on purpose, I just—"

"Jeremy." Gillian's voice was strangled, strained with hope. "Just tell the officer the number, please."

"Sure, Mum. It was 9107, sir."

Chaudri repeated the figures, offered them to Allah in a fervent prayer. "Master Steele," he said, "are you certain you have remembered correctly?"

"Yes, sir. Quite certain, sir. It was 9107, I swear it."

"Then we have him," Mahboob Chaudri exulted, his fist clenched triumphantly beneath the fire of the afternoon sun. "We have him!"

But it was not to be that easy.

An urgent telephone call to the Vehicle Registration Office of the Traffic & Licensing Directorate of the Ministry of the Interior produced the information that the automobile carrying license plate number 9107 was a 1981 Volkswagen Golf, and was registered to one Jassim Ismail Shirazi, a resident of the public housing project at Isa Town.

Jeremy Steele had seen a white man carry off baby Adam, but the owner of the vehicle with the plate number the boy had memorized had an Arabic name. Had the car been stolen? Chaudri's second call, to the Officer in Charge of the Investigation Division of the Criminal Investigation Directorate, revealed that the Volkswagen had *not*—as yet, at least—been reported missing. It was, of course, entirely possible that Jassim Shirazi had not as yet realized that it was gone.

A third call, to the Investigation Officer of the Isa Town Public Security Station, resulted in the immediate dispatch of a Land Rover and a pair of *mahsools* to Mr. Shirazi's address.

The officers found the suspect vehicle parked behind the modern six-story apartment building in which Shirazi lived. The car was pale green, not white, and its owner lay on a canvas drop cloth beneath it, busily engaged in replacing its badly rusted muffler. Several of Shirazi's neighbors were clustered around the Volkswagen, observing the work in progress and offering suggestions and encouragement.

Adiyay, the policemen demanded. How long had Shirazi been working? All day, the man vowed, since early that morning. And after a huddled conversation, the bystanders agreed that neither Shirazi nor his automobile nor its license plates had left the parking lot for many hours. Are you certain, the policemen insisted. *Aywah*, the Arabs nodded sagely. They were certain.

"*Beri pani peh geya*," Mahboob Chaudri uttered, when the news was relayed back to Sheikh's Beach. "It is wrong, all wrong. The car is the wrong color, the owner is the wrong color, everything is wrong." He wiped the sweat from his burning forehead and wished Sheikh Abdulaziz and the Steeles would turn their heads just long enough for him to empty the infuriating sand from his heavy black shoes.

* * * *

Mahboob Chaudri and Jeremy Steele stood side by side at the water's edge, staring silently out across the opalescent Gulf at the hazy brown line on the distant horizon that was the coast of Saudi Arabia and the flickering pinpoints of orange flame that were the burnoffs atop the Dharan oil refinery's smokestacks.

"Are you certain?" the Pakistani said at last. "Are you *certain* you have remembered the numbers correctly?"

The boy traced a 9 in the damp brown sand with a thin stick he had picked up as they walked the beach. "Yes, sir," he said. "It was 9107, I'm positive." He pushed the tip of the stick into the sand and pulled it toward him, adding a long 1 beside the 9 he had drawn.

Chaudri raised his head and gazed again at the infinite beauty of the Gulf. In Karachi, where his family still lived, he had often taken his children to Clifton Beach to bathe, had often stood proudly and watched Arshed and Perveen and little Javaid as they frolicked happily in the gently lapping wavelets of the Arabian Sea.

Beside him, Jeremy scratched an oval and the crooked shape of a 7 in the sand, but Chaudri's mind was elsewhere. He was thinking of his son Javaid, his youngest, whose innocent nut-brown face was the very image of his father's. Javaid was almost five, now, but the last time Chaudri had seen him, the last time he had been permitted to return to Pakistan on home leave, the child was only three, barely a year older than the poor kidnapped Adam.

If it had been Javaid who was missing, his own flesh, his own blood, would he be standing here in idleness? Of course not, the idea was absurd. Yet what was there to do? As small as the emirate was, it was much too large for him to search its every corner, far too large for the entire Public Security Force to track down an infant and a single unknown criminal who could be hiding anywhere in its capital city or its many villages or its 200 square miles of desert.

Chaudri sighed, and writhed uncomfortably within the hot confines of his olive-green uniform. He rested a hand on Jeremy Steele's shoulder and, glancing down, noticed the numerals the boy had scrawled so carefully in the sand.

He froze.

"Oh, dearie me," he breathed. "If only we are not already too late!"

* * * *

"He is, I fear, quite mad," Chaudri explained. "He resented your husband's replacing him at the British Council and determined to avenge himself by stealing away your child. By Allah's grace, however, we were able to find him before...."

He allowed the sentence to trail away unfinished.

"Would Brian have—do you really think he would have *hurt* Adam?" Gillian winced at the possibility. "He seemed like such a harmless little chap."

The Pakistani turned up his palms. "There is no way of knowing. We can only be grateful that he brought the baby directly to his home, where it was easy for us to locate them."

They were seated on plush red couches in the spacious living room of the Sheikh's beach house. The room was tastefully decorated, with deep brown carpeting on the floor and paintings by Bahraini artists on the ivory walls, brass coffee tables and a crystal chandelier and an enormous picture window offering a magnificent panorama of the Gulf.

Gillian Steele had barely noticed the furnishings or the view, though, despite her earlier interest in the interior of the house. Her entire universe at that moment extended no farther than her younger son, who sat merrily in a wooden high chair Naveen Jayasinghe had brought down from an upstairs storage room and basked in all the wonderful attention he was getting. Adam seemed none the worse for his experience, and it was clear that the kidnapper—now in custody at Jau Prison—had treated him gently.

"I myself am most entirely grateful," Sheikh Abdulaziz murmured. "But what I do not understand, *mahsool,* is how you were able to discover so quickly where the child was being held."

Chaudri smiled wryly. "What I myself am not understanding," he said, "is how I can have been so blind as not to have seen the answer much sooner. When young Master Jeremy told me that he had seen the number of the kidnapper's automobile, I asked him if he was certain that it was the Arabic numerals he had memorized."

"It *was* the Arabic numbers I saw," Jeremy cried. "But 9107 turned out to be a different car!"

"Indeed. But do you also remember, my young friend, that when you first arrived at Sheikh's Beach this morning, I was telling you that many things are different here from what you are used to in faraway England?"

"Yes, sir," the boy agreed. "You said the rules are different, and the language, and even the alphabet."

The Sheikh's eyes widened.

"Even the alphabet," Mahboob Chaudri repeated. "And even the numbers. What you in the West call Arabic numerals, you see, are not entirely the same as what we in the Arabic world call Arabic numerals. In some cases, they *are* the same: your one and your nine are the same as ours, for example. But there are also differences. Our seven looks exactly like your letter V, our eight like your V turned upside down, our zero like the period you use at the end of a sentence."

"But there was one of our zeroes and one of our sevens on the license plate!"

"And that is the oddest difference between Western 'Arabic' numbers and Arabic Arabic numbers," Chaudri nodded. "We make use of the same symbol which to you represents zero, only for us that endless oval is the numeral five. And, for us, the symbol which you call a seven stands for six."

"In that case," said Gillian, "what Jeremy thought was 9107 was actually—or, no, half a tick. There's another difference between Arabic and English, isn't there? We read our language from left to right, but you read yours from right to left. So Jeremy's 9107 turns out to be—let's see, now—6519."

"Very close, Mrs. Steele. But another of the unusual features of the Arabic language is that, although *words* are read from right to left, *numbers* are read from left to right, just the same as English. I should have realized immediately that the number your son saw was in fact 9156, but I foolishly failed to do so. It was not until I saw him trace the English numbers 9107 in the sand that I recognized my mistake and had the Vehicle Registration Office look up the owner of the automobile with plate number 9156. Who, of course, turned out to be Brian Stevens, your husband's predecessor at the British Council and still a resident of Manama."

"And the Manama Directorate sent policemen to Mr. Stevens' home," the Sheikh completed the recital, "where they found the car and the criminal ... and, most importantly, the child."

"The child," Gillian Steele beamed, "the lovely child. I—I can't thank you enough, officer, for getting him back safely. If Brian had—if Adam was—I don't know what I—"

And then she was crying, and Jeremy slid closer to her on the sofa and put his arms around her and held her. After a while, she looked up and sniffled and parted with an embarrassed laugh. "There's so much I want to say to you, officer, and I don't even know what to call you. You've mentioned your name, I'm sure, but I'm afraid I've forgotten it. It's frightfully stupid of me."

"My name is Chaudri, madam. Mahboob Chaudri. And I—"

Baby Adam banged his fists on the metal tray that held him in place in the borrowed high chair. "Boob," he yelled gaily, delighted at the sound of the word. "Boob boob boob boob boob!"

AFTERWORD

The last three Chaudri stories I wrote were all submitted to *Ellery Queen's Mystery Magazine*, and after Eleanor Sullivan turned each of them down, to *Alfred Hitchcock's Mystery Magazine*, where Cathleen Jordan did the same. I'm sure Eleanor and Cathleen must have told me why, but I don't recall—and all of our correspondence is now long gone. Rereading the stories today, it seems to me that their quality is on a par with the first seven—and, since I'm including them in this volume, I hope you'll agree!

At that time—1987—there simply *weren't* many other markets for short crime fiction. The revival of *The Saint Mystery Magazine* lasted for only three issues in 1984, the 30-year run of *Mike Shayne Mystery Magazine* ended in 1985, and, although *Espionage* was still in business and publishing me regularly, "Sheikh's Beach" was by no stretch of the imagination a spy story, so I didn't even bother sending it to editor Jackie Lewis.

Following in the footsteps of Wayne Dundee's *Hardboiled*, a semi-prozine (midway between a fanzine and a professional publication) which first appeared in 1985, Gary Lovisi launched his own semiprozine, *Detective Story Magazine*, in 1988. Partly to support what Wayne and Gary were doing and partly to find a home—be it ever so humble—for work the "big" magazines didn't want, I submitted several of my stories to each of them.

Gary ran "Sheikh's Beach" in DSM #2 (September 1988)—and in fact made it the issue's featured story. Ron Wilbur's cover illustration was an imaginative rendering of a critical scene, though he didn't do much in the way of research: that plumed hat Mahboob is wearing doesn't look like anything I ever saw during my year in Bahrain! But the numerals the child is drawing in the sand are the story's principal clue—and constitute, in fact, the most authentically Middle Eastern clue in *any* of the 10 Chaudri stories.

If I wrote this story today, the clue unfortunately wouldn't work, since Bahraini license plates nowadays show the plate number in both Western and Arabic numerals. Back in the '80s, though, only the Arabic Arabic numerals were used, as you can see in the modern (left) and older (right) photos below:

I mentioned in my Afterword to "The Night of Power" that I used the name Gillian in two consecutive Chaudri stories, that one and this one.

Perhaps you noticed that I also named characters Abdulaziz in both tales. No idea why. There are plenty of other mellifluous British and Arabic names I could have chosen!

A couple of other notes:

• In 1982, Sheikh's Beach really existed. It was open to foreigners and off-limits to Bahrainis, and was owned, not by the fictional Sheikh Abdulaziz bin Yousif al-Sayed, "one of the wealthiest men in Bahrain," but by Sheikh Isa bin Salman al-Khalifa, the country's ruler, who really *did* hang out in a beautiful beach house and invite attractive Western women to join him for tea. (After Sheikh Isa's death in 1999, the beach's ownership descended to one of the country's sheikhas, who ultimately stopped admitting foreign visitors.)

• The story of the "impertinent *natoor* from Baluchistan" that Mahboob recalls on page 166 is a story I heard told many times on American military bases while I was teaching overseas for the University of Maryland. As I heard it, it usually featured a private and a general as its main characters, and I think this repurposed version fits nicely here.

• On page 167, Gillian Steele is reading a trashy romance novel set in Bahrain. There actually *was* a trashy romance novel set in Bahrain, which someone gave me soon after I arrived in the country and which I read about 20 pages of before giving up in disgust. (It was not Lucy Caldwell's *The Meeting Point*, which came out in 2011. In 1982, Lucy Caldwell was one year old.) The description of the cover illustration is an in joke, a reference to a conversation I had with a very well known Gothic Romance writer at a Mystery Writers of America cocktail party in the early '70s. I forget if it was Phyllis Whitney or Mary Stewart, but I think it was one of those two. When I translated Piet Schreuders' *Paperbacks, USA: A Graphic History, 1939-1959* from Dutch to English for Blue Dolphin Books in 1981, I inserted this passage with Piet's permission: "One popular Gothic author tells a wonderful story about the immutability of the Gothic cover: 'Once, just to see what would happen, I wrote a story set in a suburban ranch house in a densely populated valley, with every single scene taking place in broad daylight; the heroine was a short-haired redhead who wore jeans throughout the entire book. But when the paperback came out, sure enough, there on the cover was a long-haired blonde in a flowing white dress, haring away from some frightening mansion at the top of a lonely hill in the dead of night!'"

• On page 168, Jeremy is excited about a little hut on the beach which was giving free soft drinks to the beach's visitors. That hut was really there in 1982, and it offered—as Jeremy indicates—Pepsi products only. I mentioned Pepsi not as a matter of personal preference but for the sake of accuracy. Not long after Coca-Cola opened its first bottling plant in Israel in 1966, the Arab League launched a boycott of Coke products throughout the Middle East that lasted until 1991 (except in Egypt, which ended it much earlier). So that classic line "No Coke, Pepsi!" from the recurring Olympia Café sketch on early *Saturday Night Live* was for quite a few years the reality in Bahrain.

• My first-ever college teaching job, way back in the late 1970s, was at what was then called Slippery Rock State College (and is now Slippery Rock University), in the little town of Slippery Rock, PA. Terry and Stacey Steele, who taught in the music department, graciously welcomed me to the community and the college and were my closest friends for the two years I spent at the Rock—and their young son Jeremy, who was about 5 when I met him, was my very special buddy. A few years later, I used his name in this story. Jeremy grew up to be a talented musician like his mom and dad and was a doctoral student in the biological sciences at the University of Pittsburgh when, tragically, he passed away in 2004 at the age of 30. So young, so very young....

THE IVORY BEAST

They were waiting for him at the gate that separated ASU from the outside world. A *natoor* he knew only slightly raised the thin wooden barrier for him, and then Tom Sanders was pumping his hand and Dolly Miller had wrapped her arms around him and planted a warm kiss full on his lips.

Mahboob Chaudri was mortified. He had never been kissed by a white woman before, had never been kissed on the lips by anyone other than his beloved wife Shazia.

"Oh, dearie me," he said. "I—"

"You leave go of him, now, Dolly," said Sanders, slapping the girl's shoulder lightly. "Cain't you see you're embarrassin' the man?"

Miller laughed and released him. "Jeez, it's good to see you again, Mahboob! What's it been, a couple months?"

"It has, indeed," the Pakistani agreed, straightening his tie and arranging his peaked black cap more firmly on his head. "And how have you been enjoying your stay in Bahrain, my friends?"

"We haven't had much time for enjoyment," Miller frowned. "They've been keeping us pretty busy lately, with all this fuss there's been in the Gulf."

"C'mon, Dolly, it ain't been that bad." The boy's sudden grin lit up his coal-black face like fireworks on the night of *Eid al-Fitr*. "We was out on one of them fishin' *dhows* last Friday, caught us some dynamite *hamour*. And I got some fine pictures in that little village where they make the pottery, what's it called again?"

"A'ali," Miller supplied. "But you better save the travelogue for later, boy, we're late enough as it is." She clasped Chaudri's arm in both her hands and tugged him deeper into the territory of the Administrative Support Unit.

"Where is it we are going?" the little policeman wondered. "My superiors told me only that I was expected here at two in the afternoon."

"Administration Building," Tom Sanders replied, bubbling with an inner excitement Chaudri had never seen in him before. "Cap'n's got somethin' to tell you."

* * * *

"Officer Chaudri," Captain Craft rose to greet him, "it's a pleasure to see you again. How's that head of yours?"

Chaudri smiled ruefully as he shook the captain's hand, remembering the painful lump Owais Gujarit's red plastic water jug had raised.

"Completely healed, sir," he said. "Your doctor's ministrations were most effective."

"Glad to hear it." Craft settled his lanky frame in the leather swivel chair behind his cluttered desk and waved his visitor to an armchair. Miller and Sanders remained standing on either side of the office doorway. "Officer, I know you're a busy man. Let me get right to it and tell you why I asked for you today. The US Navy's still grateful to you for uncovering the identity of our rumrunner last spring, and we've finally thought of something we can do to express our gratitude."

Chaudri raised a hand in protest, but the captain went on before he could speak.

"Now, I've talked with your Deputy Director over there at the Manama Directorate, and he tells me you've got a month off coming up, is that correct?"

"Yes, sir, in seven weeks and four days I am leaving for Pakistan."

Craft pursed his lips. "Looking forward to it, are you?"

"Oh, most definitely, sir! It has been three years since my last home leave, three years since I have seen my wife and children."

"Well, Officer, our fleet flagship, the *Coronado*, has a show-the-flag run to Karachi scheduled for the middle of next month, and your Deputy Director's agreed to move your leave up a bit so you can ride along with the ship."

Chaudri gaped at him. "I—I am most thankful for your generosity," he said, "but I have already been provided with an airplane ticket for my round-trip flight. That is one of the benefits of my position with the—"

"Don't you get it, Mahboob?" Dolly Miller burst out, then winced in pain as Sanders edged toward her and dug an elbow in her ribs. "Oh, jeez, sorry, sir."

A corner of Craft's mouth turned up. "That's quite all right, sailor. Please continue."

"Thank you, sir. Don't you see, Mahboob? If you ride home on the ship, you can cash in that ticket they gave you, and put the money towards that house of yours in Jong—damn, I never can get that name right."

"Jhang-Maghiana," the Pakistani said softly.

"Check. I bet you could get 400, 500 dollars for it, don't you think?"

THE IVORY BEAST | 133

Chaudri moistened his lips with the tip of his tongue. The ticket, he knew, was worth almost 500 *dinars*, not dollars—more than 20,000 rupees at the current rate of exchange. And with 20,000 rupees added to what he had already managed to save from his salary, he would finally have enough to make the down payment on the bungalow he yearned to build for his family in Shazia's native village.

"But the voyage," he said. "It will take several days to reach Karachi by sea, and I have only one month for my leave. That means I would—"

"No, you wouldn't," Tom Sanders interrupted eagerly. "The Cap'n done arranged all that. They're gonna give you a couple extra days, so you won't lose any time with your folks. It's all set up, Mahboob. The Cap'n got it all took care of."

Chaudri regarded the beaming expressions on his young friends' faces, then turned to their commanding officer. "I—I am overwhelmed," he stammered. "I am most absolutely grateful, Captain. I pray to Allah that I may be worthy of this honor."

"Does that mean you accept, then, Officer?"

"Accept? Oh, dearie me, yes! Yes, indeed!"

"Very well," said Captain Craft with a smile.

* * * *

"Sure wish we were going with you," said Miller wistfully, as the Pakistani guard at the entrance to Mina Sulman harbor scrutinized the photograph on her ID card.

"It saddens me to go without you," Chaudri replied. "I had hoped to be able to show you my city, and to introduce you to my family. And you *should* be going. You and Tom were as responsible for the capture of the ASU smuggler as I."

"That's as may be," Sanders shrugged. "But you know how short-handed we been on post since Adelson and Leavitt PCS'd, Dolly. Just ain't no *way* they could spare us right now."

Chaudri took back his own identity card from the gate guard and murmured a thank-you. "What is this PCS?" he asked.

Sanders shifted the olive-drab van into gear and drove on. "Permanent Change of Station. Military talk."

"Beats me why they can't just say 'move,'" Dolly complained. "You come in the service they practically make you learn a whole new language. Seems like they've always got to come up with some fancy way to say the simplest damn things."

"She's right," nodded Sanders. "My favorite's POV, for Privately Owned *Vee*-hickle. Back home we jes' say C-A-R, and that's plenty good enough for us po' black trash."

They swung around a corrugated tin warehouse, and an enormous off-white troop transport loomed into view.

"There she is," Sanders announced. "The USS *Coronado*."

Chaudri was perplexed. "I was thinking that all of your naval vessels were painted gray," he said.

"Most of 'em are," Dolly Miller confirmed. "The *Coronado*'s the flagship, though, so they want her to stand out from the crowd."

"We call her the Ivory Beast," said Sanders proudly. "The Ivory Beast of the Middle East."

* * * *

The black letters stenciled above the breast pocket of the young bosun's mate's chambray work shirt spelled JENSEN, but when the boy stooped to take charge of Mahboob Chaudri's cardboard suitcase and overnight grip, the little policeman saw a different name engraved on the thin strip of metal wrapped around his cheerful escort's tanned right wrist.

"Shall I be calling you Jensen," Chaudri asked, "or Ja*ko*vac?" The name on the silvery band was unfamiliar to him and he guessed at its pronunciation, accenting the middle syllable.

"Sir?" The youth's brow furrowed, then cleared as he nodded down at his wrist. "Oh, you mean that? This way, sir." He set off briskly along the main deck, and Chaudri had to hurry to keep up with him. "No, sir, my name's Jensen, okay. This here's a POW bracelet, I've had it on since I was a kid. I don't even hardly notice it any more."

"And what does it signify?"

"Well, sir, that's the name of an American soldier who fought in Vietnam, and underneath it is the date he was reported missing in action."

Chaudri eyed the weathered engraving as they walked. "S/SGT," he read aloud. "That is military talk, then?"

"Staff Sergeant, sir. Staff Sergeant John *Jak*ovac, missing since May 29, 1967." Jensen stressed the first syllable of the soldier's name. "It's a long time. He's probably dead, I guess, but, when I put this on, back in the fifth grade, I promised I'd wear it till they found out for sure what happened to him. He's still officially listed as missing, so I still wear the bracelet."

"You are most dedicated," said Mahboob Chaudri. "I admire that, Mr. Jensen."

The boy ducked his head. "Thank you, sir. I just do what I think is right."

They passed through an arched metal hatchway to the interior of the ship, and found themselves in a large mess hall where more than 100 sailors in work shirts and bell-bottomed dungarees sat at long tables with trays of food before them. Heads turned and the buzz of conversation abated at the sight of the Pakistani in the strange olive-green uniform, but the allures of lunch and gossip quickly reasserted themselves.

"It's just up this ladder, sir. Watch your head." Jensen led the way up a steep flight of narrow metal steps, Chaudri's heavy old suitcase seemingly weightless in his left hand, the overnight bag a feather in his right.

At the top of the stairs, a gleaming brass plaque announced: *Welcome to Officers' Country*. Jensen strode down a long corridor punctuated on both sides by framed sketches of American warships and tall doorways hung with floor-length gray curtains instead of doors.

"You'll be in here, sir." He swept a curtain to one side and waved Chaudri in ahead of him.

The cubicle was small and colorless, tightly packed with a set of bunk beds, two identical wooden writing desks and chairs, and a pair of metal lockers flanking a single sink and mirror. Sheets, a rough woolen blanket and a feather pillow lay neatly folded at the foot of each of the beds, and plain white towels hung from a chromium bar beneath the sink.

"Sorry it's so tiny, sir." Jensen lifted the larger of Chaudri's bags onto the top bunk, then swung the handgrip up beside it. "You're pretty lucky, though: most of the officers have to double up, but you've got this compartment all to yourself this trip. At least you'll have some privacy."

"I am quite content," said Chaudri. "My room at the Police Barracks in Juffair is three times this size, but I am sharing it with five other men."

The young sailor glanced around the room, switched on the overhead fan, scuffed a foot on the immaculate floor. "Well, I guess I'd best be getting back down, then. Oh, gosh, almost forgot: officers' head's down the passageway, first hatch on the port side."

"Officers' head?" Chaudri echoed. "First hatch? The port side?"

Jensen grimaced apologetically. "Bathroom and shower, sir. They're down the hall, first door on your left."

* * * *

"So tell me, *mahsool*, what's your verdict?"

Mahboob Chaudri looked up from his plate. "Sir?"

"The food," Captain Dave Buck elaborated. He was a ruddy Southerner with half a century under his ample belt, more than two decades of it in the Navy. "How are you enjoying your meal?"

The Pakistani worked his knife and fork and took another bite. The chicken was dry and bland and coated with a greasy breading. The green beans were overcooked and tasteless, the mashed potatoes lumpy. "Most excellent," he said, chewing bravely.

Captain Buck's hearty laughter led the explosion of glee which greeted this statement. Even the sober Lieutenant-Commander Meacham—who had been introduced as the captain's second-in-command and the *Coronado*'s Executive Officer, or XO—was visibly amused.

"You don't have to be polite," the bearded man across from Chaudri grinned. Like the captain and XO, like all 22 of the officers in the room, he was dressed in a simple khaki uniform; the oak leaf and single acorn on his collar identified him as the ship's doctor, the nametag pinned to his breast pocket gave his last name as Steen.

Lieutenant (JG) William Kundo, sitting next to the doctor, agreed loudly. "We all know it's garbage," he boomed, pushing away his plate and reaching for his pipe. "First night out and a guest on board, you'd think we could dish him up some decent chow."

"There's nothing wrong with the food," said Meacham, a cadaverous black man whose 18 years at sea had turned his skin to deep-lined leather. "It's that damn Crockett, that's the problem."

"Crockett?" said Chaudri.

"Seaman Apprentice Crockett, our temporary chef."

"To use the term extremely loosely." Kundo shook his head sadly and struck a match. "Our regular cookie's been confined to sick bay for, what is it, a week now?"

"Six days," said the doctor. "And it'll be a couple more before I let him out of quarantine."

"Can you believe it," the captain sighed, "the kid's 24 years old and he's got the dadburned chicken pox."

"*He's* got the chicken pox and *I've* got indigestion," Kundo groused. "I'll bet they never had to put up with this sort of bull on a pirate ship."

A chorus of groans went up.

"Don't get Kundo started on his pirate ships," warned the XO. "We'll be here all night."

Doctor Steen coughed into his fist. "Ah, tell me, *mahsool*," he said diplomatically, "what sort of food would you recommend we try while we're in Karachi?"

Chaudri welcomed the opportunity to sing his homeland's praises. "My country has many wonderful dishes," he said. "There are curries, *baryanis, masalas*, chicken *tikka*...."

A steward in an immaculate white mess jacket brought around a steaming carafe of coffee, and the tension lifted.

* * * *

The next day, the *Coronado*'s first full day at sea, was uneventful. Lt. (JG) Kundo, a jack-of-all-trades whose varied duties included public relations, took Mahboob Chaudri on an extended tour of the ship, from the sweltering depths of the engine room to the air-conditioned comfort of the radar room, where the sole illumination was provided by the pale-green glow of the vigilant screens.

The only sour note was the continued grumbling about the meals in the Officers' Mess, but even that problem was resolved at last when, after a dinner of soggy pink meatloaf, Doctor Steen stroked his gray-flecked beard and announced that the popular Seaman 2nd Peterson's condition had improved to the point that he would be permitted to return to duty in the morning.

At breakfast time, thanks to Pete, the omelets were fluffy, the toast unburnt, and it was with a full and contented stomach that Mahboob Chaudri folded his arms on the main deck aft rail and watched the *Coronado*'s frothy wake glitter with reflected sunlight.

It was just after eight, and the sun hung low in a clear blue sky not yet written on by clouds. It would soon turn hot and muggy, Chaudri knew, but at this hour the air was still pleasantly cool.

For a day and two nights they had steamed slowly to the east, and now they approached the narrow funnel of the Strait of Hormuz. The Iranian coastline, already visible two miles to the north, would draw closer as they rounded the Ras Masandam peninsula. To the south, where at present there was only the endless cobalt mystery of the sea, the United Arab Emirates would come briefly into view, then melt into the desert sands of Oman.

Chaudri cupped a hand above his eyes and gazed westward. Far beyond the black speck that punctuated the distant horizon lay the tiny Bahraini archipelago, his adopted home. He turned, and rested his back against the rail. Far ahead, far beyond the Strait and the Gulf of Oman, deep into the Arabian Sea, lay his past and his future: Pakistan, Karachi, his wife and children.

But between the little policeman and his family rose the enormous superstructure of the USS *Coronado*, with its flat-black main mast and yardarms and radars and whip antennas, and the imposing off-white of its helo hangar and stacks and flying bridge.

"The Ivory Beast," Chaudri murmured. "The Ivory Beast of the Middle East."

The *Coronado*, with all its sophisticated weaponry, was a powerful beast indeed. But was it powerful enough to keep the peace throughout its vast domain? Was it strong enough for that?

For there was another beast at large in the Gulf, Chaudri thought, a beast with many millions of heads and claws: the angry green beast of fanatic Islamic fundamentalism.

To the north, the brown hills of Iran were quiet, but their soft serenity was deceptive. Behind those hills, a government gone mad was busy planning strategies for its painful war with Iraq. The war had dragged on for years, had cost many thousands of lives, and there were no signs that it was any closer to a resolution now than it had ever been before.

Chaudri peered westward once again. The black speck on the horizon was growing larger.

At the far end of the Gulf, where Iran and Iraq shared a common border, the battle raged. And why? Because the madmen on one side of that imaginary line—that line which appeared so clearly on maps and globes, but which had in truth no more substance than a desert mirage—had forgotten the Messenger's commandment to live in peace and brotherhood with the madmen on its other side.

No, Chaudri realized, the distant spot of black was not getting bigger. It was coming closer. And it was not black, he saw now, it was gray. Haze gray.

Battleship gray.

"*Merea rabba!*" he exclaimed in horror. It was a warship, and it was closing on them with frightening speed.

The urgent cry of a siren scattered his thoughts.

"General Quarters! General Quarters!" A dozen loudspeakers screamed the alarm. "Man your battle stations!"

Instantly, the giant ship was alive with activity. A thousand sailors jumped to their positions, whipped the protective tarpaulins from torpedo tubes, clambered up the turrets of the 5mm guns to arm them and swing their barrels astern toward the rapidly approaching cruiser.

Mahboob Chaudri raced forward, his heart pounding, and scrambled up two steep ladders to the bridge. He found Captain Buck and the XO out on the deck behind it, each with a pair of field glasses raised to his eyes.

"Captain, sir," Chaudri wheezed, pressing a hand to his breast. "What is happening? Whose ship is that?"

"Don't know yet." The captain's voice was strained. "If it's Iranians and they're looking for a fight, we could have a nasty little incident on our hands here."

"Can you make out the colors of their flag, sir?"

"Just barely. Three stripes, I think. Green, white and red. Dammit, that *is* Iran, isn't it?"

Chaudri gripped his arm. "Those *are* Iran's colors," he said urgently. "But is that the order they are in, sir: green, white and red from top to bottom?"

"What the—?" Buck glared at his passenger. "What difference does it—"

"Please, sir," Chaudri insisted. "Please look again!"

A moment passed. Then the captain nodded slowly and lifted his binoculars.

"White, red and green," he said tightly, "with a vertical red stripe nearest the flagpole."

Chaudri closed his eyes and sighed, and released the officer's sleeve. "Oman," he whispered. "The Iranian flag is green, white and red, with a yellow lion centered in the middle stripe."

Captain Buck breathed deeply. "Are you sure about that, *mahsool*?"

"Oh, yes, sir. Oh, dearie me, most certainly yes. I assure you, that is the flag of Oman."

The captain stared out at the sleek gray vessel, now close enough to make out its dark-skinned crew with the naked eye. He licked his dry lips absently. He wiped the back of his hand across his forehead.

Then he made his decision, stepped through a hatchway onto the bridge and grabbed a microphone and stabbed the red button on its side.

"Now hear this," he said, and the ship's loudspeakers took his voice and turned it into thunder. "Secure from General Quarters. Secure from General Quarters."

* * * *

The emergency was over. Mahboob Chaudri had been right about the gunboat: it was Omani, sent out by a friendly government to guarantee the Americans safe passage through the troubled waters of the Strait of Hormuz.

The *Coronado* had stepped down from General Quarters and kept steadily on course, with the Omani escort off its starboard bow.

Mahboob Chaudri crossed the empty mess deck and went up the ladder to Officers' Country. His olive-green uniform blouse was drenched with the sour spoor of fear.

When he reached his compartment, he swung aside the floor-length curtain and switched on the lights and gasped.

Seaman Apprentice Jensen lay stretched out on his back on Chaudri's bunk, his head resting on the Pakistani's pillow. The young bosun's mate's throat had been cut, and the bloody straight razor that dangled from his right hand was Chaudri's own.

* * * *

"Not long. Not long at all." Doc Steen looked up from his examination of the body. "Maybe as little as 15 minutes. Certainly no longer than an hour. When did you find him, *mahsool*?"

"At 9:47, Doctor. Precisely 12 minutes ago."

"He probably did it during the alert, then," the captain mused. "But *why*, dammit? And why *here*, in your compartment?"

"Ah, excuse me, sir." Lieutenant Anthony Policastro, a swarthy New Yorker who barely cleared the Navy's minimum height requirement, was the Operations Officer assigned by the XO to prepare an official report on the circumstances of Jensen's death. "I think I can answer at least the first of those questions."

Chaudri pulled a clean white handkerchief from the hip pocket of his trousers and draped it over his palm. In the crowded compartment, he had to move carefully to avoid elbowing Captain Buck or the XO.

"The gunboat, sir," Policastro went on. "See, Jensen must have assumed they were Iranians, just like the rest of us. He figured they were on their way to blow us out of the water, so he—uh, sir? I don't think you should be messing with that."

Making sure he touched it only with his handkerchief, Chaudri gently loosened the razor from Jensen's limp fingers and wrapped it in the cloth.

Lieutenant-Commander Meacham put out a hand to hold back his deputy. "Just a second, Tony. What is it, Officer?"

"I am thinking, sir, that we should be dusting this—"

He broke off to stare at the dead boy's wrist. "Odd," he murmured. "Most decidedly odd." He knelt beside the body and pushed his hands beneath it and traced around its contours. He paused in surprise at the back of Jensen's head and examined it closely.

Policastro folded his arms across his chest and scowled. "My idea is Jensen was a damn coward, sir. He couldn't face the thought of waiting around for the Ay-rabs to get him, so he came up here and did the job himself."

Captain Buck rubbed his chin thoughtfully. "Why *here*, though? I don't like it, Tony. It doesn't make sense."

"I'll have to take him down to food storage," the doctor said, "put him in a body bag in one of the coolers. You'd think a ship this size'd have a morgue." He edged around Mahboob Chaudri, who was on his hands and knees peering beneath the bunk, and left the compartment to find two sailors to help him move the body.

"Are you looking for something, Officer?"

Chaudri drew a line in the fine white dust that powdered the floor, then studied the tip of his finger and licked it cautiously.

"*Mahsool?*" There was irritation in the captain's tone as he repeated his question.

The Pakistani glanced up, and a glint of metal caught his eye from above. A bone in his ankle crackled as he got to his feet. He dug his fingers between the mattress and frame of the upper berth.

"Dammit, man," the captain growled. "What have you found?"

"John Jakovac," Chaudri replied, holding out a misshapen silver bracelet on his palm. He accented the initial syllable, as Jensen had done two days earlier, but he was sorely puzzled when he said it.

* * * *

Though Seaman 2nd Peterson's lasagna looked perfect and smelled even better than it looked, not one of the two dozen officers whose duty schedule allowed them to gather at noon that day for lunch seemed in the mood to eat.

"Anything on Jensen, Tony?" Captain Buck demanded.

The Operations Officer cleared his throat. "Not much to report, sir. I dusted the razor for fingerprints as Mr. Chaudri suggested, but Jensen's were the only ones on it. He killed himself, Captain, there's no doubt of that. The one thing I still can't figure is what he was doing up here in the first—"

"No!" Mahboob Chaudri slammed down his silverware. "No, no, no, Captain! I am most terribly sorry to be interfering, sir, but it was *my* compartment the boy was found in, it was my very own razor that took his life, it was *I* who discovered his body. I cannot sit here and allow you to call his death a suicide. He was murdered, sir, he was most definitely murdered."

"Gentlemen!" The captain's voice rose above the immediate protest of his men, and at the sharpness of his tone they stilled as quickly as they had begun. "Murder, *mahsool*? I understand you've had some experience in these matters, but that's a very serious charge."

"Indeed, sir, it is. I am, however, quite certain I am right. I spoke with Jensen when I first came aboard this ship. He seemed to be in perfect spirits. I am convinced he would never have killed himself."

"*You're* convinced," Bill Kundo repeated, his eyebrows arched. "Well, you're gonna need a damn sight more than that to convince *me* you're right about this and Policastro's wrong, *mahsool*."

"Yes, most assuredly," Chaudri nodded. "There *is* more. When Jensen was bringing my bags up to my compartment, he carried my heavy suitcase in his left hand, my lighter grip in his right. This indicates that he—"

"Oh, come on, now," the doctor scoffed. "I can see what you're driving at, man, but it doesn't wash. You're saying Jensen was left-handed, and, since the razor was in his right hand when you found him, someone else must have slit his throat and put it there. That's detective-story stuff, Officer, not evidence."

"I'm with Doc," said Lieutenant-Commander Meacham. "Just because he carried your bag in his left hand doesn't prove he was left-handed—and, even if he *was* left-handed, there's no way to prove he couldn't have used his right hand to kill himself."

"After you left my compartment to take away Jensen's body," said Chaudri patiently, "I was not idle. I found the poor boy's bunkmates and questioned them, one by one. They were all agreed: Mr. Jensen *was* left-handed, and he shaved with his left hand, not his right."

"But what about the fingerprints?" Tony Policastro set his jaw angrily. "The only prints on that razor were Jensen's, you can't get around that."

"Precisely! But it was *my* razor, Lieutenant. I use it every morning, I used it *this* morning, before Seaman Peterson's most excellent breakfast. If Jensen truly killed himself, why in the name of the Prophet would he have wiped my fingerprints from the handle of the razor before doing so?"

"My God," the captain whispered.

"Indeed, sir. And there is further proof, should anyone require it. Doctor Steen, sir, have you had an opportunity as yet to examine the back of the boy's head?"

"The back of his head? Why—why, no, not yet. There'll have to be an autopsy, of course, but I—"

"I thought not. And with the cause of his death so evident, there was no real reason for you to have done so." He pulled a thin strip of metal from his pocket. "But when I was looking for this bracelet this morning, I found a fresh discoloration at the base of Jensen's skull. Surely he did not bruise himself by falling back on my pillow. No, sir, he was coshed, knocked out, and it was while he was unconscious that his throat was cut."

"But—but *why*, dammit?" Captain Buck pounded a fist on the table, and water sloshed from his drinking glass to dampen the crisp white tablecloth. "And what's that bracelet got to do with it?"

Chaudri leaned forward and rested his elbows on the cloth. "I will tell you how I have reconstructed the crime. This prisoner-of-war bracelet represented an important commitment to Jensen, but it had been on his wrist for so many years that he sometimes forgot he was wearing it, he told me so himself. In fact, when I questioned his bunkmates I discovered that it was one of *them* who noticed this morning that it was missing, and called its absence to Jensen's attention."

"You found it in the upper berth in your compartment," the captain recalled. "What was it doing up there?"

"I am thinking it must have pulled off his wrist when he swung my overnight grip up onto the mattress. Perhaps it caught on the handle of my bag, or on the metal frame of the bunk. In any case, Jensen did not realize it was gone until someone asked him what had happened to it. Once he knew it was missing, though, he searched his own compartment and failed to find it, and after that I would imagine he spent some time retracing his recent movements as best he could remember them, looking for it. At last he thought of my compartment and went there, but I was out on the main deck, watching the sea."

"So he went in without you?"

"It would seem so. On his hands and knees he looked beneath my bunk, and found—not his bracelet, but a packet of cocaine which had been hidden between the mattress and the spring."

"*What!*" Captain Buck was stunned. "Cocaine? On my ship? No, I'm sorry, *mahsool*, that's impossible."

Chaudri shook his head sadly. "Nevertheless, sir, I found grains of a fine white powder on the floor beneath my bunk, and I assure you it was cocaine. Of relatively poor quality, perhaps, but most assuredly cocaine."

The XO stirred restlessly in his seat. "Let's say it *was* cocaine. What was it doing in your compartment?"

"I should think that was obvious, Lieutenant-Commander. Before my arrival here, that compartment was vacant, which made it the perfect place to hide the drug so that someone could have access to it without running the risk of its being discovered in his own quarters."

"You're saying it was one of us," said Kundo slowly. "An enlisted man wouldn't stash contraband in Officers' Country, he'd keep it down in crew quarters where he could get to it whenever he wanted it."

"Are you telling me one of my *officers* has been doing coke, then? Doc," the captain roared, "I want every man in khakis tested for substance abuse. There must be some procedure you can—"

Chaudri held up a hand. "That will not be necessary, sir. I know who brought the drug aboard ship."

"You—you—"

"But of course, Captain. The cocaine belonged to the killer. During the alert, he came to my compartment to take it away, but when he reached my doorway he saw that Jensen had already found it in his search for his missing bracelet. He panicked, struck Jensen on the back of the head with his fist before the boy became aware of his presence. He looked frantically around the room, and saw my razor lying beside the sink, where I had left it after shaving this morning. So he lifted the unconscious sailor to my bed and cut his throat to silence him. Then he wiped his fingerprints—and, incidentally, mine—from the handle and pressed it into Jensen's lifeless hand, cleaned up the spilled cocaine as best he could and ran off, not noticing he had left a small amount of the drug behind him on the floor."

Bill Kundo ran his index finger along the edge of the table. "And you say you know who it was?"

"Oh, yes, indeed. You see, I asked Jensen's bunkmates when they had learned that I was to be a passenger on this voyage, and was surprised to find that they had not been told in advance of my impending arrival. One of them was in the Enlisted Men's Mess when Jensen escorted me

THE IVORY BEAST | 145

up the ladder to Officers' Country and remembers wondering who I was. The others knew nothing of my being here until Jensen told them about me, later in the day."

"We didn't see any need to make a general announcement to the crew," the captain frowned, "but what does—"

"I understand, sir. But your officers must have known I was coming?"

"Yes, of course. With you bunking up here and eating in our mess, I had to let the officers and stewards know ahead of time that you'd be traveling with us."

Chaudri smiled. "Then why," he asked, "if he was aware that I was coming, would the murderer have waited until the second day after my arrival before removing his contraband from my compartment?"

The faraway thrum of the *Coronado*'s powerful engines was the only sound in the room.

The XO was the first of them to understand. "He wouldn't have," he said. "Not unless there was something that prevented him from taking care of it until this morning."

"Oh, no," said Doctor Steen. "Oh, Christ, no."

Mahboob Chaudri lifted his knife and fork and sampled his lasagna. "Most excellent," he said, though the meal had long since gone cold. "Perhaps you would be so kind, Captain, as to ask Seaman Peterson to leave his kitchen for a moment and join us, so that we may welcome him back from his long confinement to sick bay."

* * * *

The low, dusty buildings of West Wharf lay off their port bow, the sagging warehouses of East Wharf hulked to starboard. Ahead, the broad expanse of the Custom House; behind it, shimmering in the heat, the tall minaret of the Memon Mosque and the towers of the city, Karachi, his home.

Along the quayside, hordes of brown-skinned men and women and children milled to and fro in restless excitement. Mahboob Chaudri, forward on the main deck of the Ivory Beast, leaned against its warm white railing and scanned their faces, searching, searching, his pulse racing with the sweet pain of expectancy.

And there, there in the front rank of the crowd, there they stood! Shazia, Arshed, Perveen, Javaid—his wife, his children, his family, his life!

"*Mahsool?*" The voice at his side was tentative, questioning. "Do you mind if I join you?"

Chaudri blinked in confusion, and the city before him disappeared. In its place were only cobalt and cream, the placid sea and the sky. The joyous homecoming of his daydream still lay a day and a night to the east.

"Not at all, Captain." His throat was dry, and the words emerged in a gravelly parody of his voice. "I would be most honored."

They stood there, the Pakistani and the American, side by side in silence, as the *Coronado*'s bow carved a passage through the Arabian Sea. It was late afternoon, and they had left the Strait of Hormuz and the Omani gunboat and the worst of the midday temperatures behind them.

"Drugs aboard my ship," said Captain Buck at last. "Drugs and murder." He shook his head sadly. "We're in your debt, *mahsool*."

The little policeman shrugged modestly. "You were saying it yourself, sir. I have had some experience in these matters."

"Damn good thing you were able to find the cocaine. Without that, we wouldn't have a shred of evidence against him."

A gentle breeze stirred Chaudri's neat black hair and tickled his forehead. "There was simply no time for Peterson to have spirited the contraband away from Officers' Country," he explained, "so I was certain he must have concealed it somewhere in the galley. But where? Where else but in a place where searching eyes would fail to notice it, even if they should happen to see it."

"It amazed me, the way you went straight for the right shaker. There must have been 20 of them on that tray."

"Indeed there were. But table salt is coarsely grained, sir, where Peterson's cocaine was fine. And in his haste to conceal the drug, he failed to add the grains of rice that were in all the other shakers to protect their contents from the humidity. The differences might not have been visible to one who was not looking for them—but I *was* looking for them, unhappily for Seaman Peterson." Chaudri fell silent for a moment, then faced the captain and asked a question that had been bothering him for several hours. "What will become of him, sir?"

"Of Pete? We'll hold him in our brig until we reach Karachi, and from there he'll be flown back to Bahrain under guard. He'll have a trial, of course—Captain's Mast, we call it. They'll charge him with possession and use of a controlled substance and either first- or second-degree murder. I'd say first, under the circumstances. And given his confession, I don't think there's any chance he'll avoid being court-marshaled."

"And his punishment?"

"He's going to spend a lot of years behind bars, I'm afraid. And they'll bust him down to Seaman Recruit and withhold his pay for the length of his sentence."

Mahboob Chaudri sighed, and buried his hands in the pockets of his uniform trousers. His fingers brushed cool metal. "This bracelet was quite important to young Jensen," he said. "Perhaps it should be returned to his wrist."

Captain Buck took the silver strip from the policeman's palm. "That's very thoughtful, *mahsool*. Thank you. I'll take care of it myself."

Chaudri turned back to the sea, filled his lungs with fresh sea air and exhaled it slowly.

Ahead, in the distance, the sky began to darken.

"You know," the captain said, "I suppose I really ought to be angry with you."

"Angry, sir?" Chaudri looked up in surprise, but the man at his side was smiling.

"Because of you," Buck scolded, "we're stuck with that damn Crockett's so-called cooking till they can send us out a replacement from ASU."

Young Jensen was dead, young Peterson doomed to prison—but the sea was unchanged, the sky took little notice, and the Ivory Beast sailed on.

Mahboob Chaudri's perfect teeth sparkled in the day's last rays of sunlight. "Oh, dearie me," he said.

AFTERWORD

In late November of 1982, during the heat of the Iran-Iraq War—which on the first page of this story Dolly Miller refers to as "all this fuss there's been in the Gulf" and which was known as the Gulf War until the Iraqi invasion of Kuwait in 1990 co-opted that name—I was invited to teach a remedial English class to off-duty sailors aboard the USS *Coronado* as it made what was called a "show-the-flag" cruise from Bahrain to Karachi. The first photograph in the story is the *Coronado*; I took the picture as I was being ferried out to the ship from the harbor at Mina Sulman.

I was given a compartment to myself in Officers' Country and ate three meals a day in the Officers' Mess—with Captain Dave Buck and Lieutenant (JG) Bill Kundo, who gave me permission to use their real names in the story and are presented as accurately as I could depict them, right down to Kundo's pipe and ongoing rants about how much better life would have been on a pirate ship. The names of the other officers in the story are also the names of real people, though not the names of real Navy men. By the time I wrote "The Ivory Beast," I was living in southern Germany. Gary Steen was an American guy who lived around the corner from me, Fred Meacham was a teacher at the DoDDS school on the US Army base in nearby Erlangen—and Tony Policastro was a lab technician who worked for my father when I was a kid on Long Island.

Anyway, our voyage took several days—and the incident involving the Omani gunboat happened pretty much precisely as I chronicled it in this story. From a distance, the Omani and Iranian flags do look very similar, especially when they're fluttering wildly in a sea breeze on a gunboat traveling across choppy water at full speed. Here, see for yourself. This is the Iranian flag on the top and the Omani flag on the bottom:

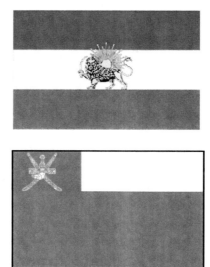

I was standing at the main deck aft rail, watching the gunboat rocket toward us, when the ship went to General Quarters—which is Navy speak for full battle alert—and I was absolutely terrified until Captain Buck, who was standing right beside me, peering at the approaching craft through powerful binoculars, finally identified the flag it was flying as Omani, not Iranian, which told him it was a friendly vessel, approaching in order to accompany us through the narrow Strait of Hormuz. I took the second picture used in the story, which shows our escort, after we stood down from General Quarters and I could breathe again.

While we were at sea, I became friendly with three of the enlisted men aboard the ship. Here's "Bear" Jensen, who not only granted permission for me to kill him off in fiction but practically *begged* me to do so:

And here are Tom Sanders (at the left) and Miller (whose first name I have sadly forgotten, although I'm pretty positive it wasn't Dolly) and me chilling out during our voyage:

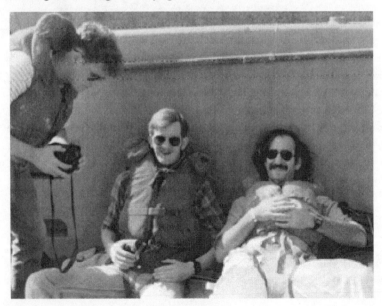

If you look closely, you can make out a thin strip of silver on my right wrist: that's a POW/MIA bracelet from the Vietnam era—and, sure enough, it bears the name S/SGT John Jakovac and the date he was reported missing in action, which was May 29, 1967. In the story, of course, the bracelet turns out to be an important clue. In the real world, I put it on my own wrist on November 11, 1972, and it remains there today.

I think it may be because the Gulf War was still being fought when I wrote the story that Eleanor at EQMM and Cathleen at AHMM turned it down. By 1993, though, *both* Gulf Wars were history, and an interesting gentleman named Charles Raisch had recently started up a new mystery magazine called, well, *New Mystery*. I submitted "The Ivory Beast" to Charles, and he featured it in Volume 2, #1, which came out early in 1994. My last name is the first name listed on the front cover (above the names of two *much* more prolific and better known of my colleagues, Henry Slesar and Jerry Kennealy), a nice photo of me with my then-six-year-old daughter Becca appears both on the inside front cover and again on the back cover, and Charles' editor's note on the first page of my story calls me "a well-known and well-liked master of the short story," at least two-thirds of which is hyperbole.

The story, I think, shows Mahboob at his most Western. It's a straightforward tale of murder and detection, with classical fair-play clues in abundance. At the time, I intended it to be part two of a trilogy; "ASU" had been the first episode, and the third was to be titled "Home Leave." My idea was that the third story would pick up where "The Ivory Beast" leaves off, as the *Coronado* enters Karachi harbor, and that Mahboob would return home to find his wife Shazia falsely accused of a murder which Mahboob would have to solve in order to prove her innocence. That story never did get written—but I still think it's a good idea, and maybe I'll tackle it, one of these days....

For those who may be interested in such things, the USS *Coronado* (AGF-11) was an Austin class amphibious transport ship. She was launched in 1966 and commissioned in 1970, and in 1980 she was redesignated an auxiliary command ship so that she could see duty as the flagship for the US Third Fleet in the Persian Gulf while the "real" Ivory Beast of the Middle East was in dry dock undergoing repairs. The *Coronado* was the first Navy combat ship to welcome female crew members—so Dolly Miller *could* in principle have at some point been assigned to her. She served in Desert Storm from January 1989 to January 1992, was decommissioned in 2006, and, on September 12, 2012, during Operation Valiant Shield, she was sunk 100 miles south of Guam in 3,045 fathoms of water as part of a live-fire training exercise.

THE SWORD OF GOD

In the neighborhood where Mahboob Chaudri grew to manhood, where his beloved wife and children still lived, in the Defense Housing Society a safe distance to the southeast of the incessant clamor of central Karachi, Westerners were an infrequent sight. Oh, dearie me, yes, occasional tourists passed through on their way to the Tuba Mosque, in horsedrawn Victorias hired for 100 *rupees* a day with driver, but otherwise the pale-skinned foreigners were scarce.

Here in Bahrain, though, Chaudri had lived among them for six years, and he had developed an amused tolerance of their curious ways. From time to time, of course, they still were able to surprise him. Take this remarkable game of theirs, this—this *golf*, they called it.

There stood Senator William Adam Harding, an eminent statesman, tall and athletic and attractively graying, one of the highest-ranking members of the American government ever to visit the emirate. Chaudri could not recall which of the 40 or 50 states the Senator represented, but it was one of the larger ones, that much he knew, one of the more powerful ones, one of the ones with oil and cowboys.

It was oil which had brought the Senator to Bahrain, where he had spent most of the last three days touring the Sitrah refinery and meeting with executives of BAPCO, the Bahrain Petroleum Company.

Yet there he stood, that distinguished gentleman, hunched over a pockmarked orange ball on a square of artificial grass in the middle of the fiery desert, waggling a long metal stick foolishly in his thick hands and fully intending to smite the little ball with the stick, to smash it away into the distance, only in order to trudge after it and place his bit of plastic sword beneath it and hit it away from him once more, again and again until at last he succeeded in tapping it into a metal cup with a flag on a pole sticking out of it, the flag now barely visible through the shimmer of heat which rose from the desert surface several hundred yards away.

This was obviously not recreation for the body, Chaudri mused, as beads of itchy sweat trickled within the blouse of his olive-green uniform. Nor, in its pointlessness, could he conceive of it as recreation for anything but the most limited of minds.

Why, then, did they bother with it, the Senator and his deferential young aide and the two exuberant BAPCO executives? Why were they still hard at it after well over an hour, with the thermometer reading in three figures and the merciless sun overhead and their idiotic balls already tapped into a dozen or more of their idiotic cups?

And how much longer would they go on before returning to the bliss of an enclosed and air-conditioned space?

And why, Chaudri marveled, why in the name of the Prophet must they attire themselves in those outrageous costumes? The Senator, whom he had previously only seen in sedate charcoal-gray suits and rich silk ties, now wore a pair of lime-green trousers, an open-necked canary-yellow shirt with a crocodile at the breast, a peaked mechanic's cap and white shoes with leather tassels flapping at every step and—incredibly—*nails* extending downward from their soles!

Chaudri shook his head sadly. He would never really understand these foreigners, never. They lived in another world; their values were hopelessly alien to him.

Which of them was right? The thought disturbed him. In his heart, he knew that neither culture was right, neither wrong. Each was what it was, neither more nor less, and perhaps this *golf* seemed as normal to the Senator as it seemed normal to Mahboob Chaudri that he should live and work and be lonely in Bahrain while his dearest ones stayed behind in Pakistan and lived in vastly greater comfort off the money he was able to send them from his monthly pay packet than they could possibly have enjoyed had he chosen to remain with them and earn perhaps a tenth as much at home.

Though these thoughts occupied his mind, Chaudri was still the first of them to notice the swirl of sand and the faint rumble of an engine in the distance.

It was a dusty Land Rover with four-wheel drive, and as it approached them the Pakistani recognized its driver as a minor functionary at the American embassy, where he had accompanied the Senator to a brief and apparently purely ceremonial meeting with the ambassador two days earlier. Ostensibly, Chaudri had been assigned to provide the Senator with personal security for the length of his stay, but—given the general peacefulness of the emirate since Saddam Hussein's forces had been pushed back out of Kuwait at the beginning of the '90s—he considered himself more of a uniformed guide than a bodyguard.

The Land Rover's rear tires swung wildly and threw up a curtain of sand as the vehicle slewed to a stop. The gentlemen from BAPCO seemed scandalized by the interruption, the Senator's aide continued to look as if he were waiting to be switched on, the Senator himself wore suit-and-tie solemnity over his ridiculous golfing garb.

"Sorry, sir," the boy from the embassy blurted, jumping from the hot Land Rover to fumble in his pockets before them. "The ambassador thought you'd want to know. The Suq-al-Khamis Mosque, sir, and four Americans. They're going crazy back there!"

The Senator stepped forward and put out a soothing hand. "Slow down, there, son," he said, his deep voice a velvet command. "What's this about four Americans?"

"Hostages!" the young man gasped. "Some group of terrorists has moved into the Suq-al-Khamis Mosque, and they're holding four Americans hostage, a doctor and three nurses from the Mission Hospital." He pulled at last a sheet of yellow flimsy from a pocket and unfolded it triumphantly. "They sent this message to Radio Bahrain and both of the national newspapers."

The Land Rover's engine ticked its disapproval and settled into silence. For a long moment, the only sound was the whisper of the heat. Then Senator Harding snatched the slip of paper and his aide handed him a pair of wire-rimmed spectacles. He hooked them over his ears and read the note aloud in the stillness of the desert afternoon.

"The decadent era of Western dominance is at an end," it said. "The Great Satan will be driven far beyond Bahrain's borders. We will re-establish a true Islamic society and return the land to its former glory as the 14th province of Iran. It is written in the Book of Books: 'As for the unbelievers, their works are as a mirage in a spacious plain which the man athirst supposes to be water, till, when he comes to it, he finds it is nothing; there indeed he finds God, and He pays him his account in full; and God is swift at the reckoning.' *Saifoullah*."

The Senator looked up. "The Great Satan," he scowled. "That's supposed to mean the U.S. of A., I reckon. But who the hell's this *Saifoullah* character? One of them damn ayatullahs, is that the idea?"

"*Saifoullah* is a what, sir," said Mahboob Chaudri, "not a who. I have heard of them before. They have been writing inflammatory letters to the Arabic media, but this is to my knowledge the first time they have been committing an act of political aggression. We are knowing very little about them, but from their demands it would seem that they are Iranians, or at least that they are sponsored by Tehran. Bahrain, you see, was a part of the Persian Empire for almost two centuries previous to 1782, when the first of the al-Khalifas was driving the invaders back to Persia. Whatever else they may be, *Saifoullah* are Shi'ite fundamentalists, and if they—"

"Whatever the hell else they may be," the Senator snarled, "*Saifoullah* are a pack of kidnappin' terrorist dogs, and if they think they can get away with holdin' four Americans hostage they damn well better think again."

"*Saifoullah*." The younger of the gentlemen from BAPCO said the word slowly, tasting it. "You know what it means, officer? I've only been here four months; my Arabic doesn't go much beyond please and thank you."

Mahboob Chaudri nodded. His nut-brown face was drawn with lines of concern. "*Saifoullah* is meaning 'the Sword of God,'" he said.

* * * *

The American Embassy in Manama was not sequestered behind concrete bunkers and grim Marines—not yet—but the windowless walls of Ambassador Paul Northfield's private office were three feet thick and made of steel; his door was as strong as that of any bank vault and opened only to those few high-ranking members of his staff who were privileged to know the combination to its sophisticated electronic locking mechanism.

Behind the state-of-the-art security, the office itself had been decorated to reflect the informal nature of its occupant. A massive mahogany desk and plush swivel chair dominated the room, two sofas at right angles around a low brass filigreed coffee table formed a pleasant conversation nook in one corner and a well-stocked wet bar stood invitingly in another, there was soft brown carpeting underfoot and an attractive arrangement of paintings on the walls.

Mahboob Chaudri sipped gratefully at the cold club soda he had been offered and studied the paintings with feigned interest. Most of them were oils by the emirate's own Abdullah al-Muharraqi, scenes of Arab life in warm reds and oranges, old men hunkered down in the *suq* with their worry beads, fishermen mending their nets by the sea, women in black *abbas* heating up their tambourines before a wedding performance. Under other circumstances, Chaudri's interest would have been genuine. But today he was far too busy eavesdropping on the argument from which he had turned his back in deferential politeness to concentrate on the primitive beauty of the artwork.

"Dammit, Mr. Ambassador," Senator Harding was saying, "I take your point, sir—but there's no way in hell you're gonna be able to hush this thing up. The local media already know exackly what's goin' on, and—what with Saddam still makin' noise up there in Eye-Rack—you got your wire-service reporters based right here in Bahrain, you got your

Time and *Newsweek* boys roamin' around lookin' for stories to file, you got—"

"I know all that, Bill." Like his office, Ambassador Northfield seemed relaxed and comfortable in the midst of chaos. He was a tall bear of a man, with steel-gray hair and a full salt-and-pepper beard and a strong handshake—but he was a tame bear, a teddy bear, not a grizzly. "All I'm saying is I think we need to stay in the background on this thing until we—"

"In the background," the Senator exploded. "But that's just exackly my point, Ambassador! Those damn journalists are on the *scene*, they are a fact of *life*, and before one hell of a lot more time elapses you're gonna have them bangin' on your door here yellin' for answers. And you and I, sir, are gonna wind up representin' the United States of America in a major media event before a global audience, so I say we damn well better have some answers, and we better have 'em right damn quick!"

Chaudri wondered if it had been with the idea of representing his country in mind that the Senator had insisted on a brief stop at the BAPCO compound in Awali before proceeding to the embassy. He had been gone for less than five minutes, but when he'd returned to the government limousine his gaudy golfing costume had vanished, replaced by the impeccable attire of the statesman.

The Ambassador smiled tightly. "A major media event, Bill? A global audience? I see what you're driving at, but I can't help thinking you're exaggerating the importance of what's going on here. I mean, it's only been a—"

"—couple of hours," the Senator finished the bear's sentence in exasperation. "And after all, Bill, we don't even know who these people *are*, just yet." He tossed down the rest of his scotch and water and marched to the bar to fix himself a refill. "Now, you lookie here, Ambassador, I *know* all that. And I know that, with the good Lord's blessin', we may well get our folks out of there before anybody winds up gettin' hurt. And I know I may be just a ignorant ol' country boy and talkin' out of turn, but I'd like to remind you of a couple of things here, Ambassador. I'd like to remind you of that little incident back in Tehran in 1979, for instance. You may remember it, because it lasted 444 days and got a lot of attention on the news. I'd also like to remind you of TWA Flight 847 over there in Beirut a couple years later; that one only lasted 17 days, but it got a fair piece of play in the media, too. Now, while you and I sit here havin' this cozy discussion over drinks, we got—"

"While you and I are having this discussion, Bill," the Ambassador said firmly, "we have four American citizens held hostage about a mile from this spot, and we're not doing a single thing to help them in their time of need."

He leaned forward and pressed a button on his intercom, and a woman's voice immediately said, "Yes, sir?"

"Carol," Ambassador Northfield instructed, "get me the State Department, would you, please? Priority One."

Senator Harding turned to his waiting aide. "Jerry," he said angrily. It was the first time Mahboob Chaudri had heard the young man's name. "Jerry, you go find yourself a secure phone and get me the White House. Mack, if you can get him; otherwise, I'll settle for the Veep. You know who I *really* want to talk to, but I reckon he's out joggin' or eatin' a Big Mac or some damn thing."

* * * *

From their vantage point atop the four-story apartment building a quarter of a mile to the south, Mahboob Chaudri and Senator Harding had an unobstructed view of the Suq-al-Khamis Mosque. Its twin minarets gleamed in the twilight, though a closer inspection would have revealed that the towers had been patchily whitewashed and the wooden balconies three-quarters of the way up the height of each spire were in poor repair.

Behind the concrete wall which ringed the compound, the mosque itself was a barren ruin—roofless, floorless, without walls. Of the once-proud temple erected almost 13 centuries in the past by the Umayyad Caliph Umar bin Abdul Aziz, nothing remained but a scattering of stone columns and crumbling archways, baked by the harsh Middle Eastern sun and scoured colorless by a thousand thousand sandstorms.

"AK-47 assault rifles," Chaudri frowned, passing his binoculars to the Senator. "Kalashnikovs, Russian-made."

An armed guard stood on each of the weathered balconies, framed by the narrow arches leading to the interior of the minarets. Both men wore long white *thobes*, their heads covered with the traditional *ghutra* and thin black *agal*. It was impossible to be sure of their nationalities, but from their set expressions and their weapons Chaudri was convinced they were Iranians.

"Mean-lookin' sons a bitches," the Senator snapped, handing the field glasses on to his aide. "Them *and* their guns. Where you reckon they're holdin' the hostages, Officer?"

Chaudri considered the question. "Inside the minarets," he said at last. "It is the only possibility. They are being held on the stone steps within the minarets, trapped between the pair of guards we can see on the balconies above and another pair at the base of the towers, hidden from us behind the wall."

Chaudri accepted the return of the binoculars and raised them again to his eyes. A dozen official vehicles were stationed at 20-yard intervals around the compound; a hundred officers in the olive-green of the Public Security Force were in position behind the buses and sedans and Land Rovers, some unarmed, others with their useless weapons held loosely, waiting.

And, as the Senator had predicted, a score of reporters milled about with their notepads and their tape recorders and their cameras. They, too, were waiting, waiting for something to happen, for tragedy or resolution, for any scrap of news or human interest with which to still the constant hunger of their editors and readers and viewers, their audience.

Among the assembled policemen, there were sharpshooters present who could easily take out the Arabs on the balconies of the Suq-al-Khamis Mosque's twin spires. Even from this distance, Chaudri could read the frustration on their faces. For, if the guards above were wounded or killed, then their brothers below would surely retaliate—and it was the four American hostages who would suffer.

No, the Public Security marksmen must wait impatiently for the situation to develop, and Mahboob Chaudri knew and shared their emotion. He, too, had used a telephone at the American embassy, not an hour before. He had phoned the Police Fort at al-Qalah and practically begged for reassignment to the team now surrounding the mosque. But his superiors had ordered him to remain with Senator Harding, and the Senator's own superiors in Washington had ordered *him* to stay clear of the scene, to leave any negotiations with the Sword of God to the Bahrainis and any contact with the press to Ambassador Northfield.

"Why the hell don't your people get in there and *do* somethin'?" the Senator demanded. "You just set around and wait for somethin' to happen—well, by God, when somethin' *does* happen, you may just find out it ain't the somethin' you was hopin' for!"

"And what would you suggest we should be doing, sir?" the Pakistani asked quietly.

Senator Harding glared at him. "Don't you patronize me, son. And, hell, *I* don't know what to do. That's why my damn gummint's got me benched here on the sidelines. Ain't you got somebody you can send in there to make nice with 'em, like Jesse Jackson sweet-talked them grunts out of Kosovo last year? Or, if this bunch's too far gone to cut a deal with, you just send your local SWAT team in and pull a Rambo—that's what I'd do if I's in charge. I'll tell you this much for free: you better do *somethin'*, 'fore them bastards in the white nighties decide to commence usin' them peashooters they're totin'."

Mahboob Chaudri understood very little of the Senator's English. He understood the feelings which boiled beneath the words, though. He understood that Senator Harding, too, was frustrated by his inability to bring a stop to this terrorist madness, to find a way to resheathe the Sword of God before innocent blood was spilled.

Chaudri understood and shared the American's sense of impotence—and wondered if the angry words were only words, or if a man of true courage stood behind them.

As the police and press stood around and did nothing, he made up his mind to find out.

"Senator, sir," he said softly, "I am thinking that perhaps it is time for you and I to talk."

* * * *

The heavy iron gates had been barred and chained by the terrorists. It was well after sunset, and the moon hung obscured behind heavy clouds—but Public Security floodlights bathed the gateway and the twin minarets towering above it in a harsh illumination which gave the mosque the artificial appearance of a disused film set.

The two armed guards stood motionless on their perches, as they had stood for hours. *Saifoullah* had issued no further demands, had not even asked for food or water to be delivered for themselves or their hostages. It was as if the scene was frozen not only in the glare of the spotlights but in time as well, as if the Sword of God awaited some word from absent leaders—some ineffable sign from its vengeful deity—before proceeding with the next step of its plan.

Behind the compound, all was dark. Mahboob Chaudri and the Senator slipped soundlessly between two government vehicles parked far enough apart to allow them to make their way to the wall surrounding the Suq-al-Khamis Mosque unobserved. They crouched there for a moment to catch their breath, backs pressed against the rapidly cooling roughness of the concrete, hearts pounding with the rush of adrenaline, listening intently to the viscous silence which enveloped them. Far away, a nightbird laughed raucously at the folly of their mission.

"You know what happens if we screw this up, don't you?" the Senator whispered fiercely.

Chaudri's nod went unnoticed in the blackness. "Indeed I do," he answered, his voice barely audible. "You and I are probably being injured, sir, quite possibly being dead—and most certainly being unemployed and disgraced. And the hostages? Our actions may be serving to further endanger their safety, rather than restoring it. Shall we be giving up and going back now, Senator?"

Harding tasted his lower lip. "Hell, no," he decided. "Not if you really think there's a chance we can keep this mess from turnin' into tie-a-yellow-ribbon-'round-the-old-oak-tree."

"I *do* think so, Senator. It is a dim chance, at best, but it is better to act and pray for success, I am thinking, than to do nothing and wait helplessly for failure."

"Them's my sentiments exackly, son. Lead on."

The two dark figures straightened and began to work their way westward in single file, the Pakistani in the lead, each of them tracing the course of their progress along the wall with the tips of his fingers. It was difficult to walk quietly on the loose pebbles which rolled beneath their feet; they took slow and cautious steps to compensate, pausing often to listen for movement around them. When the moon peeked out briefly from behind its blanket of clouds, they stopped completely, and waited without speaking until it once more hid its face from sight.

At last Mahboob Chaudri dropped back a step and put his lips close to the Senator's ear. "We are nearing the opening in the wall," he breathed.

And, at that moment, a shape appeared from the shadows before them, and the clouds parted as if on cue to let the moon show them a long white *thobe* and a pair of burning black eyes and a Kalashnikov assault rifle held at the ready.

"You have reached the opening in the wall," the Arab said coldly, in English, "and you are prisoners of the Sword of God."

O pehan yeh geya, thought Mahboob Chaudri bitterly.

"Holy Kee-rist," the Senator sighed.

They raised their hands above their heads.

* * * *

The terrorist turned away from him, the back of his *thobe* shimmering like the eyes of a cat in the night. His hands gripped the barrel of the AK-47 tightly, and he swung the rifle high over his shoulder and smashed the butt end down at the head of the figure who lay in the sand at his feet. He battered his unconscious victim again and again, and with every slashing stroke of the rifle butt he screamed, "*Saifoullah! Saifoullah! Saifoullah!*" When he lowered the thin metal golfing stick at last, the dead man's head was small and round and drenched with orange blood, its features shattered beyond recognition. The Arab looked around at last, and the face framed by the checkered *ghutra* and black *agal* was the face of Senator William Harding.

Mahboob Chaudri shuddered at the bloodlust in the Senator's eyes and awakened. It was morning, and somewhere a lone rooster was celebrating the dawn.

Chaudri squirmed around on the stone step where he had slept, trying not to disturb Dr. Apostolou two steps above him or Nurse Hewitt two steps below, but it was impossible for him to find a comfortable position. His muscles were cramped and sore from the long hours of sitting, his bottom was numb from the chill of the stone, his throat was cottony with thirst, his stomach rumbled.

"*Merea rabba*," he muttered, then cursed himself for speaking aloud when the young nurse stirred restlessly and a pained whimper escaped her. He held his breath and kept still, and was gratified to see her settle back into an uneasy slumber.

Allah, let them sleep, he prayed. Every moment they were sleeping was one less moment they would have to deal with the horror of their situation—unless, of course, they went on dealing with it, as he had, in their dreams.

Had the Arabs who were guarding the minarets been able to sleep? Had they taken turns standing watch, or had they forced themselves to remain alert throughout the night? Chaudri did not know. There was much, he found, that he did not know. What was happening in the other spire, where the other pair of terrorists was holding Senator Harding and Nurses Graham and Gaylor? What was going on outside the compound? Were negotiations to effect their release under way? Were demands being made, being met or rejected? Were his comrades on the Public Security Force aware that there were now *six* hostages within the wall surrounding the Suq-al-Khamis Mosque? And, with the Senator a captive, would the Americans finally involve themselves, or would they continue to leave the situation in the hands of the Bahrainis?

Chaudri did not know the answers to any of these questions, and it was the not-knowing which worried him more than anything else.

When he looked up from his thoughts, the doctor was awake. He was a large-boned man with the look of a boxer gone to seed, his forehead receding into what had once been a full head of thick brown hair. He regarded Chaudri through narrowed eyes, his thin lips pressed together tightly.

"What do we do now, *mahsool*?" he said. His voice was hoarse from disuse. They had spoken together the night before, when Chaudri was first brought into the minaret, and the American's story had been quickly told.

Dr. Apostolou had suggested an afternoon expedition to the Suq-al-Khamis ruins to his colleagues at the American Mission Hospital. Three of the nurses on his shift had agreed to accompany him. The foursome had explored the compound for perhaps half an hour, but the day was hot and there was little to see, and they were on their way back to the doctor's car when the four *Saifoullah* Arabs had burst through the iron gates. There had been much shouting and waving of weaponry, and eventually he and Nurse Hewitt had been deposited halfway up the minaret steps with guards stationed above and below them. The doctor was not sure what had become of the other two women, but there had been no gunfire, and he hoped they were safe within the second tower. It had all happened around three the previous afternoon; it was now almost seven in the morning, and they had been given neither food nor water in all that time. After the initial encounter, they had seen only one of their captors and him only once, when Chaudri had been brought in to join them.

"What do we do now?" Dr. Apostolou asked, and the sound awakened Nurse Hewitt, who stretched luxuriously and opened her eyes and shrank back in on herself as she remembered where she was, and why.

"I do not know," said Chaudri, watching helplessly as the pretty young Western woman's shoulders shook with the effort to hold back tears. She seemed about the same age as Shazia, his own dear wife, and—though her complexion was pale and tinged a delicate pink by the sun, where his wife's was a rich and beautiful brown—she had Shazia's jet-black hair and bottomless wide black eyes. His heart went out to her, and to the doctor, and to the other women he had not yet seen. "We must wait and pray," he said, but the words seemed hollow and empty in the narrow confines of the minaret.

"I'm not frightened," Nurse Hewitt insisted. "If they were going to—to hurt us, they'd have done it by now, wouldn't they?" She folded her thin arms across her chest and hugged herself. "I just wish they'd settle whatever it is they have to settle and let us out of here. If I don't get a hot shower and a decent meal sometime soon, I'm going to scream."

Dr. Apostolou grinned and reached down from his place on the step above her to touch her shoulder reassuringly. "You're a trooper, Kate," he said. "I hope Jessie and Sarah are holding up as well as you are."

She pressed his hand and returned his smile, and Chaudri found himself wondering if their relationship was entirely a professional one.

There was no opportunity for him to pursue the thought. The sound of sandals scuffing on stone reached him from below, and the guard who had captured him and the Senator the night before came into view as he ascended the spiral steps toward them. It was difficult to see the man clearly in the dimness of the tower, but it seemed to Chaudri that his expression was less threatening than it had been. His mouth had slackened, his eyelids drooped, his curly black hair was oily and streaked with dust, the Kalashnikov he held cradled in his arms seemed to have taken on extra weight.

He has not slept, the Pakistani realized, and he filed that knowledge away for possible future use.

"*Mahsool,*" the terrorist addressed him in liquid Arabic, "I must speak with you."

Perhaps it was only the strain of the long hours of imprisonment, but Chaudri thought he could read a plea in the Arab's penetrating gaze. A plea for what? It was the Sword of God which had the weapons, the Sword of God which controlled the situation. What could they possibly want from *him,* their captive?

"If you must be speaking, then I must be listening," Chaudri replied.

The Arab glanced briefly at the two Americans. He was really no more than a boy, Chaudri saw, at most 19 or 20 years of age. But even at 19 or 20, he was old enough to carry a rifle, old enough to know how to use it. He was old enough for that.

"We must have food and water," the boy announced suddenly, "but your government does not approach us. How are we to communicate with them and let them know our demands?"

"What's he saying?" Nurse Hewitt whispered, and the doctor squeezed her shoulder to quiet her, afraid the guard might harm her for interfering.

But the guard ignored them both, his attention fixed on Mahboob Chaudri.

They have no plan, Chaudri recognized, and the thought astounded him. *In the passion of their religious fervor, they determined to take over the Suq-al-Khamis Mosque, but they did not anticipate having to deal with hostages. Now they are holding the shrine, but they are stuck with us as well. This is the first time the Sword of God is doing anything more than writing angry letters to the press, and they have no idea how to proceed.*

Interesting, he thought, *most highly interesting. Does this often lie beneath the heartless exterior of terrorism—this uncertainty, this confusion, this doubt? Is this the way it was aboard the Achille Lauro, aboard Flight 847, at the American embassy in Tehran? Is it possible that the Shi'ite extremists are as much the victims of their madness as they are its agents?*

"You ask me to help you," said Mahboob Chaudri slowly, "but how can I be helping you when you treat me as if I am your enemy? I am not your enemy. I am your brother, and these Americans are your brother and sisters."

"You lie," the boy spat. "America is not my brother. America is the Great Satan, the despoiler of Islam, the—"

"I am not speaking of America. I am speaking of these innocent Americans, who came to Bahrain to heal the sick—not just their own people, but all who are in need of their skills. What have they done to deserve your anger, your threats?"

Nurse Hewitt reached for the doctor's hand and held it tightly. A silence hung heavily in the air.

"This is wartime," the Arab boy said at last. "And, in wartime, the innocent must suffer for the sins of their governments. This country was a model of Islamic purity until—"

Chaudri shook his head. "But this is not the answer. I am a Muslim myself, and I am agreeing with you that there are problems in the world, problems here in the Gulf, in Bahrain, problems which can and must be solved. But this"—he indicated the Kalashnikov with a gesture—"this violence, this terrorism, this fanaticism, this is not the answer. Perhaps we have been done injustice, but is it Allah's will that we should be repaying the injustices of others with injustice of our own?" He sighed deeply. "No, that is not the way. As it is written in the Holy Quran, 'Direct us in the right path, in the path of those to whom Thou hast been gracious; not of those against whom Thou art incensed, nor of those who go astray.' Put down your gun, my friend, put it down. Let us find another path to peace."

Again it was silent, and the absence of sound was a living thing which wrapped itself around them and held them for a timeless interval. The doctor, the nurse, the Pakistani, the Arab—the silence entered into each of them and touched them and told them its secrets.

Mahboob Chaudri listened to the beating of his heart, and with great serenity put out his hands to the terrorist, his brother.

The Arab boy licked dry lips and swallowed his uncertainty. "My name is Hamid," he said.

* * * *

The sun beat down fiercely from its perch in the ivory sky, sucking rivulets of perspiration from Chaudri's forehead and armpits. The columns and archways of the Suq-al-Khamis Mosque squatted patiently in the heat, the twin minarets pointing impassive fingers at Heaven's vastness.

Chaudri stood alone between the spires, his only companions the sun and stone, the oppressive warmth and choking dust. The wooden balconies above were empty; Yousif Falamarzi was waiting with Hamid Yacoob and the two Americans within the tower that had been Chaudri's prison, and the remaining pair of terrorists was hidden from his view on the far side of the second minaret. His Public Security Force comrades and the Western reporters waited beyond the compound wall; although Chaudri could not see them from where he stood, he knew that they were still out there, that they would remain at their posts until the confrontation with *Saifoullah* wound its way to a conclusion.

The Pakistani moved slowly toward the second minaret, the olive-green material of his uniform chafing his arms and legs with every step. Hamid and Yousif had wanted to accompany him, but he had decided it would be best to go alone. If there was trouble, if there was gunfire, he must face it by himself. Uncomfortable as it might be in the summer heat, Chaudri's uniform gave him that obligation.

The Americans had wanted him to take one of the Kalashnikovs, but again he had demurred. He would go alone, he had told them firmly, and he would go unarmed. They had tried to change his mind, had tried to convince him that he was taking too many risks, but Chaudri had been resolute. Alone, he had repeated, and unarmed. That was the way it must be.

A determined fly buzzed circles around his head as he crept closer to his destination, alighting momentarily on his ears, his nose, his lips, then flitting off to safety as he slapped at it uselessly.

He reached the stone base of the minaret and paused for a moment to listen. The heat and the silence closed in on him and made the drawing of every breath an arduous task. Chaudri was tempted just to stand there, to wait, yet he knew that there was nothing to be gained by waiting. He had waited long enough already.

Courage, Mr. Chaudri, he told himself. He raised his hands in the gesture of surrender he had used the night before—and realized with clinical interest that the Arabic word for "surrender" is "Islam."

Islam, the surrender to God's will, the surrender to destiny.

With surrender in his heart, he stepped around the base of the minaret and gasped in sudden fear to find himself staring down the barrel of an AK-47.

* * * *

An eternity passed before he recognized that the rifle was in the hands of Senator William Adam Harding, and one of the two remaining members of the Sword of God lay motionless in the dust at his feet, his *thobe* and *ghutra* in disarray.

"Well, hot damn," the Senator roared, "it's you!" He flung aside the Kalashnikov and pounded Chaudri gleefully on the back. "I shore am glad to see your ugly mug again, there, son. I's afraid they might've—"

"What—?" Chaudri stammered. "How—? How did you—?"

"Well, hell, son, there was only two of 'em," the Senator beamed. "It's not like they had thesselves a damn army or nothin'. I took out this here downstairs one first, while he's around this side of the tower and out of sight of the rest of 'em, anen I snuck upstairs and whomped the other'n. I's just on my way over to take care of your two when you walked into my gun and like to scare the pants offa me." He looked Chaudri up and down with admiration. "But I guess you handled your boys okay on your own, there, din't you? I thought you was kind of runty for a police officer, if you'll excuse me for sayin' so, but you done good, son. I'm right proud of you."

Chaudri looked down at the body lying crumpled and motionless in the dust. "Is he—?"

"Dead?" The Senator chuckled. "Hell, no, he's just takin' hisself a li'l nap, that's all. I din't hardly hit him hard enough to raise a lump. And don't you fret none about the one upstairs, neither. He'll be back on his feet afore the ladies in there stop bawlin'."

"They are not hurt?"

"Naw, they're fine and dandy, son." He jerked his head toward the entrance. "They're inside there havin' thesselves a good old-fashioned cry, but they ain't been hurt none."

Chaudri put a hand to his heart. They were all alive, then, and it was over.

He shook his head in disbelief. It could so very easily have ended in bloodshed and horror. The Senator's solution had been unbelievably rash, had been taken without sufficient thought, had endangered all their lives.

And yet....

And yet the man had succeeded, praise Allah, and no one had been hurt.

They were a strange people, these Westerners, and the Americans were the strangest of them all. As strange, in their own way, as that small minority of Muslims who fervently believed that violence was the behavior God demanded of them.

And yet it seemed clear to Mahboob Chaudri that, in a world rocked with acts of senseless terrorism, it was perhaps possible after all for his culture and the Senator's to work together toward the goal of peace. And, if it was possible to live in harmony with the Westerners, then perhaps it might be possible to live in harmony with the likes of *Saifoullah* as well.

Insh'Allah. If only God was willing.

And that, Chaudri decided, as he found the ring of keys in the pocket of the fallen Arab's *thobe* and moved through brilliant sunshine to the gate in the wall which surrounded the Suq-al-Khamis Mosque, would be a very good thing.

Oh, dearie me, yes, that would be a very good thing indeed.

AFTERWORD

I originally wrote this tenth Mahboob Chaudri story in 1988, but EQMM and AHMM both turned it down, both editors explaining that, given the Middle Eastern geopolitics of that time, it was *too* true-to-life for their readerships, who read crime fiction to *escape* the headlines, not to get a look at the realities which lie behind them.

In my own opinion, though, this was one of the best stories in the series, and I was disappointed not to be able to share it with Mahboob's—and my—readers. Some 20 years after I wrote it, British anthologist Maxim Jakubowski paid me to translate several Dutch crime stories into English for *The Mammoth Book of Best International Crime*, a collection he was editing. I agreed, and asked him if he'd be willing to consider one of my own stories for inclusion in the book. *He* agreed, I sent him "The Sword of God," and he bought it.

Although Senator William Harding is an entirely fictional character, American Ambassador Paul Northfield is loosely modeled on Peter Sutherland, who was the American Ambassador to Bahrain from 1980 to 1983. Partly because the American community in Bahrain was small and therefore tightly knit and partly because his wife Carol was a member of the informal "Welcome Wagon" which looked after visiting University of Maryland faculty members, Ambassador Sutherland would sometimes call me up late at night and invite me over to the embassy residence to drink a beer and listen to him play jazz piano. Peter and Carol were good people, and I wonder where they are now. Google for once has let me down when it comes to locating them.

The Suq-al-Khamis Mosque remains a Bahraini tourist attraction today. It is one of the oldest mosques in the country—some sources say *the* oldest—with a foundation dating back to the 11th century or possibly even earlier. In this photograph, you can see the twin minarets described in the story—which, by the way, don't seem to have been part of the original mosque, but were added when the structure was rebuilt in the 15th century—and the stone wall which surrounds the compound:

Abdullah al-Muharraqi (b. 1939) was when I was in Bahrain and remains today the emirate's most important and best-known modern artist—and certainly one of the most important and best-known throughout the Gulf region. I still have a copy of his *Scenes from the Gulf*, a gorgeous volume containing 56 full-color reproductions of his paintings, and the description of Aiysha, Hassan al-Shama's first wife, which appears near the end of "The Tree of Life" is very closely based on one of the paintings which appears in that book. Here's another painting, titled "The War Generation," which I think goes well with the subject matter of "The Sword of God."

Scenes from the Gulf is long out of print, but you can sometimes find a used copy on Amazon or Abebooks.com, and you can find more of al-Muharraqi's work online by Googling his name.

As I write this Afterword in 2015, I seem to once again have picked up the threads of a "career" as a writer. My non-series story "Police Navidad" was in the January 2015 issue of *EQMM*, and another one-off, "Selfie," is scheduled to come out later in the year—which will make this the first time I've had two of my own stories appear in the pages of *EQMM* in the same year since 1986, when *three* of the stories you've just read all debuted ("ASU" in April, "Jemaa el Fna" in June, and "The Night of Power" in September). And in November 2015, Simon 451 (a new speculative imprint of Simon & Schuster) will publish *Styx*, a zombie cop novel on which I collaborated with Belgian writer Bavo Dhooge. In principle, Bavo and I will be doing two sequels to *Styx* together, and I'm also working collaboratively with another Belgian, Dirk Vanderlinden, on what's intended to be a 10-volume series of thrillers, the first of which is titled *The Fiandre Brotherhood*.

Will Mahboob Chaudri ever return? Perhaps.

The year 2018 will mark the 50th anniversary of the publication of my first short story, "E.Q. Griffen Earns His Name," in the December 1968 issue of *EQMM*. I've already begun work on a special story to mark the occasion. I'm calling it "50," and it features E.Q. Griffen, the hero of that first story, all growed up and thinking back on a case he failed to solve as a teenager.

Revisiting my old friend E.Q. has got me thinking nostalgically of my old friend Mahboob. It would be fun to spend some more time in his world, all these years after he and I first got to know each other. And, hey, there's still "Home Leave"—part three of the trilogy that began with "ASU" and continued with "The Ivory Beast"—to be written.

So perhaps Mahboob will be back.

Insh'Allah....

PUBLICATION INFORMATION

"The Dilmun Exchange" originally appeared in *Ellery Queen's Mystery Magazine* (July 1984). Reprinted in *The Year's Best Mystery and Suspense Stories* (Walker & Co, 1985).

"The Beer Drinkers" originally appeared in *Ellery Queen's Mystery Magazine* (December 1984). Reprinted in *The Ethnic Detectives* (Dodd, Mead & Company, 1985).

"The Tree of Life" originally appeared in *Ellery Queen's Mystery Magazine* (Mid-December 1985).

"The Qatar Causeway" originally appeared in *Alfred Hitchcock's Mystery Magazine* (January 1986).

"ASU" originally appeared in *Ellery Queen's Mystery Magazine* (April 1986).

"Jemaa el Fna" originally appeared in *Ellery Queen's Mystery Magazine* as "The Exchange" (June 1986).

"The Night of Power" originally appeared in *Ellery Queen's Mystery Magazine* (September 1986). Reprinted in *The Year's Best Mystery and Suspense Stories* (Walker & Co, 1987). Reprinted in *Murder Intercontinental* (Carroll & Graf, 1996).

"Sheikh's Beach" originally appeared in *Detective Story Magazine* (Issue #2, 1988).

"The Ivory Beast" originally appeared in *New Mystery* (Vol. 2, #1, 1993).

"The Sword of God" originally appeared in *The Mammoth Book of Best International Crime* (Robinson, 2009). Reprinted in *The Mammoth Book of the World's Best Crime Stories* (Running Press, 2009).

ACKNOWLEDGMENTS

The illustration of the Beer Drinkers was drawn by Dutch graphic artist Piet Schreuders from a photograph taken by Josh Pachter. It is copyright © 1984 and is reproduced here with the permission of the artist. For more information about Piet Schreuders, please visit his website at www.pietschreuders.com.

The photograph which appears in the Afterword to "The Tree of Life" was taken by Harold Laudeus and is reprinted with his permission. You can find more of his photography at www.flickr.com/photos/haerold/.

The illustration which appears in the Afterword to "The Tree of Life" was drawn by Jim Odbert and was originally published in the January 1986 issue of *Alfred Hitchcock's Mystery Magazine*. It is copyright © 1986 and is reproduced here with the permission of the artist. For more information about Jim Odbert, please visit his website at www.nyborart.com/about.html.

The illustration which appears in the Afterword to "The Qatar Causeway" was drawn by Ron Wilbur. Both the magazine cover and illustration are copyright © 1988 and are reproduced here with the permission of *DSM* publisher Gary Lovisi. For more information about *Detective Story Magazine* and its later reincarnation as *Hardboiled Detective Story Magazine*, please visit Gary Lovisi's website at www.gryphonbooks.com.

The reproduction of Abdullah al-Muharraqi's painting which appears in the Afterword to "The Sword of God" is used with the permission of the artist.

All other photographs in this book were either taken by Josh Pachter or found online. An attempt has been made to identify the photographers and to request permission to reproduce their work here. If you took one of these pictures, please contact Josh Pachter or Wildside Press, so that you can be given appropriate credit for your work in subsequent editions of this book.

ABOUT THE AUTHOR

Josh Pachter is the author of some 70 short crime stories, which have appeared in *Ellery Queen's Mystery Magazine*, *Alfred Hitchcock's Mystery Magazine*, and many other periodicals and anthologies in the US and around the world. He translates novels and short stories from Dutch and Flemish into English. *Styx*, a zombie cop novel on which he collaborated with Belgian author Bavo Dhooge, will be published by Simon 451, an imprint of Simon & Schuster, in 2015, and he's currently working with another Belgian writer, Dirk Vanderlinden, on *The Fiandre Brotherhood*, the first book in a projected series.

In his day job, Josh is the assistant dean for communication studies and theater at Northern Virginia Community College's Loudoun Campus. He is an avid traveler, bike rider and photographer. His wife Laurie is a writer/editor for a Federal agency in Washington, DC, and his daughter Rebecca is an attorney in Arizona. He lives in Herndon, Virginia, with Laurie and their dog Tessa.

CPSIA information can be obtained at www.ICGtesting.com
Printed in the USA
BVOW02s1135300715

411145BV00001B/23/P